The
Coffee
Cartel

The
Coffee
Cartel

Paul H. Barrett

THE COFFEE CARTEL

iUniverse books may be ordered through booksellers or by contacting:

iUniverse
1663 Liberty Drive
Bloomington, IN 47403
www.iuniverse.com
1-800-Authors (1-800-288-4677)

ISBN: 978-1-5320-8475-1 (sc)
ISBN: 978-1-5320-8476-8 (e)

Print information available on the last page.

iUniverse rev. date: 10/08/2019

Contents

Part One: Deep Sea Intrusion 1

Part Two: Ebony Angel 27

Part Three: Suriname...117

Part Four: Isiolo, Kenya 141

Part Five: Terasina, Brazil 209

Part Six: Washington, DC 275

PART ONE

Deep Sea Intrusion

It must have been a twist of fate or pure coincidence that put me in this aquatic setting at this time. As the sun set it lit up the sky in a crimson panorama unequalled in any place but the Straits of Florida. A hard day of deep sea fishing preceded the brilliance of the setting sun.

My friend Carl and I were held nearly stationary by our sea anchor, about 20 miles from Cuba. There was a slight drift with the waves as evidenced by the Simrad GPS unit aboard. Carl and I rotated watch duties for the night; you never know what's going to happen at sea, so night watches were essential. I slept the first leg. All was calm until a loud unmistakable sound of gunfire shook me.

"What the hell!", shouted Carl! Someone had apparently shot at Carl? I was sleeping soundly in the master suite when I heard the blast. Without stopping to put pants on, I ran out to see a dark-skinned man climbing over the gunnel into the cockpit. I ran back to my bedroom to get my shotgun from the bulkhead locker; it was always loaded with 12-gage shells. When I got back to the salon I caught a glimpse of Carl hitting the intruder, who then tried to get in the Salon door. I shot through the door, taking the intruder and the door out! I also saw a second man coming over the transom. Carl, who had been knocked down by the first intruder, grabbed him. I was trying to get a shot at the second man but he and Carl were fighting and revolving, so a clear shot was improbable. The wind had picked up so the boat was wobbling, making a clear shot even more unlikely. Finally, a "7th wave," pretty big, tossed the boat enough to knock the unwanted guest against the fighting chair, and I let him have it. Thank God we had stopped them, really stopped them, as they both appeared dead.

What the hell were we going to do now? What in the hell were these two (apparently Cuban) after in the first place? Carl went up the ladder to the flying bridge to see if there were any other visitors around? We both looked around everywhere, but the only thing we could see was the smaller boat our visitors came in; it was floating about 10 yards away. We figured, since we had scanned the dimly lit horizon that we were safe to secure their boat to ours, rather than deal with the dead bodies onboard first.

I went to the bedroom to put a pair of pants on. I then took note of the battery status and instruments before firing up our main engines. Letting them warm up, I asked Carl to run up on the bow and retrieve the sea-anchor. Sea-anchor secure, we slowly went to the intruder's boat. As we got near, I took the BFB out of gear and Carl caught their boat with a boat hook. He secured it to our port side while I shut down the engines and blowers.

We both went into the salon and sat on the couch to try and figure out what to do next? We had two dead bodies on board and an unwanted boat about 25 feet long. We decided to look on their bodies and see if they had credentials or anything to figure out why they boarded us. Maybe they were just thieves or pirates? We found driver's licenses and determined that they were thirty something Cubans. One had a passport and a photo. The passport jived with the license and the photo was of a boat. On second glance, it looked like the boat was like ours. In fact, it was a 55' Hatteras, just like mine. We tried to figure out what they were after? Maybe, or even probably, they boarded the wrong Hatteras. It certainly looked like the photo, one of them had! They could have boarded what they thought were friendlies, been caught by surprise, and shot at Carl. What could the Hatteras they thought they were boarding have had? "Several unanswered questions," we said. But we had to dispose of the two bodies and the towed boat and clean up the shattered teak from the salon door, and the blood all over the cockpit deck and salon carpet. Unanswered questions would have to wait. We decided to tie lead ballast weights to them and let the fish have them, after we opened their entrails and eyeballs to prevent flotation, if the ballast weights came off. It wasn't easy, but we got them both thrown over the gunnel. All this was after discussing whether-or-not to call the Coast Guard and explain to them about the illegal boarding and shot that was fired before boarding. Should we call our Coastguard or the Cuban Coastguard? The attendant interrogation wouldn't be fun, so we decided to just throw them over; they quickly disappeared below the dark waves. We then untied the line securing the boat and let it drift. We assumed the boat would ultimately drift to the Florida Keys, like so many Cuban refugee crafts. The Coastguard would likely intercept it before it made it to shore, as it was routine for them to look for refugees and drugs.

We had a hell of a mess to clean up; blood on the cockpit deck, shattered teak from the salon door, blood all over the salon carpet, and so on. Carl started on the cockpit, I started in the salon. The carpet was the worst. I had to soak with soap and water, retry, soak again until visually clean. There were small splatters of blood everywhere. A challenge, but I got her done. Carl was equally successful outside. We looked "shipshape," except for the gaping hole in the Salon door. I found a thin sheet of starboard and secured it to the door with glue and stainless screws. Feeling somewhat recovered, we got a drink and sat down on the salon couch to figure out our next move. I said to Carl, "Those guys were looking for a 55' Hatteras that had someone or something they wanted." Carl said, "Maybe they were looking for someone to take hostage or kill?" "Who knows," I said.

We had another drink and decided to hit the hay. I asked Carl to deploy the sea-anchor, and I went below.

I lay on the bed thinking that those intruders were looking for a Hatteras that they thought was in this area. Either the Florida Straits, The Keys, or Cuba. Havana was a likely candidate since we were so close, and these guys were Cuban and Obama had recently softened the restrictions for visiting Cuba before he left office.

I got up around eight and made coffee. After consuming one cup, I made another and went to the engine room, turned on the heaters, checked the fuel, batteries, sea cocks, strainers and fuel filters; I felt all was A-Okay to go to Cuba. I started up the generator and mains. We were now about 21 miles from the Cuban Coastline, so I pointed the BFB southward after the sea-anchor was retrieved by Carl.

My Simrad GPS and charts gave me a true vector to the marina's sea buoy, so I engaged the auto-pilot and throttled up. It was an almost due South heading, and the sea and horizon was clear ahead. The seas were about two feet and we were heading into the waves at a 40-degree angle, so full steam ahead was the order of the day. As we cruised along, I couldn't get our unwanted and now deceased visitors and their intrusion out of my head. We were making 20 knots, so we should be seeing land on the horizon in about 50 minutes. The weather was super, and the waves seemed to be getting smaller (1 -2 feet).

In a few minutes we could make out irregular features on the horizon and after consulting the chart-plotter, it had to be Havana. In a few more minutes the sea buoy that headed the Channel to the Hemingway Marina was sighted. In another few more minutes I hailed the Marina on Channel 16 to get a slip. They requested I move to channel 22, which I did. After giving my name and the vessel's name, they asked how long I would be staying? I said, "Indeterminant." Well, that was a mistake. They said again, "How long are you here for?" I said, "Several days, I don't know exactly?" They returned, "You have to tell us how long, Senõr!" I said, "Seven days, por favor, and all was well. "Si Senõr," the voice on the radio said. I called back and said, "Slip numero, por favor?" "Ciete Cinco," the voice said. We found slip 75 and backed in slowly without incident. We secured the boat, shut down mains, generator and blowers, and attached shore power. Carl went inside and got two Cervezas. I said, "What a great trip here, huh?" Carl said, "Finest kind." After a beer I checked the voltage, as I'd become accustomed to, and it read 200 volts. The only problem was that it should be 220 volts to run air conditioners, refrigerators and freezers. I called the Dock Master who said, "It was the way it was, and the power company couldn't do anything about it." "Figures," I said. Slip number 75 wasn't the only one with low voltage, it seemed. So, I told Carl, "We are in a foreign country, aren't we?" I installed a filter and small softener on the water and started washing the salt off our boat. I had heard the water in Cuban marinas needs a filter. By the time we'd finished washing her off we were hungry, very hungry, but had to check into the Marina and fill out their paperwork for visiting vessels.

I went to the office and got their form; Captain – Paul Pilot, Vessel type – Hatteras, Length – 55 ft, Beam – 19 ft, length of stay – 7 days (who knew)?

We walked down the pier to see if they had a restaurant, or grill, or someplace to get a bite? We found a little place at the end of the dock that appeared to have tapas and cerveza, at least. "Mucho Tapas, por favor" I said, and the barmaid went in the back. Hopefully to get us something to eat! In a while a plate of Flautas and a plate of Jalapeno poppers showed up. They were fabulistic! After another beer we decided to look around the marina to check things out and see if there might be another Hatteras like ours? There was the predictable Sea Ray party on one boat. Most of the boats were cabin cruisers or trawlers not fishing vessels, although there were several Hatteras'. We kept walking and it looked like another area had a group of fishing boats. We made our way to that section and there were several fishing boats. An impressive Viking drew our attention and the mate was busy rigging ballyhoo for the next day. As we walked and talked we spied a Hatteras nearly like ours but unlike others, there wasn't anyone there. We asked neighbors about it, appearing as if we might be interested in buying a boat like this. We learned that it was owned by a couple from Miami. They came down periodically to fish and dine in Havana. The man was an avid bill fisherman. The people we talked to said that he was a good fisherman and had caught several sails and a few marlin. Was this a "front" for something more nefarious or not? Probably not, I thought. It seemed innocent enough, so we moved on. We walked the entire marina and had come across only two boats close to ours. We found another 55 Hatteras near the end of a row of fishing boats. It was the same eggshell color as mine and was outfitted to the max with outriggers, downriggers, fighting chair, center rigger, extra rod holders and "top of the line" Instruments. We asked about the owners and found that it was a tournament boat with a 25 to 35-year-old crew. A very successful boat and crew headed by a Captain named Glen. The people said that Glen and the crew had gone to a bar on the Paseo Del Prado, near Havana. They also said that, "There's no telling when they might come back to the boat." We continued to look the boat over, dubbed "High Stakes," as in big poker games. The name was painted in large Gothic gold swirl letters on the stern. Carl remarked that the name was certainly apropos, like gaining a reputation for winning high stake's tournaments. A few tournaments have a top prize of $1,000,000. We'd have to look up Captain Glen later, unless we might find that bar they were talking about. We'd seen a lot of boats this afternoon, with a couple fitting the bill, but we decided to go back to the BFB.

We got back to our boat and poured a stiff drink. What happens now, I thought. Both boats we saw were like ours, but they both seemed innocent. But innocent of what exactly? We didn't really know if those two marauders that boarded us at sea were getting on the wrong boat or not? Maybe they were just pirates going for what they could steal from a nice big boat like mine.

Pirates like these know that boats like mine are usually owned by wealthy people. I had to admit that it was merely a hunch that they were looking for a boat like mine. The photo I found was the real reason I maintained this theory. We poured another drink and agreed that our best move was to continue looking for a boat exactly like ours! It had been a long day, but a good one, and it was coming to an end because I was tired.

I woke with a start, dreaming of killing those two bastards that got on the wrong boat! Perspiration salt burned my eyes! As I woke up I wondered if our lead ballast weight ties would hold until aquatic inhabitants consumed our visitors? Gradually, I fell back into the peaceful twilight of awareness preceding sleep.

I awoke in the morning to the gentle lapping of waves on the hull. Like a baby rocking in a cradle listening to the subtle slapping of waves. Reality set in and I went to the head, relieved myself, got dressed, and headed up the stairs to the Salon. Carl was still in the guest suite's bunk. I made coffee and climbed up to the bridge to wake up with one of God's greatest phenomenon's, the sunrise. Key West and Havana were both famous for their sunsets, and the sunrises were also great! Here again the two killers that boarded our boat kept interfering with my thought process. Yes, they were killers, I thought. They had shot at Carl first with a gun. We really needed to find out what the hell is going on.

I remembered that I had the photo I found on one of the killers; it was on my nightstand. I got the picture and a magnifying glass and took the picture to the head for a strong light. It was an askew shot of the boat, and not a clear shot at that. I could see, however, and the name of the boat appeared to be "Café Negro." Black Coffee, I thought, a good name for a boat. Maybe the boat was documented with the Coast Guard, or maybe just noted in marina clients. That's when a light went on in my mind. I had a good friend and an agent in the FBI, and I knew that he could and would help us. He and I had been agents for the same sector three years ago. His name was Jack, and I thought Jack may have access to the Photography division. I dug his phone number out of my cellphone's contact list and dialed it. "Jack Warner," he said. I said, "Paul Pilot here." Jack laughed, "How are you, Paul?" he joshed. "I'm good, but we've (Carl and I) run into a big mess." "What kind of mess?" he said. "Two pirates boarded our boat in the middle of the Florida Straits and I killed them," I offered. "How can I help?" he responded. "I found a picture of a boat like mine on one of the marauders," I said. "I looked at the picture with a magnifying glass and could see 'Café Negro' and a very blurred number in the upper right-hand corner of the transom that perhaps will identify this vessel," I said. Jack responded by saying, "I'll get it figured out, we have technology here that no one would ever believe." I said, "I'll text you the picture in as high a definition as possible." I texted the picture to Jack.

Carl got up and started breakfast; although late in the morning, I thanked him for making breakfast and made my daily coffee. "Two cups a day keeps the intruders away," I said. Carl chuckled. I explained that I'd sent Jack a high definition photo of the photo that I'd found on the Cuban. He agreed that Jack might find out something about the sister vessel that could help us. After digesting this new plan and my breakfast, we decided to look for other locations here in Cuba that would accommodate a 5-foot draft like mine. There were several. The Marina Marlin Tarara was next door, so we thought we'd look at those boats. We walked and walked, but nothing like mine was there. The Varadero Yacht Charters Marina was about three hours to the East through Matanzas. We proceeded to look for and rent a vehicle to drive. We found a Jeep, rented it, and drove to Varadero. The road was just ok, with a few pot holes and asphalt fissures. Evidence of poor Cubans and the ever-present cars from the 1950's. It is amazing what necessity can generate. The improvisation and ingenuity it took to keep these old vehicles running was impressive; either keep the old cars running or go without transportation, I guessed. One '51 Chevy slowed us down a bit due to smoke and speed. The smoke probably indicative of the need for a valve and "ring-job," and the speed for. . .who knows? From the road, on a slight hill, we could see down to the marina and boats were visible. We arrived, found a parking place, and parked the Jeep. We walked to the closest boardwalk with predominantly fishing vessels; a few Vikings, a Bertram, a Sea Ray and an Ocean Yacht. The Sea Ray reminded me of a story. "Have you seen the New Sea Ray? No why? Well, it's got a glass bottom this year! Why? So they can see last year's model (LOL)." We were lucky that so many commercial fishing boats were here, but the 25-knot winds today kept them in. Carl struck up a conversation with a blond-haired beauty on a 60′ Viking. She seemed taken with him. As they seemed to be getting along well, I walked down to a crew rigging fishing gear. I told them that we were looking for an early eighties Hatteras. They couldn't understand why, since there were so many new features on newer boats? I explained that Hatteras made a thicker hull and several other structural over-spec advantages in the early eighties. All boat manufacturers in the nineties started getting closer and closer to specifications that would just do the job, no more! A Jack Hargrave designed hull was probably the best, seaworthy, and the fastest fisher ever designed! One of the crew said, "I saw a nice, well-kept Hatteras on the south side of the Island near Trinidad." "It was probably an '82 or '83," he added. I said, "Thanks, that sounds just like what I'm looking for." I introduced myself to Carl's new acquaintance, "I'm Pilot, Paul Pilot." She said, "Me Nombre Gonzales, Etana Gonzales." Since Carl was so taken with this girl I told him, "I'll go on to the next stop if you don't mind but first, is there another cerveza in there?" The girl got me a Corona from inside the Viking, which was named "Reel Fun." Carl was telling her about some of the places we had fished. He said, "Bimini was a great place to fish, but there wasn't much else there." She said, "I agree, but they are building a pretty big Casino there, which should change things quite a bit." "No Vegas, but more than just "The Big Game Club," she added. I finished my beer, told Carl that I was going to a little-known place called Gaviota that had some kind of diving club, and it might have a Hatteras like the one we are searching.

A nice trip to Gaviota, near Puerto Vita, except for having to stop for fuel; I felt I got ripped off. He charged me the entire $20 bill for $16.50 on the meter. He said, "meter fichas," which I think meant fuck you in Spanish! It was what it was. I was now about 50 kilometers from Marina Hemingway, but we were on a quest. Although little known to the average American tourista, this marina was a big deal in the diving community. I parked the Jeep and walked down to the dock. There were a half dozen well-equipped diving boats. Most of them were privately made with wide open cockpits rimmed with air bottles on wooden racks. Quite a place, but these type boats were not what I was looking for. I talked to a couple of Captains about the availability of a 55' boat? No one knew, except a guy named Carlos. He said he knew of one on the other side of the island; probably the same one that the crewmember at Varadero told me about. This guy added, "The owner was a recluse of sorts." "It is said that the owner must be into something bad, since his big, beautiful estate was well guarded," Carlos added. "That is the only place in Cuba that has a covered slip for the boat," he went on. "Interesting," I said. "I will have to go see if his boat is for sale." I said, "Tell me where it's located again, por favor." Carlos said, "It is very near a place called Playa Ancon, near Trinidad." I told him, "Muchas' Gracias, Senõr," and went to my Jeep.

I thought that a phone call might be the best first approach, since I didn't even know the man's name. I also thought that I'd better get back to Varadero and see what Carl was up to. A short drive later I pulled back into the Marina at Veradero. I went back where I'd left Carl, but no Carl. I asked around and found out that he and others had gone to a bar called Cable 62. After finding the place and parking, I could hear voices, and one of them was Carl. He had had a few by now and sounded a little belligerent. "Oh Boy," I said out loud. He was playing pool and when money was involved Carl could be aggressive, even sober. Carl, booze and pool rarely ended well, I thought. Etana, the blond beauty that Carl met back on the Viking, was attentive to Carl and visibly concerned about his belligerence. Carl and his opponent had both had too much to drink and things went south quickly. Carl had just won the game and he was boasting way too much. "Andale Pues," he said, which was too much for his opponent. He went for Carl and fists flew! What to do? I thought. Yes, Carl would help me if I got into this kind of situation but that would never happen. Anyway, I had to help my friend! I grabbed a cue from the wall holder and hit Carl's rival on the neck and broke the cue. "Que hacer dano," he said, as he turned his attention to me. He came at me, but I'd put the table between us. We darted back and forth, to and fro. Carl, seeing the jostling for position, grabbed another cue and "cold cocked" the guy on the head. Thank God the bystanders didn't interfere and apparently didn't think much of Carl's opponent. I looked at Carl, he looked at me, and we both ran like hell for the front door. Out on the street we looked for any structure to hide behind, in case the bartender called the Policía. We ran behind a repair shop to catch our breath and hide. I had left the Jeep next to the Marina's Ship's Store, so after a few hand signals we both sprinted to the Jeep.

We made it to the Jeep and pulled out, just when the Policía pulled in. Thankfully they ignored us. So I drove all the way back to Hemingway Marina and the BFB, parked, then jumped out of the Jeep, ran down the dock to the BFB, jumped on boat, unlocked and opened the Salon door, ran to the galley cabinets, got some scotch, a glass and went to the ice maker, got ice in my glass, poured the Macallan 18 and sat down on the couch. Carl finally got there after I'd finished half of my drink! Carl, although slow, had picked up on something I'd missed coming in so fast. Someone had left a note on the bridge ladder. The note said, "Found what you were asking about," signed Jack. Immediately we knew that Jack (my friend from the FBI) had found something important about the Hatteras in the picture found on the intruder. I called Jack on my sat phone, but a message said that he'd left for the day. It was late DC time, so I'd have to wait till tomorrow to call and find out what he'd found. I was anxious to know what Jack had found. His answer would likely tell us our next move in this strange, distressing true life mystery. Carl made an unorthodox early retirement, nursing a very bad hangover and lamenting over his pool brawl. I nursed a second scotch, while contemplating our next move and listening to Antonia Carlos Jobim.

I awoke and thought I'd make coffee and call Jack, ASAP. I started calling Jack as soon as I thought he'd be at his office, 9 am. I finally got him at 9:15 with sat interference, but he said he'd have to call back at his coffee break; which I assumed was ten o'clock, or there about. He called back at 10:10 and said, "Paul?" I said, "Yes." He said, "That Hatteras had been documented, but it had elapsed. The hull ID was determined by The Super Photographers, as HATBM38TM85A." The Hull ID confirmed that it was a Hatteras and that it was an '85 Model. That boat would be easily mistaken for my BFB. Jack went on, "The managing owner back in 1995 was William H. Black and his address of record at that time was 112 So. Hammock, High Rock on Grand Bahama Island." "Anything else," I asked. Jack responded, "Not at this time," indicating, I thought, that he must be working on something more.

A lot to digest! One thing for sure, that Hat had moved around. But really, it was only 350 miles from Grand Bahama to Cuba. A Hat like that would likely have a range of 600 miles or more. Anyway, it had moved around and was in Cuban waters where the two marauders came in, I guess? But what the hell were they looking for? Carl and I decided to strikeout first by looking at the North eastern Cuban marinas, remembering the lead that Carlos had given us a day or so ago. Carlos was one of the Captains we met at the Diving Marina at Puerto Vita. I planned to take the Jeep to the residence of the man mentioned by Carlos on the south side of Cuba near Playa Ancon. We didn't know the owner's name at this point, but we did know that he had a Hatteras, like mine, under a covered slip at his plush residence.

It was 10:30 a.m., so we headed for Playa Ancon or Trinidad about six hours away, per our hand-held GPS. We packed a few things, including our pistolas. Thank God the Policía had not found us or Carl's pool opponent. As we packed Carl said, "Since we won't get there until about 6 p.m., shouldn't we try to find a place to stay?" I agreed. I'll go see the Dock Master and see if he knows of a place? "Right on," Carl said. I walked down to see Enrique, the Dock Master. He immediately said that he had friends that lived there who had a bungalow called "Casa Morales," and that he would call the Morales' and make arrangements. I went back, told Carl about the lodging, and we got off about 11:15 a.m.

It was a beautiful countryside road with farms along the road, some looking like the Tobacco farms in North Carolina. Some had coffee, some tobacco and corn. Another field looked like potatoes. Cuban tobacco, I think, usually went into Cigars, where our North Carolina tobacco was going into cigarettes. I thought, I must get a Cohiba since I'm here. Cohiba was Fidel Castro's cigar and although I didn't like Castro, I did like his cigar!

We finally made it to Trinidad and Enrique had given me directions to the "Casa Morales." A small bungalow was set back by itself, very unlike the hotels in Havana. We were greeted by Concetta Morales. She was very cordial and walked us to the hacienda. We entered; it was great, kitchen, fridge, dinette table, couch, two bedrooms. All the comforts of home, away from home. We got somewhat settled in at 6:30 p.m. and I checked my weather App. The sunset was slated for 7:05 today. It was too late to go check out the Hatteras today; we needed to be on top of our game when we did. Carl took the Jeep to see if he could find a grocery to get food.

He came back and said he found a Mercado and had gotten, chips, salsa, chorizo, queso, mescal and Tecate; a wholesome repast, if I say so myself. I wouldn't be caught dead drinking mescal, but Carl was going for it. We chowed down on chips, chorizo, cheese and salsa; with me drinking beer and Carl sipping mescal. Another long day came to an end, so we went to our separate bedrooms.

We arose the next morning about the same time, got our Café Negro and opened our eyes. Carl was a little hung over from his dinner drinks and neither of us felt like cooking. Hell, we didn't have anything to cook anyway! We both got a second cup of Java, put on some threads and went to the Jeep. We drove around and found a small restaurant in central Trinidad that looked nice (maybe a local's breakfast place). We went in and ordered coffee, Huevos Rancheros, Papas and several warmed tortillas with butter. Carl said, "This is great, especially after mescal last night." I agreed, it was a wonderful breakfast, but now we had to find out about this Hatteras that looked like mine. It might be the answer to our mystery?

We drove to the Hacienda that had our sister vessel. But it wasn't a hacienda, it was a damn Plantation! It was just out of Trinidad near the Playa Ancon. We pulled up a safe distance away, but near the gate to the walled-in estate (about 50 acres, it appeared). We got out of the Jeep and walked up to the gate. A speaker on the right side had a button to press, so I said, "Hola, Hola." After the sixth Hola a voice said, "Que Quedas." Unfortunately, neither of us knew much Spanish. We tried to tell them we were interested in their Hatteras. Their English was as bad as our Spanish, but we persisted. "Me queda un barco preya on la Aqua." Silence. It was our best attempt to tell them we were interested in their boat on the water. "Me queda procure la barco, por favor," I offered again. More silence. Soon, two tough looking Cubans carrying AR-15's and appearing hostile came to the inside of the gate and stood with threatening postures. We got the message and went back to the Jeep. Carl said, "That went well." I said, "It didn't look like a serene, friendly place did it?"

We drove back to Casa Morales and grabbed a couple of Tecates. The grandeur of and the greeting from this plantation led to the unmistakable conclusion that this was the residence of a ruthless owner that thought he was above the law or something. We had an innocent inquiry about buying his boat and were met with hostility. Something illegal was going on behind this wall on this plantation, and we were going to find out what it was. The Estate reminded me of the southern plantations in the states that grew cotton, when cotton was King. This plantation also had adjacent fields, but it was coffee, not cotton. I wondered what some of the locals thought or could tell us about this place? We left and went to the first gas station we could find to fill up and ask about this place? I asked the attendant, "Que tipo de plantacion es la que esta al oeste de aqui, con la pared, por favor" (I did acquire another App last night that I'd forgotten about that converts English to Spanish). Although there are dialectical differences, it was a hell of a lot better than trying to remember high school Spanish. "Reo que solo recaudan y venen café," he said. Which meant, "I think they just raise and sell coffee." Coffee was a big crop in this latitude, but usually at higher elevations. They were doing so much gnome alterations these days that we weren't surprised that coffee could be raised at sea level. The attendant added before we left that their coffee was not sold locally, it was all shipped out somewhere?

I still wanted to find out about this place and my sister ship. A boat like he had on the water might be the cause of this whole incident. Then again, it might not. It was an enigma for sure. On the way back we decided we had to get to this Hatteras another way, but how? AR-15's are not very inviting to a visitor wanting to buy a damn boat. Carl and I discussed several plans and finally decided on an aquatic approach. The biggest concern was how it was guarded. Based on our greeting, the plantation was heavily guarded; most likely both electronic and human security, and probably around the clock. The walls were simple, but what measures had been taken at water's edge or around his covered dock? We decided to make a list of all the implements we could need to gain knowledge about their security. We needed binoculars to get a closeup view of the Hatteras and slip as well as night vision glasses for low light or night situations, a small boat (10' or so), oars for silent power and a small motor to get us close, line, snorkels, foot fins and firearms. There might be more, but right now that seemed to be a complete list. We drove around to several places to buy the items on our list and after asking questions, were accumulating most of them. A marina had a small Caribe inflatable boat about 10', which we bought along with a 7.5 HP Honda motor (very quiet), line and snorkel gear. We couldn't find binoculars or the other gear, so we decided to go with what we had rather than go back to Havana to find the remainder.

We loaded the uninflated boat and other items in the back of the Jeep and headed back to Casa Morales. We felt we could pretend to be boating tourists or even fishermen. Yes, we needed to go find a couple of fishing poles and some shrimp to round out our arsenal. If we were tourist fishermen, we might get away with getting close and appear innocent. Carl went back to a Tackle Shop he'd seen. I poured myself a nice Macallan 18 while Carl was gone. He came back in a few with two cheap rods and reels to help carry out the charade. We had also seen a nice restaurant in our earlier shopping trips, so we decided to try it. We both took a badly needed shower (fear perspiration seems more pungent than other forms). We put on our best clothes, which wasn't much. Carl seemed bound and determined to get lucky tonight, which was not a departure from his normal outlook; especially if there was the slightest hint that the "getting" presented itself.

It was a short drive to the Restauranté San José, which looked nice from the exterior. We walked in, and indeed it was nicer than expected. Florida Lobster was the dish of the day and the showcase preceding the main restaurant confirmed that the lobsters did not have claws. So our mouths were salivating, and the wine list was decent. I ordered a Silverado Sauvignon Blanc that should pair with the lobster quite nicely, and a Glenlivet Scotch and water beforehand. Everything went well and the room had a definite, tropical, Cuban atmosphere. The lobster came and was done perfectly; not cooked too long. A nice flan with a port capped off a great meal.

During the meal the waiter had told us that the band would start at 9 p.m. and after all those drinks we thought that might be good, especially in view of Carl's romantic drive. We were still early, so I nursed the port and Carl ordered another Rum and coke. It was going to be an Afro-Cuban Band, so I started thinking about Cuban history. Slavery was rampant in Cuba, particularly on this coast with farming as the prevailing stimulant to the economy, other than fishing. This mixing of Africans and Cubans gave rise to the unique and sexual rhythms of Afro-Cuban music. We thought of the nice bar we saw on the way in and decided to take our drinks there. I finally ran out of Port, so ordered another Glenlivet and water. Carl was on his own. The night was young and we thought we were too. Carl seemed like he was getting a little aggressive, or maybe just strongly assertive. He was ready to go back to Veradero and try and find Etana, the blonde beauty he'd connected with there at the Marina. That was too long of a drive, chiefly because he couldn't drive around the block at this juncture. His attention was quickly averted when another tanned doll with muy Grande Chi-Chi's sashayed in and sat at the bar. It was about two minutes before Carl was putting on the charm, albeit, slightly inebriated. He'd been there before, and I could see he was trying to be polite and put restraints on his desire.

PART TWO

Ebony Angel

Then, almost as if I'd asked a higher power, a second ebony angel came in and casually sat beside me. Although I'd been drinking almost as much as Carl, I couldn't resist saying, "Hola, Buenos tardes," while hoisting my drink in a "cheers" gesture. "Como esta, ce soir?" I said. She looked strangely, so I wondered what was wrong. Then I realized I had mixed Spanish and French in an effort to be debonair and suave. She laughed but didn't put me off. There was an unmistakable gleam in her eyes that I knew well. Quickly, before she could order, I asked the Bartender to get her whatever she wanted. "Como te llamas," I said. The bartender said, "At least you said it correctly, but I do speak English." So what's your name, pretty woman?" I offered. "Sara," she said. A little strange for a Cuban, but what did I know. Cuban's have many strange monikers. This one's like Sara-ndipity. She said,

"What's your name, guapo?" I said, as much as I could sound like James Bond, "Pilot, Paul Pilot." She seemed to understand English better than I did, so communications refocused on English only. In fact, it wasn't even English that prevailed; it was gestures, facial expressions, body movement, eye contact and a touch or two that said it all. She ordered another Lemon Drop while I nursed my scotch, knowing that if I were to get lucky, sober was better. She, on the other hand, had only had one drink. So, nurse I did. She was a beauty and smart, and this might be an eventful encounter, I hoped. In the meantime, Carl was progressing with a girl named Margarita. I say progressing, but it would have moved in a positive direction much quicker if the alcohol wasn't helping so much. All four of us were having a good time. I asked the Bartender if he had any playing cards, as I loved to do card tricks after a couple of drinks to astound acquaintances with dexterity and puzzling tricks. I had learned magic at an early age in Junior High School. A little Zinc Stearate powder would allow them to slide easily to facilitate fanning. No stearate here, but I did manage to fan them. Sara seemed impressed, which was all I wanted anyway.

"Another drink?" I said, "or would you rather leave this place." "Where would we go, Pablo?" "Maybe the Casa Morales," I said. "What's that?" she quickly added. "That's the Morales bungalow were staying at," I said. "That seems ok," she said. I said, "Excuse me for a minute, El Bano Calls." Sara laughed at what I said and how I said it, I guess? I walked by Carl and told him not to come home tonight, if he could help it. "Get a cab or sleep in the Jeep, if you have to," I said, and went to the restroom.

Sara and I left grasping one another's waist. We got in the Jeep and headed for Casa Morales.

We went in and I offered her another drink, it was either Tecate Cerveza or Mescal, as that was all I had. She didn't want anything but water. I'd already had too much to drink, so I got both of us "Agua con hielo," and we sat on the edge of the bed. Small talk with little linguistic confusion led to lying back on the bed and embracing. I was really turned on by this ebony beauty, so we both gently disrobed the other. Slow and caring foreplay was and always will be the most gratifying.

Needless to say, we were both satisfied, gratified and pleased with the sensations of the preceding fifteen minutes or so and anticipation for two and half hours.

I lie there thinking about what has happened with our plan to get up early to go investigate the enigmatic Hatteras from the water. Another day would have to suffice, since it was already 2 a.m. and I was intoxicated and tired, and God knows where Carl was? Another day, when we were rested and sober, would be much better than going this morning. We both fell asleep.

A glint of light came through the window and all of a sudden, I knew that we had missed our opportunity to surreptitiously get up close and personal to the "look alike" vessel docked six miles away.

Sara was gone, so I checked my wallet, money clip and cellphone, all were okay. This had been a pleasant and rewarding night for both of us. I didn't even know her last name or where she lived. Well, she knew where I was staying and what would be, would be.

Carl was missing. I assumed that he too had a successful encounter and had gone to her place or another "Casa Motel." I proceeded to make coffee and figure out where to go from here.

Another cup of java and pangs of hunger ensued. I decided to jump in the Jeep and go get breakfast. The Jeep was just where I left it. But before I saw it, I didn't truthfully remember where I'd left it. I was just pulling out when an old 1950 Chevy pulled up . . . Carl was in the backseat. He looked like hell. I told him to get in and we would go get some breakfast, since we both fucked up our plans to sneak up on the perplexing Hatteras down the road. Carl waved goodbye to Margarita and jumped in my Jeep.

Huevos rancheros was the dish of the morning with mucho bacon and mas Café Negro. We discussed the situation, although Carl's attention span was short, and decided to give it a go even thought it would be light and late morning when we would get there.

Our ten-foot inflatable boat, motor and other gear were still in the back of the Jeep, so we set out from the restaurant to see where we might put the boat in. We found a probable point of entry on our cellphone's Maps App and proceeded in that direction. The potential point of entry was about one mile east of the plantation. We also found the name of the plantation estate on the Map App. It said, "Padron Plantation." We assumed that the Hatteras' owner's name was Padron. On the way, we stopped and asked the cashier in a "Quick Stop," about the plantation. She confirmed that the estate was owned by Pascal Padron, and it was a mystery just what went on there, aside from coffee raising, harvesting and distribution.

We proceeded to the entry point but would have to walk a while to get to the water. Carl and I rigged a line that would give us a sling to share the weight of the motor, gas tank and inflatable, which were tied together. We only had to stop once to unload and rest a moment. The entry point was a little rocky, but easy enough. A small handpump slowly inflated the boat. Once in the water we secured the 7.5 HP motor to the stern, threw in the snorkel gear, and confirmed our location relative to Plantation Padron with our phone's global positioning site. All was good, as the surf was calm. Carl got out to push the boat and me out past the small breakers; he struggled to get in and we were off.

We got close enough to see the bow, complete with dinghy, bow-box and bumpers. We went closer and closer until an alarm sounded. We assumed we had crossed a radar activated perimeter. In just a couple of minutes, guards walked out to the end of the dock adjacent to the boat and shouted (through a megaphone), "DETENER, DETENER, POR FAVOR." We guessed that meant stop or halt, so we did. We reversed course to deeper water and headed back to the entry point. We had successfully determined that there was a peripheral intrusion alarm somehow radar detected. This told us that a night, underwater access might be more successful.

We made our way back to where we entered and stowed the deflated dingy and motor between rocks and covered it with grass and sand. A little shook, we headed back to the jeep over the sand and grass called "Swallenia;" the same grass that we covered our dingy with.

We had to stop and get something at the Mercado on the way back; shrimp and grits with Queso sounded good and to our surprise they had everything. The white cheese down here was fantastic. Also picked up more Cervesa, cornflakes and Leche.

Made it back to Casa Morales and got ourselves a beer, while stowing the groceries. An early morning, like 3 a.m., was our next operational plan. We would go to the entry point, inflate our raft and head toward the Padron Plantation.

We sat down, had a drink and went to bed, set our cellphone alarms for 2:30 a.m. and tried to go to sleep.

Buzz, Buzz, Buzz, Buzz – the alarms went off. We got up, dressed, made and gulped down coffee, and headed for the Jeep. We drove to the site closest to where we could access the entry point and walked to the grass covered raft; inflated it and put it in the water.

We could see the lights of the Padron Plantation in the distance. The seas had a light chop, which seemed like ideal conditions for our encroachment. The Honda was very quiet, so our short voyage was hopefully undetectable. We remembered the distance away from the Hatteras that radar detected us yesterday and stayed well back. We anchored and donned our scuba gear.

We had discussed previously that there was no way that radar could detect us under water. We slipped in the water and swam towards the enigmatic Hatteras.

Swimming near to the surface, so our snorkel could get air, we managed to get all the way to the end of the structure sheltering the boat, with finger piers on either side of the vessel. No sounds or alarms threatened our mission. I carefully and slowly pulled myself out of the water and up on the pier. I could see motion detectors on each side of the boat, so I moved ever so slowly.

I whispered to Carl to carefully join me. We then slowly slipped back to the stern of the boat. So far, so good! Whispering again, we wondered if we could slip aboard without detection and that we would run and dive in if detection ensued.

I grabbed the side of the gunnel and pulled myself into the cockpit. No alarms sounded! I rolled over to the fighting chair to give Carl room to join me. I then, on my knees, went to the salon door and saw that it was locked, but had the old original Schlage lock on the door. Our presence was still undetected, although we could see a camera oscillating back and forth . . . maybe the viewer was not watching closely or was asleep. Thank goodness I had put a paper clip in my outfit for just this occasion. I picked the lock and gently opened the door. They must have thought that the radar, motion detector and cameras could suffice, as no alarm sounded when I opened the door.

The salon appeared conventional and had a nice layout; couch, coffee table, desk, TV, etc. The galley was on the starboard side with normal setup; oven, stove and refrigerator, nothing out of the ordinary. But upon looking further, a door enclosed a great cavity filled with (of all things) coffee. The entire hull of this large 55' boat was filled with nothing but coffee? The aroma of coffee beans filled the air and there was a hint of a scent unfamiliar. The unknown scent was almost undetectable, but still there – a hint of lilac; that's what it smelled like.

We looked at each other in awe and whispered to slowly get the hell out of there. As we left the boat and slivered onto the pier, we saw a building about twenty yards away. It appeared unremarkable and had concrete block construction. We gestured and slowly crept up to the building. We opened the door to see a large table with nothing but cardboard boxes filled with bills. There must have been millions of dollars. There was a laboratory beyond the table filled with money; there were beakers, Bunsen burners, microscopes, etc.

The problem was, when we opened the door the alarm went off. It only took a fraction of a second to see the money table and lab. So after that sight had registered, we both ran like hell back to the pier and jumped off the end. We swam underwater as long as we could hold our breath, surfacing only long enough to catch our breath and hear the rattling of automatic weapons. There were zings and whistles of bullets hitting the water all around us, but we swam underwater as fast as we could. Carl got hit in the leg by one bullet but thank God the bullet's velocity was severely dampened by the water and didn't enter his leg.

We made it back to our anchored inflatable and pulled ourselves on. Our boat was beyond the range of several guards firing at us, so we cranked up the Honda and escaped out of harm's way. We opened up the throttle and got back to our point of entry. No one had followed, thank God!

We just left the boat on the rocks, covered it with grass, and headed for our Jeep. We got in and, without hesitation, headed back to Casa Morales.

We got back, wanted a drink, but I made coffee. We sat down staring at each other. "What the hell just happened?" said Carl. I said, "We just got the shit scared out of us." We concluded that we had found out a lot more about the enigmatic Hatteras, but what had we really found out? There was no question that this plantation was hiding something big, really big. Otherwise, it would not have had all the security, guards and assault weaponry. Especially around that Hatteras. It was outwardly only a fishing yacht, but inside it was filled with coffee? There must be something about this coffee that eluded us? Coffee is a worldwide source of addictive caffeine. Coffee is the world's most widely consumed psychoactive drug. It is legal and unregulated in the entire world, a stimulant that gets the entire world going in the morning. But what the hell was the Hatteras filled with coffee hiding? Coffee is legal!

The only thing we could come up with was to get some of that coffee and analyze it chemically. There had to be a reason a legal substance was guarded so considerably. But given the reception we got while checking out the elusive Hatteras gave us pause. Was the mystery of the coffee, Hatteras, Padron Plantation and the two "pirates" that boarded our boat in the middle of the Florida straits enough to subject ourselves to possibly getting killed? Being killed was a real possibility, or as Carl said, "Getting killed fucking around with this coffee-filled boat is a very high probability." Was it worth it?

We were already in up to our assholes. We had killed two people at sea and severely hurt Carl's pool opponent in the bar brawl, both of which would have the local Police, Coast Guard, and who knows who coming after us. We had almost been killed twice. Once at sea and another at the Padron Plantation. Should we stop now? Could we stop now?

No, we couldn't stop! The baffling mystery of the impenetrable plantation was too much. What would we do anyway? Go back fishing in some of the world's most productive waters? Go back to the nearly mundane pursuit of the "Man in the Blue Suit" (Marlin). No, we would have to figure out how in the hell to get some of that coffee and have it analized.

We were exhausted and went back to bed.

I awoke with a start, due to the dream I had about the Padron guards or henchmen coming to our place and confronting us with guns. It took a few seconds to realize that it was a dream and that all was well at Casa Morales.

In some strange way, the excitement of the close encounter with death stimulated my desire for sexuality.

How could I find Sara again? She had left after our eventful evening and I didn't even know her last name? My only recourse would be to return to Restauranté San José and see if I could track her down.

Carl was still asleep, so I got a cup of Java and walked outside. The wind was blowing about twenty-five knots, and it looked like rain was in the offing this afternoon. Cumulus clouds were building to Nimbus and I was glad we weren't where all this shit started, the Straits of Florida between Key West and Havana, Cuba.

Carl came outside to join me and I told him I was thinking about two things; how I could connect with my ebony acquaintance Sara again, and how the hell could we get a sample of the coffee from our sister ship, "Café-Negro." Yes, I'd taken note of the name just prior to boarding early this morning. A fitting name, given its hull was black and the damn thing was filled with coffee.

We both said, "Forget it." Let's get another nap and get up and go look for Sara and Margarita again this evening. We each went to our separate beds to mull over what just happened at the Padron Plantation?

We got some three hours of "shuteye" and got up to make coffee again. We both expressed we would like to see Sara and Margarita; not so much for sex, but rather have companionship with someone other than each other.

We shit, showered and shaved, then put on our glad rags (classic Cuban, vertically pleated, white, untucked shirt on top of Levi's). Ready to roll, we headed to the Jeep. The Restauranté San José was only a short distance away and we were eager to have a drink, look for the girls and escape from the saga of the coffee beans.

Dinners were being served. We got a nice table and decided on a good cut of beef and a salad, especially since we both had had Florida lobster the last time. After ordering, I went to the bar and asked if he remembered us and the girls we left with. He remembered all of us. He said those girls were BFF's and only occasionally came in, they usually just to have a couple of drinks at the bar and leave. He thought Sara's last name was Sonata and didn't know Margarita's last name.

We ate a great steak, had Crème Brûlée and a nice Taylor Fladgate Port. Well satisfied, we headed for the bar, but still no girls. If this kept up, I'd have to resort to the phonebook. Did they even have phonebooks in Trinidad, Cuba? Yes, they did, the bartender said. We ordered our drinks, Glenlivet and water for me and a Bacardi and coke for Carl.

After the second round, I decided to look up Sara in the phonebook. No payphone here, just a phone at the end of the bar (the restaurant's) and a phonebook nearby. Pepe, the bartender that I'd spoken to earlier, gladly brought me the phonebook and I eagerly thumbed by the K's and M's to get to S. There were five Sonata's and who knew which one, since Sara was not to be found. Pepe didn't know if she was married, lived with parents or relatives, or what. I was at an impasse, two impasses in one day, one about Pascal Padron and the other about Sara Sonata. Oh well, it is what it is, I thought.

One more was enough to prompt a return to Casa Morales and more sack time. We were both exhausted, well-fueled, full, and hit the hay.

I awoke at 3 a.m., probably because we'd gotten up early to investigate the "Café Negro," and because I had a revelation about how to get the coffee sample from it. We needed to get some black (flat black) paint to paint the inflatable, the motor, everything. A black wetsuit was also required. In addition, we needed a hole drill bit (1 ½ inch diameter) and a battery-operated drill, and heavy-duty batteries (one or two extra) in case drilling was tough. Also needed, a rubber gasketed Mason jar to contain the sample. I figured the Mason jar, drill, batteries, wetsuit, drill bit and spray paint were all available locally at the local la Ferretería or hardware store.

My plan was to spray paint the entire inflatable boat, motor and everything; including chrome enhancements to render it almost invisible at night. At least I hoped so.

We would anchor in the dark far enough away to avoid radar detection. I would enter the water after anchoring, swim submerged up to the bow of the "Café Negro," and drill a 1 ½ inch hole above the waterline and hope that coffee would pour out, since it had appeared that the forward two-thirds of the vessel was an empty hull filled with nothing but coffee. I would carry a sack with the Mason jar to carefully store the coffee, uncontaminated, and extra batteries for the drill as the fiberglass hull of that model was thick, probably three quarters of an inch thick or more.

Since I would only go to the bow of the boat, I was sure that the motion alarms would not go off.

"Sounds like a plan," Carl said. Thank God we had been there before and knew about the radar, motion sensors and security guards. Hopefully, nothing new or unknown would surface.

Tonight, or early tomorrow morning would be as good as any to go for it.

Thinking ahead to analysis, I called Jack Warner (my friend with the FBI that used their equipment to enhance the photo I took from one of the intruders that boarded our boat at sea). Jack said that there was certainly no reason to be so secretive about plain old coffee. He gave me an address in Washington to send the coffee to. He'd have it analyzed for everything since we didn't know what to look for; explosives, drugs, poison, Gnomes, bacteria, chemical agents. We knew one result we'd get – caffeine!

We anticipated going to bed early, in order to get up at about 2 a.m. and get to the "Café Negro" about 3 a.m. Perfect, with only a sliver of moon showing last night. I still had a desire to find Sara, even if I couldn't see her tonight. So I went to see if Concetta Morales, the owner's wife, could loan me a telephone book or at least let me copy down five numbers. I asked her if she knew any of the Sonatas in or around Trinidad. She didn't. I wrote down the five Sonata numbers and went back to our bungalow to make some calls.

I struggled to come up with an approach on the phone, not knowing whether Sara was even married or not? I had gotten the distinct impression that she wasn't married by her straight forward demeanor. At this point, I really hoped she was single. I decided to go with telling whomever answered the phone that I had found some keys and the feminine fob had the initials SAS. A bartender had suggested that they would probably belong to a woman called Sara Sonata. So, I was calling to return her keys.

The first two phone calls were fruitless, but the third hit pay dirt. I called and her distinctive voice said, "Hola, En qué te puedo ayudar?" Instantly relieved, I said, "Sara, is that you?" She said, "Yes, Pablo baby, it's me." I said, "I've called all over Cuba to see if I could find you again. Don't get me wrong, I just felt obligated. You were a wonderful diversion from some of the strange developments on my trip to your country." She said, "Thanks, I wondered why I didn't tell you where to find me, or given you a phone number, or something. You too were a nice diversion."

"That's a relief, I didn't know if you were married, in a relationship, or anything; except that there was really something, a connection." I said, "Is there some way I can see you again?" She said, "Sure." I told her that I would be turning in early tonight because Carl and I had an engagement early in the morning, but maybe tomorrow night? She said, "Maybe, call me tomorrow evening about 5 o'clock." "Alright then," I jubilantly responded.

As planned, we hit the hay at 8 p.m. But as one might guess, we couldn't get to sleep quickly at such an early hour, but we must have dozed off as the alarm went off at 2 a.m.

I shook Carl and quickly made coffee; ironically, my favorite, "Café Negro." I had a few gulps, climbed into pants, donned a sweatshirt and that was it; everything else was already at the inflatable's hiding place and I had a bag full of paint, wetsuit, drill, 1 ½ inch drill bit, Mason jar, and extra batteries.

We dragged ourselves off to the Jeep and proceeded to the site.

Got there, dragged out the inflatable, scuba gear and gas can. Sprayed the entire boat, motor and everything with quick drying flat black paint. If some paint came off on us, what-the-hell! Right! We jettisoned the craft and got in, the Honda started right up and we were off.

The moon was just a sliver of light, seas were a light chop; perfect for our mission. Southern winds prevailed for this time of year, and gently pushed inshore. We slowly cruised along to the proposed anchoring point and anchored.

I got my bag of goodies ready and entered the water. Carl would stay behind. The gentle waves were just right for this approach, even though I would swim underwater to avoid detection.

Got to the bow of the boat, starboard side. I tried to get aft of the anchor chamber, which would be like my boat. I retrieved the drill bit and started drilling a hole about one foot above the waterline. It was hard to get the bit centered and started, as the gentle waves still caused unsteady drilling. Once the bit was seated, things went quickly, although one battery change was required. The bit finally lost all resistance and as I retrieved it, coffee started pouring out, as planned. I got my Mason jar, filled it, carefully placed the rubber gasket, and sealed it. I then bagged everything and started back to Carl.

I surfaced for a moment after swimming for some fifty yards. All was quiet, no guards, guns or alarms. All was good. All I had to do now was get back to the boat, pull anchor and slip off.

I reached the boat, handed the bag with contents to Carl, got in, crawled up and headed back to the same old entry point. Our plan had worked without a hitch, so far. Now to get back and mail the coffee sample back to Jack in DC.

We got back to shore and decided to hide the black beauty and cover it with grass, as we had before; although another voyage was not anticipated.

We took everything we needed to the Jeep and headed again for Casa Morales. Carl asked on the way, "What if the 'Café Negro' sinks from your hole?" I said, "Only large waves could cause water to enter the 1 ½ inch hole and then it would take a very long time to fill the bow. Holes below the waterline were a different story." "Our hole will take a very long time to discover," I went on. It was still dark when we got back to our bungalow. Time to get a couple hours sleep before packaging and overnighting the beans to Jack.

Unlike last night, I was quickly fast asleep.

A couple of hours shuteye turned into five; but it was still only 10:30 a.m. and I awoke rested.

'Café Negro', once again as I tried to figure out just how to package the Mason jar. Lots of bubble wrap in a strong, correctly sized cardboard box should do it. After another cup of coffee, I told Carl I was going to find packaging and mail the package, overnight if possible.

I found bubble wrap, tape and a box at the Cuban equivalent of a K-Mart and wrapped the jar in the front seat of the Jeep. Then off to the Post Office. They said they could promise three days, but not overnight. It was what it was, so I paid up and asked them to put fragile on the box to:

> Jack Murray, Special Agent
> 935 Pennsylvania Avenue, NW
> Washington, D.C. 20535

Our interim mission had been accomplished and was in limbo until Jack got back with me.

I decided to go back to Casa Morales and take a nap to regenerate before calling Sara at 5 p.m. this evening to see if we could go out this evening. Carl was on his own! Set my cellphone alarm for 4:30 p.m.

Deep sleep jolted to an awake reality by an electronic alarm; 4:30 came quickly, but the shock of leaving REM sleep was too abrupt. Struggled to go make coffee for caffeine fix. Wow! Where was I? Okay, deep in the heart of Cuba looking for answers. A friendly fishing trip had turned into a nightmare, except for my meeting Sara. That encounter brought a glimmer of light in the darkness of this conundrum.

One cup almost cured my foggy perspective. I was really looking forward to being with Sara again. As I mentioned before, Carl was on his own. I started to make a second cup of dark magic that would help regain normal awareness. Cuba was a country lost in the fifties, even the phones were the circular numeric-dial type, right out of the 1950's.

I dialed her number, as it was five o'clock. It rang six times, but no response. Now what? I didn't know where she lived, so the only connection was via telephone. All I could do was wait a while and call again. No more coffee needed, I was acutely aware of what was going on.

I re-dialed her number – one ring, two rings, three rings and she answered. "Hola," she said. I said, "Hello Sara." She said, "Hola, guapo." I thought, what a short succinct way of saying "hello handsome," with a spicy Cuban flair. "Would you be available for dinner this evening?" I said. She said, "Absolutely." "Great, what time, and is Restauranté San José okay?" "Yes," she said, "Make reservations for 7 p.m. and we'll have a drink at the bar at 6:30 or so, okay." I said, "Perfecta mundo, see you then," and hung up.

Perfect, I had over an hour to get ready and get to the restaurant. I eagerly set out my white shirt and slacks on the bed, turned on the shower, stripped, and stepped into the shower. I then shaved, brushed my hair, deodorant, after shave, a shot of pheromone fragrance and off we go. Got dressed and told Carl, I was off to see the Princess of Trinidad. Got to Restauranté San José at about 6:20 p.m. Only one person was at the bar, a rough looking local guy that looked as though he'd just walked out of a field of coffee. He was quietly consuming his drink, while taking a peek at the new visitor (me).

Another five minutes passed and you guessed it, he sauntered over my way. "You just visiting?" he said. I wondered if this was just a chance meeting or if he was an undercover guy with Padron? I thought, he couldn't have known that I was coming here, but nevertheless I was a little skeptical after all we'd been through. I said, "Yes, just a visit. Un Tourista." He said, "Muy bien, Señor." "Disfruta tu estancia," he added. As rough as he looked, he was soft spoken and apparently innocent enough.

Sara walked in and said, "Como esta Señor Pablo." I said, "Muy bien Senorita Sonata." Enough Spanish; hell, Sara was more fluent in English than I was.

"It's very nice to see you again," I said, and added, "I felt like we really connected the other night." She concurred, "We did, yes we did." Connected, was a poor choice of words maybe, but that is exactly what we did, both emotionally and physically. "I'd like a lemon drop martini," she said. My scotch was still half full, so I called the bartender, "Una gota de limon martini, por favor."

We resumed conversation as though longtime friends. She wondered how long I would be here. I told her I just didn't know, which I didn't. I told her we were looking at a boat similar to mine for Carl. He loved my boat so much he wanted one built just like it. They don't make Hatteras like they did in the early eighties. She didn't know I had a boat in the first place. I said, "Yes, my boat is on the other side of the island at Marina

Hemingway. Carl and I were on a dual mission: to catch a big Blue Marlin and to come to Cuba to find a boat." We got another drink and transferred from the bar to a nice table by the window.

"Lobster," she said, "I love Florida Lobster." I went for deep sea scallops and a nice Cakebread Cellars Sauvignon Blanc. Pairs perfectly with lobster or scallops.

We talked, laughed, ate, drank and truly enjoyed our repast. We paid and moved back to the bar for a nightcap. I ordered Taylor Fladgate 20 and Sara ordered Tia Maria. She asked again, "When you leave, will you come back? I'm starting to like you a lot." "I understand, and I feel the same way," I whispered. I just couldn't figure out how in the world this woman hadn't been married, no children, no dramatic ties, a nice job, and was free and beautiful.

We went to her place this time and just had apple juice and talked somemore. Soon we were under the covers of her bed and loving it, and one another.

An orgasmic exchange ensued. Wow! This is what sensuality is supposed to be; intimate copulation mixed with caring affection.

Spent, we both lie there thinking and drifting to another dimension.

And then there was light gently shining through her curtain. I carefully and gently got out of bed, while she was still sleeping, and looked for coffee. Funny how my life was starting to completely revolve around coffee. Who knew?

I found the coffee maker, the old drip kind, but I'd been there before. Sara woke to the aroma of Columbian java and joined me in the kitchen. No regrets, and a unique compatibility prevailed as the sun shown bright at the kitchen window above the sink. A beautiful day was just evolving, it seemed.

We talked while she got bacon and eggs from the fridge. "Queda PaPas?" she said. I said, "Ce." So she sliced a potato in slices like three times the thickness of potato chips and boiled them. Bacon fried, then the potatoes went from the pot to the bacon grease. Scrambled eggs followed and we enjoyed a beautiful breakfast.

We kissed and I told her I'd call her later, if that was okay. She replied, "Abso-fucking-lutely." I left walking on air and got in the Jeep, which needed petrol.

Got to a gas station and struck up a conversation with the attendant. I asked if he knew anything about the Padron Plantation. He replied, "Muy misterioso, me compadre." "There's a lot of speculation, but I don't think it's legal," he said. "Nobody knows, but the local workers are all scared to death and won't say anything about what's going on there; except that they raise and sell coffee." This guy just strengthened the speculation of something really criminal or egregious going on at the Padron Plantation.

Got back to the bungalow and just sat thinking about all that had transpired over the past week. Unbelievable! I was thinking, due to circumstances, I'd just have to wait on Jack's coffee analysis. Carl came in and immediately asked, "What the hell happens now, Paul?" I said, "I don't know what happens now, Carl. I guess we'll just wait on Jack Murray, won't we." "Maybe you want to go back to the main gate and deal with guards and guns!" Carl said. I said, "Not really, I just could not think of any other approach; above, under, sideways, head-on? How could we find out anymore than we knew already? The Padron Plantation raised coffee, and something apparently very profitable was going on as well. The laboratory that we found, the money, the Hatteras filled with coffee, and an extremely well-guarded operation." This wasn't a small insignificant operation. We had stumbled onto something big!

We agreed that there wasn't anything else we could do to attain more information on Patron, at this point, so we would just wait for Jack's feedback.

There really wasn't anything keeping us here. We had done everything we could to find information on Padron. The only thing, really, that might make me want to stay was Sara. She had a job at a local shopping center. I toyed with the idea of asking her to come with us but decided to just tell her that I had to go back to my boat and stop renting the Morales bungalow. Yes, we'd just go back to the BFB! People always ask what those initials stand for and if they're children. I say, "Big Fishing Boat." But if it's adults, it's the "Big Fucking Boat!"

I decided to call Sara and tell her of our latest plan. I called her phone and got her. She was expecting a client and couldn't talk too long, so I just said, "Carl and I really need to go back to our boat in Havana." She said, "No, Pablo, I was just getting to know you." I said, "I know, I know, but the boat needs checking on. There could be a faulty bilge pump, an electrical problem or something.

There's always something with a big fucking boat!" "I understand," she said, "but will you come back?" Havana and Marina Hemingway was about three and half hours away by the shortest route possible. I said, "Yes, I can come back, but you could come to the BFB as well." "Okay," she said, "You do what you have to do, but this isn't over between us." I concurred and said, "Goodbye for now."

Carl had been listening, so he knew what I had told Sara. He didn't have the same feelings for Margarita, but understood that I really cared for Sara.

We got our belongings, put them in the Jeep and I told Mrs. Morales that we had to leave and paid her.

We got in the Jeep and started the trip back to Marina Hemingway. We got on Highway 12 to Cienfuegos. It was a nice drive, scenic to say the least. We would go over central Cuba, unlike our trip to Trinidad, and we filled up in Cienfuegos and got lunch at a small café called, "Comedero Casita." The Chicken taquitos looked good, with refried beans and rice; and they were.

Quite a haul back to the marina, but we kept driving and finally made it; parked the Jeep, got our stuff and walked back to the BFB, which was still floating just where we left it. After a quick inspection, all seemed shipshape. There was one problem, however, the incoming 50-amp power still only registered 200 volts on the voltmeter gage on our breaker panel.

I asked a neighbor if he'd noticed the incoming voltage and he said, "Yes, it's always this low, but nothing we can do about it." The same story I'd gotten from Enrique, the dockmaster, the day we got there.

It was good to be back in familiar territory, as the BFB was my home. I started up the generator and mains to make sure everything was A-OK. I'd gotten into the habit of starting the generator and mains every couple of weeks just to keep up. All was well on the BFB.

It took us four hours to get here and already I wanted to go back for Sara. But no, I was really glad to be back and so far, no Federales, Policía or the like had tracked us down. We only had a few problems that might draw attention: Killing two apparent Cubans on our boat and casting them off with weights to the sea, two fights with broken bar equipment and one seriously injured smartass, trespassing or more on a very large Plantation. Well, that was enough!

Carl and I decided we'd just chill for this evening, but maybe go fishing tomorrow. I went down the dock and Captain Glen (from the first day here, a tournament Captain) asked if I'd found a boat yet. I told him, "Maybe, there was a nice one just out of Trinidad across the Island." "How much," he said. I told him "500K," as it was an easier thing to say. "Alright then," he said. I told him I was just going down to see if the marina had any Ballyhoo. He said, "I've got some for you." "They've been frozen a couple of days, but should be good," he went on. "My crew only uses fresh if possible, just to improve our chances," he said. "A couple dozen do ya?" he said. I said, "Yes Sir Captain."

What a nice guy, I thought. I walked down the dock a little farther, saying hello where appropriate. At the Marina office, I thought I'd better get back and put these "hoo" in the bait freezer in the cockpit.

Got rods and reels; 50W Penn should be perfect for sailfish, tuna, etc., unless we hooked a Marlin (80's would be needed then). On second thought, I decided to get a couple of 80's, if we saw a "free jumper" or something? I took the gear to the cockpit and checked lines, tension, guides and drags. Carl joined me with two Corona's, and we turned on some Reggae to round out this prep period.

Two new members from one of the boats stopped by and asked if we would be going out tomorrow. "Yes," we said simultaneously. "We went yesterday and caught two Wahoo trolling deep at about 20 feet," one said. Okay, Wahoo were super fish, to fight or consume. "Thanks," I said. I'd have to get the downrigger out and rig it. We sure didn't want to miss out on Wahoo! We could run one downrigger line for Wahoo and another five for whatever surface level fish there might be. My recollection was that Cuban rules only allowed six lines trolling anyway. I'd have to check with the dockmaster to make sure we went by all Cuban fishing regulations. We sure didn't want to break any Cuban rules, nor did we (ha, ha, after killing two of what we thought were their countrymen).

I went down to see Enrique, the dockmaster. Enrique said he would collect the $100 for our boat to fish. I gave him the $100, but he didn't give me a license or anything. He said, "I write down your boat's name in my register and if questioned, tell them I have your fee and your license number is 669, okay?" "Muy Bien," I said and left. Unorthodox licensing, but everything else here had been unorthodox, as well.

I walked back to the BFB and Carl was finishing the rigging for our trip. A fishing trip would be a welcome intermission in our Cuban adventure. We both got a Glenlivet and water and struck up a Cohiba, purchased by Carl from the Marina as soon as we had gotten there. Carl had also picked up some grass while I was doing other things and a toke or two was enough to cap off our scotch and cigars.

A beautiful evening and the sunset, gorgeous! "Red sky at night, Sailor's delight." Tomorrow should be good fishing and reasonable seas, we thought. Some chips, frescas and frijoles, and more scotch rounded out the evening in the cockpit on the BFB.

We went to our beds; I slept in the master suite (since it was my boat) and Carl slept in the guest quarters. I set the alarm for 6 a.m. to get an early start. I know, I know, fish eat when they're hungry and go where food is probable, independent of time, unless light is required.

The alarm went off and I got up, relieved myself, put on clothes and went to the engine room to turn the heaters on. Many people have told me that in this climate that's unnecessary, but I've always thought that a happy diesel is a hot diesel and why wear out the starters and drain batteries when engine heaters are installed and working. Went back in the galley and started coffee. We had Cuban pastries that Mrs. Morales had given us earlier. A cup and pastries, in between carrying all the rods and reels to the cockpit. I attached the downrigger and attached the lead ball with a fin to the stainless-steel line. Carl stuck a post-it note to the GPS, which had coordinates he'd gotten from Captain Glen earlier. It looked like we should head for a location called "La Valle" or "The Valley." Keys in the ignition, blowers on, generator running and switched from shore power; all that remained were the lines. The way the wind was blowing the stern lines came off first, then the port spring lines and port bow line, and finally the starboard springs and bow. We were off! The channel out of the marina was smooth and markers were very visible, although the sun wasn't quite up yet.

The quest, the excitement, the anticipation. Fishing was almost as good as sex. The hope to entice an aquatic species to eat the lure you placed out and drag behind the boat is exhilarating. You never know what might eat your lure.

The trip out was great; one to two-foot waves, 8 knots, SW wind. The wind in our face at 18 knots was invigorating, to say the least. As we went, Carl and I lowered both outriggers. I put the BFB on autopilot and checked the engine room; the water pumps to see if they were cool to the touch, inlet valves and strainers to detect leaks, and the engine instruments to assure oil pressures and temperatures. All were good. Life was good.

We reached "The Valley" area and slowed to 7 knots. Carl had readied the outriggers, trailing two lures on each. The downrigger was loaded and lowered, and the center-rigger was clipped and sent back about a hundred yards. The water looked "FISHY"! That sounds crazy, but there is a seventh sense in play here. I looked for any sign of life; any birds swooping down to pluck a small fish out of the waves, a floating board or piece of debris under which a fish could find shade (as the sun had come up and was brilliant), a grass-line formed by underwater currents that also gave shade; a Frigate bird gliding over the water high in the sky. The Frigate was a great thing to see because their laser like sight could see fish under the surface. Upon spying a likely meal, the Frigate would fold his wings and dive at a high velocity to seize its prey.

I caught a glimpse of birds feeding and confirmed their presence with my Simrad radar. The radar's sensitivity was superb, and feeding birds prompted small blips on the screen. I approached the area and sure enough, birds were feeding on something, and that something would attract bigger somethings. And there you go!

Perfect. On the first pass the left outrigger snapped and the reel screamed. "Fish on," Carl screamed, "Fish on!" I kept the boat at 7 knots to keep tension on the line that had been attacked. The reel roared! It was still in the rod holder when I took the boat out of gear. Carl took the reel out of the holder and pulled, the reel continued screaming. Soon the spool of line on the reel stopped and Carl applied a steady strong pressure. This fish was hooked! This fish was big! This was what it's all about! I put the BFB on autopilot, at minimum rpm and climbed down the ladder to hurriedly get the other lines in out of the way. I pulled the outriggers up to just dangle lures above the water, cleared the others and scrambled back up the ladder to concentrate on the direction of Carl's line into the water.

Carl applied steady pressure, but no line came in. Carl pulled back, sat in the fighting chair and clipped his back pad to the reel. The reel was already attached to a small, heavy line to save it if the rod and reel was pulled out of his hands. The fight was on! Steady pressure, steady pressure, and no line came in. Carl said, "Oh boy, this is a big boy!"

After about fifteen minutes, Carl made a little progress. He retrieved a little line and started the "Pull Up, Reel Down" scenario. The only way to make progress on a big fish was to pull up on the rod and at the apex, lower the reel and reel in while lowering. This is repeated until something gives, either you get the fish to the boat or you don't.

I had to back down on the target, taking note of the line's direction. There was so much line out that the fish could be pulling down in the water at one place and it was in a much different location, as was confirmed when Carl's fish blasted out of the water, maybe eight hundred yards away. "Marlin, Marlin," Carl shouted. Yes, it looked like the "Man in the Blue Suit" to me as well. We settled in for the fight.

I engaged the appropriate engine, in reverse, while focusing on the line's orientation. The wind had picked up slightly and whitecaps were forming.

Carl was making some progress, but his groaning didn't really help. Keeping tension on a big fish was exhausting, as your arms get tired and perspiration appeared. Backing, fighting, pulling, reeling, resting, reeling . . . the fight went on. We were about an hour in when, after jumping a half-dozen times the fish went down, sounding like a submarine locomotive. Carl had made a lot of progress before the fish sounded and simultaneously, the line went back out and the reel screamed as it had at the beginning of the battle. "Oh brother," I said, encouraging Carl to keep it tight, as now I had to go forward to try and keep in front of the Marlin so the line wouldn't be chewed up in the prop or cut by the rudders.

Slowly, ever so slowly, the line started coming in again. The rod was bent into an upside down "C" shape and thank God for graphite rods that would withstand such torture. "Pull up, Reel down," was routine. Carl said, "I need water, Paul."

I didn't have water, but a Gatorade would suffice. I took the BFB out of gear, climbed down the ladder, got a water out of the cooler to give Carl a drink. I held the bottle to his mouth and although a little shaky, he managed to swallow. "Sweet Jesus," he said. "More," he uttered. After a few swigs he thanked me with a facial gesture and head shaking.

I climbed back up the ladder and reoriented the direction of the line, bumped the boat forward, and now Carl was gaining on the fish. Up and down the rod went, and slowly but surely the line was recovered. Full spool restoration was the goal, but Carl was fatigued. He kept tension with his back and legs, while trying to rest his arms. "My arms are on fire," he said. "Try to relax, Carl, you're making great progress," I said.

An hour and a half had passed, as I glanced at my Rolex. I took note of our position, made a 360° turn to make sure nothing or another boat was approaching. All was good, we were alone fighting a big fucking Marlin! The sun was bright and it glistened in the water's reflection. What a gorgeous day, I thought. It doesn't get any better than this. Yes, this experience is a close second to the thrill of sex.

Carl kept pulling, on his fourth wind, so to speak. The line kept coming; when it went aft and up. The beautiful beast jumped again, flailing to rid itself of the thing pulling on its mouth. Carl let the line go slack, as the behemoth aired itself. Sometimes, if you pull when he's out of the water flailing about, you can pull the hook.

After the last jump, Carl was really making progress. Slowly, steadily, line came on the reel. Coming, coming; we could see the leader about fifteen feet ahead of the big Blue. "Come on in Buddy", we won't hurt you, we just want to get you in and momentarily defeat you. The swivel was now at the roller bearing at the end of the rod. I went down as Carl got out of the chair after unclipping himself. He walked backwards to get the monster close to the gunnel and I grabbed, carefully grabbed, his bill. Always to the side, I said to myself, as a great fish like this can flip his tail and the bill would go right through you!

We had it! I couldn't pull him up, but Carl sat the rod down and took several pictures with his cellphone. What a grand specimen! His eyes staring at me as I tried to remove the hook from the side of his mouth. Got it out. A couple more pictures with Carl holding his catch, and I went to the helm and engaged at 500 rpm (as slow as it will go). Carl held the monstrous demon in the water to flush water through his gills. After a little while, life and strength returned to the beast, and Carl let him swim off to contemplate the thrill of what just happened.

It was amazing! We had just been trolling for about five minutes, saw the birds and hooked him immediately. First catch, "Winner, Winner, Chicken Dinner," I said. Carl agreed, "What a fight, I'm exhausted. Can we go back now?" I said, "Sure, how could we top this catch."

I put the Simrad Autopilot curser on the Sea Buoy and engaged the throttle. Up-planing at 20 knots, and life was good.

Carl drank two more Gatorades while resting in the fighting chair, for a change. The rooster tail was large and shimmering and a "vena contracta" was formed in the wake.

We headed in the channel at Marina Hemingway feeling that Earnest couldn't have done or felt any better when he entered this very channel after catching a Marlin, or maybe two. Carl hoisted a Marlin flag and we triumphantly docked our old hat.

Hell, it was only 10:30 a.m. but after shutting down, tying up, and getting shore power, we got two Coronas with Lime and we're exhausted after our short day's performance. Such a contrast from the horrific nightmare we'd been through a few days ago, and the torment of not knowing the exact motivation of those two deceased marauders that boarded us at sea. We knew one thing, it all revolved around the sister ship "Café Negro" and the "Coffee Cartel," as we began to call it.

Another Corona and it was almost time for lunch. A proud walk down the pier and some saying, "Good Day, Huh." "We saw your flag." "How big was it?" I said, "A grander!" "Here, look at these pictures," I said. I showed the monster, not believing we would have had such a great morning trip. It seemed to make everything okay. In fact, a hell of a lot more than okay!

We went back to the BFB after walking the pier and gloating a bit, to take a nap. What a glorious experience, I thought, as I lie there. Around and around, the mind's video replayed the hookup, fighting, Gatorade gulp, backing down, diving and landing of the biggest fish I'd ever snagged.

I slept almost three hours and it appeared that Carl was still cutting some zz's. I got up, made a cup of coffee, and sat on the salon lounge. The extremes of life, I thought, all in the past week from horrifically bad to spectacularly good.

Then my thoughts drifted to Sara. That beautiful bronze babe. It would take four hours to get to her, but it was tempting. I didn't want her to think I was trying too hard. Leave her alone, I thought, "Absence makes the heart grow fonder." But my heart was certainly fond enough already, beyond fond.

I turned on some Antonio Carlos Jobim and chilled, playing pool on my cellphone with gamers from all over the globe. Each player was rated after so much play and it was rewarding to win over someone with a number much bigger than mine. I took my Bose speakers and iPad up on the flybridge to chill further, while enjoying the breeze and ocean air.

The sun was gradually edging its way to the western horizon, when Captain Glen came by and congratulated me on the grander. I said, "Thanks, Captain. Yes, it was amazing and thanks for giving us the "hoo." "One of those babies hooked our big boy!" I went on. "It's not often that you can go out in the morning, catch a grander and be back before noon. "Finest kind!" he said.

It was again time for a toddy of some kind. A Macallan 25 would fit the bill, exactly. The sun was getting closer and closer to the horizon, indicating another great day tomorrow; but what could be better than today, this morning in fact. The scarlet sky shined. Whispers of red, cherry, ruby were brushed through an orange canvas. God's beauty was everywhere, but this sky was outstanding.

Time for bed. No alarm tonight!

The next morning was calm, clear and serene. Nothing like making coffee and going back up on the bridge to wake up with God and coffee. A couple of fishing boats were making ready for today's challenge. You never know what will happen when you get out there, the thrills in the quest! That's why I say, "It's all about the journey."

I consumed my cup of coffee and walked down the dock wishing the fishermen and women good luck. One of the boat's mates on the "On Course," said, "No one could do better than you did yesterday!" I thanked them and strolled along the now bustling marina, talked a bit more while passing by, and shuffled back to the BFB to make another cup of coffee.

Back up to the bridge and the pure solitude. Thoughts darted between boat maintenance and Sara. I really needed to check battery water levels and the hydraulic reservoir level. The BFB was equipped with eight batteries at 32-volts DC and ten batteries at 12-volts for all the users. Engine startup, instruments, lights, satellite phone, cameras and radios. Almost all require distilled water to fill them to operating level. After the second cup of coffee, I went to the engine room to check and top off the batteries. All went well, until I ran out of distilled water.

I walked down the dock to the ship's store, located adjacent to the dockmaster's office. Surprisingly, they did have gallons of distilled water, so I got three and trudged back to the engine room and finished filling all batteries.

Carl joined me as I finished with the batteries and asked, "Did you fill the main engine water?" I said, "No, I didn't." He proceeded to fill each one. Carl checked oil and transmission levels and all was good. The only thing remaining was to clean the saltwater inlet strainers on each engine, generator and air conditioners. All were partially plugged with seaweed, small barnacles and flora and fauna. Strainers were all cleaned and replaced. Our checklist done, we decided to walk the docks and maybe get lunch and a cerveza or two.

Boat owners and fishermen have a common bond, like motorcyclists or antique car owners. A mutual respect borne out of symbiotic challenges. We all had to fight the corrosivity of saltwater, the growth on the underwater hulls, the pumps, etc. We all knew what the other had gone through in just routine boat maintenance and/or fishing challenges.

Jack called, "I expedited analysis on your coffee and you won't believe what they found." "Your sample was not contaminated and analysis accuracy was at 98.6%," he said. "A curious variation of cocaine molecules was present. Cocaine was normally a simple covalent combination of carbon, hydrogen and nitrogen. The basic elements of life as we know it," he went on. "Instead of 17 carbon atoms and 21 hydrogen atoms, your coke had 18 carbon, 24 hydrogen and the normal nitrogen oxide component, NO_4," he said. "This variation on cocaine promotes absorption characteristics, according to the research doctors here, so the cocaine is easily absorbed by the coffee beans and easily released when the coffee is brewed, as then demonstrated in the lab," Jack said. "Thank God you had a large sample, which allowed multiple analyses to be performed, as well as simply brewing coffee." "The molecular alteration of the cocaine also made it slightly more addictive," he went on. "We've concluded that this substance, when absorbed by the coffee bean and those beans are consumed as coffee, that the consumer will be instantly addicted to two components, caffeine and cocaine. Interestingly, all addictive compounds end with the suffix INE, but I digress," Jack said.

"If these beans are distributed worldwide, the world would be addicted and demand this brand of coffee only," he said. "Coffee is universally consumed as a morning stimulant and the demand for this coffee would be intense, potentially bringing the entire planet to its knees due to the altered coffee." "If enough of these modified coffee beans could be produced, the world would become hopelessly addicted and the producer would become not only extremely wealthy but, in essence, would control the world through addiction," he added. "You've stumbled on to the biggest threat the world may have ever known! My associates at the FBI are in awe of the magnitude of this threat and all are convinced that it must be stopped in its tracks," Jack added.

"Wow," I said. "I have the feeling that there are surely other operations in nearby countries, say; Dominican Republic, Cuba, Guatemala, Nicaragua and on and on," I said. "What does the FBI think?" I asked Jack. Jack said, "We just got the analysis done this morning, so the appropriate personnel directors have not been notified, but this is BIG!" "I predict that an extremely large number of strike forces would be assembled and all deployed to assess the extent of this threat," Jack said. "My supervisors want you recruited to lead the group there in Cuba," he said. "You must help us eradicate this threat to mankind," he said. "I will serve my country and the moral ethics within my soul," I said. "Keep in close touch; I'll be sending you a special phone with built in encryption."

"We'll be able to talk freely without fear of detection," he said. "If other sites are reality, I'll have to arrange access approval from the respective governments. Given the reason, it might be relatively easy to get their permission to conduct raids or interventions, but some governments are difficult at times. We'll see?", Jack added.

I had felt this nefarious operation was bad, but the potential threat of world domination via coffee addiction was breathtaking. I feared that the Padron Plantation was only one of many addictive bean operations.

On reflection, those two intruders that boarded my boat must have been looking for beans? They must have thought that we were the "Café Negro" (Padron's Hatteras) and knew of the Plantation's operating methods. Vessels of all types could transport beans everywhere, virtually undetected. A task force sufficiently armed could easily shut down the Padron Plantation operation, but how many others were there? They must all be stopped and that was not possible until their locations were determined. I'd have to let Jack and the FBI worry about all that, since I would have my hands full here in Cuba.

Carl and I could not believe that we had stumbled into this; maybe the biggest threat to mankind that has ever been known! The unique simplicity of altered coffee beans that could dominate the world through addiction was awesome! I asked Carl if he would help me on the mission that Jack had assigned and he said, "Sure. Hell, I've been on this mission since we killed those two marauders two weeks ago." From fishermen to FBI law enforcement agents in a flash, I thought. I wasn't sure, however, how Jack would feel about Carl's recruitment? Where do we go from here? How will they (the FBI) determine just how pervasive this threat is? Capturing Pascal Padron and subsequent interrogation might or might not be successful. That may well be the next step, but strategy would be left to the FBI, CIA and potentially others.

Carl and I just sat in awe. This was nuts! It was not only bigger than us, it was the biggest hostile action ever undertaken, especially for profit. At least the profit motive must have prompted the chemistry and atomic mechanics to achieve enough dependence on a product that people couldn't live without it.

The profit motive was erroneous, as world dependency would be a catastrophe and create a demand for this coffee that would be impossible to satisfy. Utter chaos would ensue if people couldn't get their coffee. Pandemonium would prevail and cause as much destruction as the asteroid that hit the earth and wiped out the dinosaurs some sixty-five million years ago.

No wonder guards and security electronics protected the Padron Plantation. We'd just sit tight until Jack got back to us. It was way past lunch time by now, so we went to the bar and grill for Tapas and Cerveza. One beer and my thoughts turned away from modified cocaine laced coffee to Sara; imagine that. After the second beer and several taquitos and salsa, I thought I should call Sara and see what she was doing. I knew she was still probably at the shopping mall. She wasn't shopping. She had told me before that she was the Mall Manager at the "Galleria Commercial Universo" in Trinidad. I know she was probably at work but if I didn't call now, it wouldn't be possible to drive over there this evening. I called and a man answered. "Galleria Commercial, puedo ayudarte." "Puedo hablar con Sara Sonata, por favor," I told him after a few moments to compose my answer. "Un momento," he said.

The next voice I heard was like a bird, "Si, Que Quedos?" "You," I said. She laughed and said, "Hi there Pablo." "You got back to Havana safely?" she went on. "Yes, and we had a great fishing trip, caught a big Blue Marlin," I said. "I know you're working, but are you busy this evening?" I said. After a moment, she said, "No, I'm not busy. What did you have in mind?" I said, "Well, if I drove over there to take you to dinner, could I stay the night and drive back here tomorrow?" Again, hesitation, "Sure, why the quick trip?" "There have been developments, I'll tell you about it tonight, but I will have to get back here. I just wanted to be with you," I said. "Great, what time will I see you?" she said. "It's 2:30 now, I could get ready and be on the road by 3:30; say 7:30 p.m. there?" I said. "Perfecta mundo. Do you want to try a different restaurant, we have several good ones? I'll make reservations at "Crafters,' my favorite, for 7:45 or so," she said. "Okay, see you at 7:30 p.m.," I said.

Almost as high as I was getting the Blue, I started to get ready. A shower, different clothes, a shot of afternoon coffee (again, the coffee), and I told Carl what I was going to do. He said, "I'll just screw around here and maybe go to a bar or something. You never know, I might get lucky myself!" he added.

I got in the Jeep and took off. At least the road would be familiar to me and expedite my return to Trinidad. As I neared Guanabacoa, I thought . . . was there anything I could or should do for Jack Warner since I would be free tomorrow morning and near the Padron Plantation? So, I called Jack on the cellphone. "Jack Warner," he answered. I said, "Jack, this is Paul. I'm going back to Trinidad this afternoon and wondered if there was anything you wanted me to do, since I'd be close to the Padron Plantation?" I said. Jack said, "Why are you going back to Trinidad, Paul?" I said. "Because I've got a girlfriend there, okay?" "Okay," he said. "We're sending a helicopter from the Naval Air Station in Key West to take pictures; infrared, thermographic, Schmidt reflex, Rapatronic; the whole nine yards of the latest photographic technology. No, there's nothing you should do and don't call me again till you get the phone I sent you," he curtly replied. "Alrighty then," I said, and hung up.

On second thought, I probably shouldn't have called him until I got his special encrypted telephone. But, I was anxious to help. A little later, in Güines, I stopped for gas and bottled water. The guy at the counter said, "Treinta Cinco." "But the pump meter said thirty-one?" I said, "Esta pumpa say Trienta Uno?" "No," he said, "No bien Trienta Cinco, por favor!" I said, "Okay," and gave him thirty-five dollars. Hell, the bottle of water cost $3.00!?

It was a long drive, but it would be well worth it, so I drove on. The Jeep wasn't the best vehicle to drive a long distance on roads that had seen better days, and the shock absorbers had also been bumped 10,000 times, but onward. I thought about Jack's comment. I guess that all those cameras would be able to detect how many people were on the property, as well as buildings, etc. I really didn't know what they could ascertain from a flyover? How could they learn if and how many other similar operations there were? I thought that there was only one way and that was interrogation of the top people, or better yet, Padron himself. A team of Special Forces would have to gain entry and carefully secure the complex without harming Pascal Padron. Waterboarding and enhanced interrogation techniques were forbidden in our country but when saving the world was at stake, it would be stupid not to employ all ways possible to learn pertinent information. A dilemma, but one that had to be dealt with! And it had to be dealt with in short order.

The area after Cienfuegos was beautiful. I kept driving and thinking . . . this situation was beyond horrible but thank God I had my fishing and Sara to keep my sanity. The countryside was captivating and I pulled over on a hill to stop and appreciate the view. Gorgeous, to say the least. I took several cellphone pictures. I couldn't stop long, as I had a dinner date with an ebony angel.

I got back in the Jeep and plodded on. I finally got to Trinidad, but didn't know where Crafters Steak House was? I had to stop and ask. "A dónde Crafters Steak Casa?" I asked a man on the corner. "Paya," he said, while pointing straight ahead on this street. Fortunately for me I finally saw the sign. It was 7:37, so Sara should already be inside. I parked the damned Jeep (my butt and back hurt) and walked toward the entrance. It was a strange Gothic design, but a great looking place inside.

I was greeted by a host and I said, "I'm looking for an ebony angel." He said, "Muy Bien, Vamous Paya," and walked off. He went into a room for two and there she was. She looked better and better each time I saw her anew. Black hair glistening in the candlelight; the white of her brown eyes, as bright as quartz next to gold. "Cientata, por favor," the host said. "Mucho Gracious," I said, staring at Sara's bronze, unblemished face. "How was your trip over?" Sara said. "Okay, I think I got ripped off at the gas station in Güines and my back and bottom hurt, but other than that, it went fine," I said. "I'm glad you came, Pablito," she said. "You are stunning," I said, as I moved my hand to hers. Her skin was soft and subtle. She must bathe in Olive oil, I thought. "I guess it's steak," I said. She said, "Yes, this is the best steak house in Cuba, I think." "I'm going for the filet, 8 oz.," I said. She, on the other hand said, "It's a ribeye for me." I still couldn't help feeling very fortunate because Sara had not been married, wasn't in a relationship, had no children, was extremely intelligent, no ties to bind her locally and was the most beautiful woman God ever created!

The waiter came and asked if we would like a drink? We did and Sara ordered her "Lemon Drop" and I ordered a Macallan 25," feeling like a King next to a queen. The waiter left and we talked. "What were you going to tell me about?" she said. "I think you said there were developments." "Yes, developments!" I said. "I used to work for the FBI and an old acquaintance there called me and wants me back on active duty," I continued. "There is a very big threat brewing," I said, thinking about the irony of saying brewing when coffee was the concern. "Yes," I said, and "It's right under your nose." "That Padron Plantation is causing great concern," I said. "I've known and all the locals know that something nefarious is going on there," she said. "There is absolutely no reason to heavily guard a coffee plantation, like they do," she added. "Yes, they are into drug addiction big time," I said. "The FBI and I are charged with stopping their threat of pervasive addiction to their coffee." She said, "Be careful, my dear, those people won't hesitate to kill you." "I'm just on hold, waiting for instructions from Jack, my superior at the FBI in D.C.," I said.

The waiter returned with two beautifully etched glass drinks. We saluted to each other and drank. Wow, the environment seemed to enhance the quality of this scotch, but without a doubt it was the best sip of whiskey I'd ever had. I also thought, she was the most beautiful and intelligent woman I'd ever had by my side.

We ordered a filet and ribeye, medium rare and went on talking. "What happens now," she said. "Well, as I mentioned, I'm on hold until I hear from Jack," I said. "I'm expecting delivery of an encrypted telephone so I can communicate without fear of detection by anyone hacking the airwaves," I said. "That's why I have to go back to the Marina tomorrow." "Okay, let's just enjoy the evening," she said. A small trio had started playing in the large dining area, adjacent to our secluded room.

They played Latin-like tunes, like Cal Tjader played. The guitar player was very good and it sounded like the unelectrified old style, 6-string, acoustic guitar. The band sounded great, probably because of the setting and the fact that I was sitting with an ebony angel.

The steaks came, looked amazing and after a taste, they were. Our eyes showed our appreciation for a great steak. A great filet, paired with smoked Gouda mac and cheese and asparagus, along with the Caymus Reserve 1985 that I'd ordered earlier. What a super supper! Ha, Ha, a play on words. But it was spectacular and the wine wonderful. It doesn't get better than this!

We finished the fine repast and I left a 25% tip for Alphonso, the waiter, and we were off to her place. On the way, she said, "Want to go listen to a great band with me?" I said, "Absolutely." So we went to a place called "Disco Ayala." It was a jumping place and the band great. They played reggae with a Cuban flare, maybe reggaetón. We both had a cocktail and enjoyed ourselves and the music.

There was a small spot for dancing. So when one song caught our attention, I knew I should ask her to dance. I just looked at her, got up, and she did too. We walked to the dance spot and began our shift and sway. Nice! "Easy, old guy," I thought. Yes, Sara was much younger than I but we seemed to be in sync. Neither of us seemed to have ulterior motives, so it was what it was. I put it in God's hands; we were brought together under his watch and loving arms. I was never a good dancer, although I had rhythm and had played drums earlier in my life. But I felt it tonight, and I think others did as well. It really didn't matter what others thought, my feelings were created by my mind only and not affected by others. Okay, back to shuffling and being with Sara.

We listened, danced, had another drink and left. We both drove our own vehicles since she and I drove to and met at Crafters Steak House. I followed her, in her '51 Chevy (ironically the same car my father bought me as my first car). But, again, I digress. We arrived at her casita and I parked behind her car.

We walked into her well-appointed, although small, living room. The kitchen was adjacent to the living room and we walked there. I sat at the kitchen counter while she asked if I wanted anything. "Just you," I replied. Well, maybe some water as well.

She said, "You know I'm really starting to care for you, don't you?" I replied, "Yes, I feel you and I you." "Well, I've had a little too much to drink; could we just go to bed and hold each other without anything else?" she said. I said, "Sure, I've had mucho scotches."

We went to her bed, hugged and fell off into a dream. Our relationship was beginning to be much more than sex, I thought. What better way to show her my affection than to lie next to her, unclothed, just sleeping. I woke up at 3 a.m. to go to the restroom, and quietly returned without flushing so that I didn't wake her.

I awoke again at 8:15 a.m., but Sara was gone again. Oh Shit! I forgot the entire time that she ran the Mall and would have to work today. Then I found a note on the kitchen counter. "I have to go to work," it said, and a postscript added, "My darling Pablo."

Okay, I was hooked now, just like the big marlin we caught the day before yesterday. I found some cereal and leche and had breakfast. I looked around her place, not sneaking, just wanting to get to know her better. There were pictures of her family. She was on the high school track team and boxed for the school. She had won a couple of trophies for boxing and I thought how could a soft, loving creature like this box? Her face was unblemished and her nose certainly hadn't been broken, like many boxers. She never ceased to amaze.

I went out to the Jeep and started on the long haul back to Hemingway Marina. I had a great night with Sara. This is going somewhere, I thought. The long drive was much longer this time, for some obvious reason. It's all good, I said to myself.

An uneventful trip and a hell of a long one came to an end when I reached the entrance to Hemingway Marina. It was 2:30 p.m. and I thought I'd get a nap when I got back to the BFB. No one was on the boat when I got there; I could only imagine what Carl was up to while I was gone.

Well, so far so good. I managed to get to the master suite and turn the air conditioner down. Next were the clothes and I pulled myself in bed and closed my eyes.

It was 5 o'clock when I woke up and I said to myself, "It's 5 o'clock somewhere." Thank goodness I got to take a nap; it seemed twice as long coming back as it was going.

I made a cup of coffee to wake up a little and walked out to the cockpit. Glancing around, I saw a note that I had missed coming in stuck on the ladder to the bridge. It said, "Package received for Paul." Okay, I thought, it must be the phone from Jack.

I walked down to the dockmaster's office and got the package. I walked back to the BFB and went inside before opening it. Yes, as I thought, it was a cellphone with an extra section plugged into the charge port, and it had a charge port on it. I proceeded to call Jack, as he was probably still at work. "Jack," I said, "I got your phone and what's next?" "Yes, Paul, thanks for waiting to call me," he said. "We've taken the aerials and there appear to be 36 souls at that Plantation." "We're guessing about ten farmhands, four or five principals, including Pascal, and the rest guards," he went on. "You were right on when you suggested that a raid followed by careful interrogation would be the best way to find out if other operations existed," Jack said. "So, what's the next step for me?" I asked. "Hang tight, but you will be joining a task force of twelve Special Forces to take down and carefully capture Pascal Padron and his top associates," he said. "It will be your job, along with Armando Ortega, to interrogate Pascal and the principals," he added. "Okay, so when will they arrive and where?" I said. "They are assembling now, in Key West and will fly out of the NAS there. Armando is fluent in Spanish, Portuguese and several dialects (a well-schooled and competent partner to have) and can interpret, if needed. They'll take a Sikorsky Super Stallion to the field next to the Plantation and land at 3 a.m. tomorrow," he said. "Coordinates are 21.83°N, 79.6° W," he said. "Okay, I'll be there, and I'll wait for them to land," I said. Jack came back, "I'll notify Armando that you'll join in the field and to give arms to you." Again, Jack repeated, "You and Armando are crucial to the operation and you must take Pascal unharmed!" "Roger," I said, "I'll be there at 3 a.m."

Well, shit! I just got back from there. I could have stayed at Sara's until tonight and leisurely met the plane at 3 a.m. Now, I just had time to get back there. If I left at 7 p.m. I could get there by 11:30, drive to the field, park way away (so as to remain undetected) and get on the field with an hour or so to spare. I told myself that I'd signed up for this, so suck it up and get ready, and reminding myself that this may be the worst threat to mankind ever. Jack said that Armando would have a firearm for me; I guessed I didn't need anything else. I packed a little; shaving gear, shirt, pants, medicine, etc. just in case.

Got in the Jeep and off again on this same damn road to Trinidad! As I pulled out I thought, okay more gas and a cafe negro or two was required. Also, I thought that I would not contact Sara, as she would never know that I was in town. On the other hand, I needed to let Carl know, since Jack had not asked for him. I wondered where in the hell he was. I called and Carl said he was at Lupita's. I said, "Who in the hell is Lupita?" He said, "A new friend of mine I met on the 'Do It Now,' a big Horizon!" "How big?" I asked. "A hundred-footer and as gorgeous as Lupita is," he said. Carl was something else. I

78

said, "Carl, I've been given orders to go back to Trinidad, can't go into details but I'll keep you advised." "Have a good time with Lupita," I said.

I drove by Cienfuegos for the fifth time in the past few days and felt like I knew the gas station manager personally. Thank God, I got my little two-hour nap earlier, I'd need it before this night was over. I might catch a little shuteye after I got there, if I hurried, since I'd probably be up all night looking capture and interrogation in the face. I picked up speed, as I didn't recall ever seeing a speed limit sign on this road.

I arrived in Trinidad about 11:15 and decided to find an appropriate place near the field and take a nap. I set the cellphone alarm for 2:15 to give me enough time to get reasonably close to the field, park and make my way to the GPS coordinates that Jack had given me.

God! Almost three hours sleep; I'm ready! Okay, I've got to get my mind right, taking note of the absolute severity of this night's (morning's?) encounter!

I got out of the Jeep and knew I had quite a walk to get to those coordinates. I softly walked along the road and thought, what if a car goes by? I quickly went into the field. Coffee plants were well laid out and were about four feet tall and provided good cover. I went on the row heading to the center of the field, in agreement with my phone's GPS. The phone that Jack gave me also had GPS tracking. I simply entered the coordinates and automatically, I had the equivalent of SIRI without the voice. Closer and closer, and finally an opening. I thought, they must have left an opening for tractor or equipment repairs. I stopped short of getting in the open and waited in cover at the edge. The opening was just large enough for a Sikorsky Stallion helicopter. The clock said 2:48 a.m., so I had fifteen minutes until the Stallion lands. I just kneeled quietly, listening to the wind rustling the coffee plants. Then the whirring, pulsing sound of rotors approaching. Louder and louder until the massive copter sat down. Its rear end let down and the task force filed out, one by one, until all twelve had evacuated the beast. I approached and skeptically the force allowed me to come. Armando knew I'd be there and handed me an AR-18; it was light as a feather. Armando said softly, "Okay Paul, this is it." "The Plantation is to our west, let's go," I said. "Vámonos."

The brigade followed as we quietly made our way through the coffee rows. A fence loomed up and it was substantial. Anticipating the fence's structure, one of the men started cutting the heavy wire, making an opening with his 24" bolt cutter. One by one, stealthily, we went through and proceeded (now in the open) toward the east side of the complex. I warned Armando about the electronic surveillance and motion detectors, but we had to proceed, regardless. Creeping, we made it to a wall without detection and slid along the wall to the rear entrance of the grand structure. As we stepped up the stairs to the door, an alarm sounded. It was full blast from then on. Knocking the door open, guns in hand, shots were fired at guards inside. More guards, more shots. We knew there were more guards from the infrared count Jack had given us from the flyover. The other guards must have been sleeping. Then activated by the alarm they started coming, although in their underwear, carrying automatic rifles.

Armando motioned to climb the stairs, as Pascal and others were probably upstairs in bedrooms. Pascal was in his bedroom, probably relying on his guards to take out intruders, but we fooled him and quickly bound his arms behind him. We knew it was Pascal from a high school picture that The FBI had found and Jack had forwarded to both Armando and me. Other rooms were entered by other soldiers, and those thought to be "players" were cuffed or bound. The early morning raid had been successful and we subtly rejoiced by hand gestures with a vertical thumb.

While others contained a few women and children, we took Pascal and three cohorts back to the helicopter. Armando told me that the others would be taken care of back at the Plantation and that they would be evacuated separately. We were to batten down and escort Pascal and his henchmen back to NAS Key West, a mere ninety-five miles or less than an hour away in the Stallion helicopter.

The engines were started and the whirring of the blades got louder until liftoff, and we were underway. Armando and I discussed our approach to interrogation, while observing that our guests were securely bound and incapacitated. Armando said that, "Digit removal usually works for me." "Waterboarding or sirens are also fruitful," he added. It didn't hurt that Pascal and the other hostages heard us talking about interrogation techniques. I said, "Electric current or less than fatal electrocution can be good as well."

We were confident that we would find out what we wanted.

We arrived at the air station and escorted our hostages to a building prepared for us adjacent to the airfield. I remembered being there once before, for the Blue Angels Air Show. The famous Budweiser Clydesdales were stalled just south of the building we were entering. Well, back to less pleasing business! Others took the three other prisoners to different rooms and Armando and I took Pascal to another room prepared for us by experts. There were two large tables; one empty and another full of surgical implements, instruments and bottles of liquids.

We sat our subject down at the empty table and started in. "What is your operation about?" I asked. No response. "Como es en operación sobre?" Armando asked. Silence, not even a facial expression change. Without hesitation Armando started for the implement table and grabbed what looked like long-bladed wire cutters. He went to Pascal and without hesitation cut off his little finger. Pascal whaled in agony, and his facial expression certainly changed as a result of losing his little finger. Armando said, "One down, nine to go." "No comprende?" Pascal uttered. "Uno abajo, nueve para ir," Armando said again. He then said, "Como es su operacion sobre?" "What does your operation do?" I thought. I hope this guy can speak English as I will be in the dark half the time, but it didn't look like he spoke English at all. Pascal's appearance was calm, cool and collected until he lost his finger; that got his attention. "We grow coffee," Pascal said. At least he was talking, I thought. "You do more than that," I said. "We grow coffee and sell it," Pascal uttered, while grimacing. "What about the chemically altered cocaine in it?" I said. Pascal looked astonished that we knew. Armando grabbed his cutter and cut off another finger. Pascal screamed in agony, while we hoped this would unlock information about his and maybe other similar operations. Sure enough, Pascal said, "We modified the beans to cause addiction by whoever drinks its coffee." Pascal was in agony. It was working, I thought, and he spoke English. "Are there other operations like yours?" Armando asked. No response, so Armando started for his cutters again and Pascal said, "Yes." Please, no mas, por favor," he went on. "There are others treating their coffee beans, but I don't know how many," Pascal groaned. Armando had gone to get hot water with soap in it to soothe Pascal's left hand. "You are right handed, aren't you?" Armando said. "Si," said Pascal. "Soak your hand, it will feel better," Armando said. "Ahh," Pascal yelled, "Caliente, Caliente." We let him soak a little and asked again, "How many and where?" "I know of six like mine, but there are more," Pascal uttered. "I'm not in charge, I only head my operation outside of Trinidad." "Who's in charge," Armando asked. Pascal hesitated, so Armando grabbed his cutters again. "Okay, okay," Pascal whined. There is one more in Cuba on the west side of the island and two in Guatemala," he added. "What about the other two that you know of?" I asked, gesturing to Armando for cutters. Pascal whined some more, "Nicaragua and Costa Rica, but I think there are more that I don't know about; there is a bigger boss! This is going to be a multi-million-dollar concern and very profitable for all of us involved. Almost everyone drinks coffee now and it would be more in the future," he said, not wanting to lose any more fingers. "Who's in charge then if you're not?" I asked. Silence, then more silence. It was apparent that Pascal feared for his life, if he divulged the name of the head man. Armando picked up the other hand, after removing the hot water bowl, and with his cutter threatened to cut off the index finger of his right hand this time. A serious dilemma for Pascal. "Okay, okay," he said. "All I know is that he goes by El Patron." Ironic, a man called Padron calling out a man called Patron. "So where is El Patron located?" I said. Pascal said, "I don't know, I swear I don't." "How does he control you?" I asked. "He calls on the sat phone," he said. "Do you have his number?" Armando asked. "No, he just calls," Pascal responded. "Where's your sat phone?" I said. "Back at the plantation," he said, "Don't you ever call him?" I said again. "No!" "Here's my damn sat phone." Pascal said and he pulls it out from his boot compartment. "That's bull Pascal, what if something goes wrong that affects your ability to carry out his agenda?" Armando asked. Pascal responded with an arm and shoulder shrug, saying, "I don't know." Armando went for the cutter.

I was trying to see if there was any call log available on the satellite phone. I couldn't figure it out so I called Jack on my encrypted phone. "Jack Murphy," he answered.

I said, "Jack, we're making progress with Pascal but he won't tell us who, where or anything about another guy called 'El Patron,' whom Pascal says heads up the entire operation. Pascal says he knows of six similar operations but no specifics, and there are more but he didn't know where." "I'll tell you more, but right now I'm trying to identify 'El Patron.' Pascal says he never calls him (which is probably a lie), that Patron always calls Padron. I know it's confusing. I've got the satellite phone that Pascal receives his calls and uses, but I can't figure out how to get a call log." Jack said, "Can you identify the phone?" "Yes," I responded, it says 'KVH TRACPHONE' on it." "Okay, I'll make some serious calls to KVH, as we have the exact coordinates of the Padron Plantation," Jack said. "We'll talk later," he concluded.

We had to find out the extent of this threat and it sounded like "El Patron" was the answer, if we could find him.

Armando had continued with the interrogation and poor old Pascal had lost another finger from his right hand and Pascal admitted that he posts a code word on the internet at certain time of the week; Monday, Wednesday or Friday at 5 p.m. exactly. Pascal posts a different pair of words for each day (M, W, F). It wasn't that complicated. If the news warrants, then El Patron calls Pascal on the sat phone; Good news or bad.

"Good work, Armando," I said. "I wonder what Congress or John McCain would say about your techniques?" "They would be insane if they knew the end of the world might be imminent if we didn't find out how to stop it," I said. Armando said, "I think we've got as much as we can out of Pascal."

It appeared again that it might be up to Jack to find out where the calls from El Patron emanated from. Armando got more hot water and soap and some bandages for Pascal but left him tied to his chair.

We confirmed that Pascal's story was pretty accurate by talking to his direct reports. As expected, they didn't know anything about posted codes but did know that El Patron controlled everything from somewhere and that he called Pascal periodically.

We told our guards to lock them all up and get a doctor for Pascal. The lost fingers were the key to getting this far so quickly, no matter what congress would say. It looked like the interrogation phase was over for now. It was 9 a.m. at the NAS near Key West, so I decided to drive down to my favorite deli for breakfast, but my Jeep was parked along the road in Trinidad. I called Sara to help. "Sara, can you please get my Jeep from the side of the road near the Padron Plantation?" "What, how?" she said. "It's a long story, but please get someone to hotwire it and move it to your place, por favor," I said. "I didn't think to hide a key for you, but please take it to your place for me," I went on. "Okay Pablo," she said. "When will I see you again?" she added. "As soon as possible, honey babe," I said. "Okay," she said, and hung up.

I'd either have to borrow a vehicle or call a cab or Uber. I checked with the sector leader and he said they could loan me a sedan from the carpool, so happily I picked one out and checked out.

It was a short drive (about twelve miles) from the air station to Goldman's Deli. Key West was a welcome sight. It had been a while and I felt like this was a homecoming of sorts.

I drove to the shopping center that the Deli was in, parked and walked in. Breakfast was being served. I ordered two eggs, over medium, bacon and home fries and a bagel (they made their own). The owner said, "Welcome back Paul, you've been gone for a while." I said, "Yes, on a big fishing trip." "Catch much?" she said. "Yes, a great trip, my friend Carl caught a grander," I concluded. I saw a couple of familiar faces and said, "Hi." Checked my cellphone and Jack had called. I said to myself, "Okay, I'm eating before I call Jack back." I was hungry as hell. The breakfast came and I enjoyed the pseudo-homecooked breakfast.

I left the Deli, got in my blue Chevy sedan from the pool, and called Jack on my special cellphone. "Jack Warner," he answered. "Paul here," I said. "Okay Paul, we called KVH and after a little bullshit they traced the calls to Pascal. They came from Costa Rica, a small town called Jaco in the Puntarenas Province. We deployed another force to that location, hoping to take down 'El Patron.' There's a small airport there and local officials were on board. The helicopter will land at that airfield, and Andy Pellerito will survey the lay of the land around the Patron complex," Jack said. "Do you remember Andy?" Jack asked. "Yes, he was a good agent and a hell of a marksman," I said. "Yes, he and two others will pretend to be tourists and dress like beach bums to check out Patron's digs," he said. "Jaco is a beach town, so that's what we came up with," he said. "Sounds like a plan," I said. "I'll just be standing by here in Key West until you advise," I added. I missed Sara, but it was over 200 miles from me to her and I was on standby mode for the FBI.

I decided to get a room at an old home in "Old Town" Key West. A place called, "The Conch House," owned by a friend of mine. This was perfect for me and only two blocks from Duval Street. I checked in and hit the bed. It had been a long, exciting and exhausting night.

I woke up again at 7 p.m. and thought, "Okay, I have no clothes, toiletries or anything except what I have on." I made some coffee, took a shower and put my soiled clothes back on afterwards. Time to shop, but stores would be closed. Oh well.

Hungry again, I walked down to Simonton and then to Abbondanza, a local Italian restaurant and ordered Chicken Parmesan with a nice Chianti. Things had been hectic and I hoped that Andy was successful in Jaco. The wine put me at ease a little and the parmesan was good! When I finished it was nearly 9 p.m.; too late to call Sara? No, I walked back to the Conch House and called her. "Hola," she said. "It's Pablo," I said. "I'm glad you called me. I got Juan, my friend from the mall to jump your Jeep and drive it to my place. When will you return?" she said. "Not sure," I said. "We've taken Pascal Padron to Key West and made some progress, but the threat was bigger than Padron.," I continued. "I'm in Key West after spending all morning interrogating Senõr Padron. I'm staying at a friend of mine's bed and breakfast called

88

'Conch House,' and I'll keep you posted," I said. "I think I really care for you," she said. "Be careful, those people are criminals." "I'm by myself now, waiting on Jack for further orders," I said. "Bye for now."

I still had no toiletries or clothes. I went to a 24-hour CVS and got shaving gear, deodorant, Tums, toothpaste, toothbrush and mouthwash. Feeling a little relieved, I walked back to the Conch House and conked out! I laid down on a beautiful bed; which was firm, the way I like it. Good night!

The next morning was leisurely; woke up at 9:15 a.m. Thank God I have a Keurig coffee maker and Breakfast Blend Colombian coffee. I made a cup and wondered what the hell was happening in Washington with Jack. What's more, what was happening with El Patron! I knew that Pascal had been put out of business, but the head of this threat and how many others were still going strong? What would happen when El Patron called on the sat phone for Pascal and one of our agents answered? Our agents were good and one on standby at the Padron Plantation was Cuban and had recordings of Pascal to learn and imitate for that phone call, according to Jack in a text message on my new phone.

I felt very proud that I had stumbled on this dilemma with my friend Carl, and that it was a boat like mine that was being used for preliminary shipments of altered cocaine-laced coffee and that it appeared as though it might be the largest threat the world has ever known. What a remarkable world for this to have happened to me, just because two thugs jumped on my boat in the middle of the night and one of them had a picture of a boat like mine. It was an awesome feeling to be a key agent to combat this threat.

I walked down to Duval Street to get breakfast, although the B & B provided some.

Initially, there was a "Denny's" on Duval that caught my eye. It wasn't gourmet, but it was damn good. Sausage, bacon, eggs, hash browns, all the bad stuff that tasted Sooo good. They had fruit also, but I always passed it by.

A satisfying breakfast was followed by a stroll down Duval Street. There were numerous tourist traps and 101 T-shirt stores, but there were also notable artist galleries. For example, Wyland, the famous sea creature artist had a large gallery. Alan Maltz, Peter Lik, Amanda Johnson and others had galleries there. There were water sports, sunset tours, a Ripley's Believe It or Not museum and the smallest bar in the world. Quite a diversion from the past couple of days. I walked and walked, enjoying the shops, sights and wandering tourists (two cruise ships were docked, and Who Let the Dog's Out?). I walked all the way to the Pier House at the north end of Duval. On the way back on the other side of the street, I noted a topless veranda on the second floor of a place called "The Bull." This is Key West, and a sign read, "Clothing Optional." This sign reminded me that I badly needed clothes. I stopped at the next shop that might have clothes and purchased two pairs of pants, two shirts and some Sketcher slip on shoes.

I walked on and noted that there were more bars and restaurants on this street than anywhere I'd ever visited and the competition must be tough as hell! Tough competition usually means more for your money/ both quality and quantity. Again, I digress.

I got back to the Conch House and sat down and turned on the TV. I was tired, must have walked six miles or so. The news channel was talking about how China was ripping us off on trade differentials and that North Korea was firing off more missiles. If the world only knew about the "Coffee Cartel," they would not be concerned about trade differentials nearly as much. I guess that is what we were facing, a "Coffee Cartel," although it just jumped into my stream of consciousness. Somewhat depressed, I turned off the TV and turned on some Thelonious Monk; "Round Midnight" was one of my favorites.

I laid down on the coach and drifted off, thinking about Sara. The way we hit it off was too good to be true, I thought.

I wondered what she was doing now. She was probably finishing lunch in the lunchroom at the Mall she managed. When can I see her again? It all was contingent upon Jack's next directive.

I awoke at the request of my cellphone ringtone and knew in an instant that it was Jack calling. "Hello," I said. "Paul, there has been a development," he said. "Andy Pellerito has assessed the complex outside of Jaco, Costa Rica and has suggested a course of action similar in functionality as the Padron takedown, only this time a larger task force will be deployed to assure that El Patron is captured alive," he said. "Similar tactics will be employed since the raid on the Padron Plantation was so successful. A 3 a.m. assault would ensue and any guards quickly eliminated. Armando Ortega will join Andy for the raid and you will be at NAS Key West to receive and interrogate El Patron. The assault is planned for tomorrow morning and I'll let you know when to be at NAS," Jack concluded.

I sat back and prayed that the assault would be successful and that we could find out just what El Patron's Coffee Cartel controlled and where. Thank God, it appeared as though we had caught the Cartel's actions in its infancy and that we thought only a few deliveries of tainted coffee had been delivered. This according to Pascal during his interrogation. But Paul was a Lieutenant and El Patron was the top dog. Would he break in interrogation? I then texted Jack and told him that I hoped Armando would accompany El Patron back here to NAS and help in the interrogation process. Jack replied in the affirmative. I'd have to go to bed early in order to get up in time to get to NAS Key West by 5 a.m. It all depended on the strike force's ability to capture El Patron without harming him, and then fly him to Key West.

It was again naptime, I thought, being in limbo until tomorrow morning. Again, I lie there thinking of Sara. I think once all this Coffee Cartel business is over (I pray it will) it will get real serious between us. What a beautiful smile and charismatic aura she had about her. Her laugh was so utterly cute, the way it ended in a little giggle. Roll over and try to get her out of my mind – not possible!

Couldn't sleep after thinking about Sara, I wouldn't stop thinking about this Coffee Cartel and its threat to the world by involuntary addiction and subsequent domination.

I was back up at 6 p.m. and thought I might be able to get another nap before interrogation, if I had a little wine. I drank half a bottle of Caymus '89 and got hungry for a steak. I'd heard about a good steak place from someone and thought it was Prime 951; couldn't remember? Looked it up in the room's phonebook and it was Prime 951, ironically, at 951 Caroline Street in Key West, toward the Key West Bight from here. I decided to take a shower, shave and call a cab. A few minutes later I called Five Sixes, a local company. He'd pick me up in five minutes, which became fifteen. Then all the way to the steak house the driver complained about Uber and Lyft taking all their business, and the corrupt City Council that had approved them. Needless to say, I hesitated giving him a 20% tip, but did anyway.

The restaurant was located at the top of another restaurant with a large adjacent pool with a sexy metal mermaid blowing a stream of water from her mouth. Pretty impressive, and a lot of people swimming for 8:30 at night.

The menu and wine list were as impressive and believe it or not, they had the same wine and vintage that I loved drinking, but I had to buy a full bottle; so, I did. I got asparagus, smoked Gouda mac and cheese and a bone-in ribeye. A superb repast and vino for sure!

A cab back to the Conch House and to bed; set the alarm for 3 a.m. so I could be at the NAS to receive Andy, Armando and El Patron. Made my coffee, ate a Cinnabon, and got ready. The carpool Chevy got me to NAS, and I waited in the annex next to the landing strip.

I hoped that all went well with the seizure but was out of that picture for this one. Andy and Armando were both very experienced and competent agents. Time elapsed; more time waiting, anticipation, concern, prayers, more time passed. I was becoming concerned, since it was 6 a.m. and the raid was supposed to be 3 a.m. I thought, "Hell, this is not bad. It takes some three hours to fly directly, and it wouldn't be a helicopter this time; all was good. An hour for the raid, get to the airport, fly directly and I was looking at 7 a.m." If I'd thought this through earlier, I could have stayed in bed another couple of hours. Oh well, it was what it is!

I received word that the plane was nearing, probable ETA 7:10 a.m. I got a cup of coffee from the mess hall and sat back down to figure out what to ask El Patron. I'm sure Armando has things in mind; the finger technique had certainly worked on Pascal, I thought.

I hear the plane! "De Plane, De Plane," I thought to myself. Pretty stupid, when so much was at stake in just a few. Finally, it hit the runway and started to taxi this way. It slowly stopped within fifty feet of my building and I went out to meet it. Three troupers came out first, followed by El Patron and Andy. El Patron was cuffed behind his back and Armando followed close behind. Other soldiers followed them.

They reached my building and took him to the 10' x 10' interrogation room. Only a table and two chairs were in the room, but a plethora of interrogation appurtenances were in the room next door. Andy sat El Patron down and stood by with Armando. I sat down across from him and asked, "Where are your other operations?" He stared at me in a condescending manner. Armando added, "Donde eston tus otras operaciones?" El Patron just stared at both of us in disdain. Armando said, "Let me ask the son of a bitch!" I said, "Should we remove his attitude along with a few fingers?" Armando agreed and said, "Si." "Let's try a more humane approach with Senor Patron," I said. "Get the truth serum Armando," I said. Armando went next door and brought a syringe filled with "Sodium and Potassium Thiopental" (a more potent variation of Sodium Pentothal). Armando administered about half of the 100-cc. syringe in Patron's left arm vein and it went to work immediately. Some people are completely uninhibited when given this drug and easily tell the truth, without reservation. Was El Patron one of them?

I asked again, "Where are your other operations?" Senior Patron didn't hesitate and said, "En Todos Lados." I looked at Armando and said, "What the hell does that mean?" Armando said, "Everywhere, everywhere." I then asked Patron, "Can you be more specific?" A stare ensued, but without the disdain as before. He hesitated but reluctantly said, "Mostly South America." "More specific," I said. "Mas Especifico," Armando added. "Mas Especifico, por favor." "Nicaragua, Colombia, Costa

Rica, Venezuela, Equador, Suriname, Panamá, Cuba and Guatemala," he said

This was scary. Evidently, they had a coffee strain that was prolific enough to be grown in this large temperate zone. It was larger than we thought. I excused myself, went out to the hall and called Jack. "Jack Warner," he said. I said, "Jack, El Patron says there are operations all over Cuba and South America." Jack said, "Remember, Pascal said he knew of six; two in Cuba, one in Costa Rica, one in Nicaragua and two in Guatemala." "That jives with Pascal, but Patron added Panama, Suriname, Ecuador, Venezuela and Colombia. If my math is correct, that's almost a dozen places growing, processing and altering coffee!" I said. "Okay Paul, will check it out," he said, showing El Patron his "Finger Nail, uh Finger Clippers."

Thank God, the truth serum worked so well on Patron, but the threat was even bigger than we imagined! Nearly every country in Northern South America had a tobacco farm and processing facility, it sounded like.

I wondered at what stages each location was and if and how much tainted coffee was already out there? I'm sure Jack was thinking the same thing, and just how did we narrow down exact locations for each?

I went back into the interrogation room and Armando had thought the same thing. He had asked, "Where in each country." El Patron had responded by asking for un lápiz (a pencil) so he could write it down. But he didn't, so Armando administered more serum. It was apparent that El Patron was a little groggy and not lucid. Maybe he was faking or maybe the second shot was too much. I asked Petron again, "Please write down the specific locations of the different operations." He started to write and then faded. Okay, this was too serious. I told Armando to get his bolt cutters, or something. He agreed and a little finger did the touch. It brought life and agony simultaneously. Armando told El Patron, "Escribir, Sonso, Escribir!" El Patron started scribbling, since Armando had cut off his left little finger, hoping he was right handed. He wrote Cuba, Pascal Padron, near Trinidad. Orlando Rojas in Cuba, near Las Tunas, Eastern Central Cuba. Oscar Almeda in Venezuela near Barinos. On and on until all twelve were named. What a scary list. El Patron was subdued by the serum, in combination with losing a little finger, and we were jubilant that this combination had worked so successfully!

After apparent success, and before we locked El Patron up, I called Jack immediately to give him the information. "Jack Warner," he said. "Jack, we, or I should say Armando, got El Patron to give us the names and locations of all the other concerns comprising the Coffee Cartel," I said. I added, "At least he said that the ones he gave us were all of them, and under the circumstances of being under the extra dose of serum and losing a finger, I have no reason to doubt him." Jack said, "You are probably correct, but these are big time conspirators. All we can do is hope he's giving us all the entities and activate one of the largest combined task forces ever known to stop operations in all eleven sites as soon as possible!" I texted him a copy of the paper on which El

Patron had handwritten the other coffee enterprises. I got my confirmation of conveyance and went back to El Patron. Armando was still prodding him and found out that there were other operations in addition to his and the ten others. There was another one starting in Costa Rica, and yet another in Venezuela. Both were in their infancy, just tilling farmland, and neither had crops or completed facilities.

"Do you think that is now all?" I asked Armando, "I think so, this Patron is one submissive puppy dog." I hoped we had all of them, now all we could do was hope that Jack could verify the existence of all of these coffee operations."

The FBI and CIA had both skyrocketed recently, say the last decade, in technology to uncover and observe threats to the United States. Thermographic computational imaging and photography, as well as audio electronics and sound measuring technology have catapulted crime detection and elimination to new heights.

I remembered the flyovers above Padron's Plantation and the accurate human count that it produced using thermographic photography. It was all up to Jack and all that technology at this point.

Armando, Andy and I continued to quiz El Patron, but he was visibly beaten and very tired. We mutually agreed that we had gotten all we could from him, at least for now. We asked other agents, backing us up, to look after El Patron after they locked him in the isolation cell. Then we all said in unison, "Job well done!!"

I was hungry as hell and asked Armando and Andy, "You guys as hungry as I am?" They said again, in unison, "Yes!" "The base mess hall was only a quarter mile away," one of the two attendant agents said. It was about 10 a.m. by this time, so a late breakfast or brunch would be in order. The three of us got in my carpool Chevy and went to the mess hall for breakfast.

It had been forever since I'd ordered "Shit on a Shingle," but good memories of my time in the Navy prior to agent status. I got mine topped with two eggs over medium and a side of Applewood bacon. "Super breakfast," I said, and Andy and Armando shook their heads in agreement.

Meanwhile, in D.C., Jack was frantically coordinating with sectors all over the globe to corroborate El Patron's offerings, and then to eradicate the facilities and farms. A dozen flyovers were dispatched from strategic locations in and around South America and Florida. The flyover would tell us (law enforcement) exactly where the tainted coffee concerns were, how many people were there, and even the existence of weaponry and laboratories. It would take some time to dispatch all the flyovers and task forces, so I told Andy and Armando that I would be in touch should our joint services be summoned by the FBI.

I took them back to the interrogation facilities and said, "Good luck guys," as they got out of the car. I left to head back to the Conch House and regroup. Another eventful and successful morning, I thought as I drove back to Old Town Key West.

I arrived at the Conch House, mentally and physically exhausted. I went directly to bed, did "not pass go," just flopped. It was 7 p.m. when I awoke. Wow, I was tired! Got my cup and thinking to myself, "Hope this isn't an El Patron altered one."

As I became more active and aware, my thoughts again turned to Sara. Was it too late to call? No! It was only 7:30 p.m. and she was home from work, probably eating dinner. I called; the voice on the other end said, "Hola." I said, "Sara, my angel." She said, "Pablo, my Pablito, how are you?" "I'm good, just missing you," I said. "Me too," she said, "Just finished dinner myself." I said, "I think I will be on a break, but on-call 24/7." "Do you think I could come visit you for a while?" I offered. "Of course," she said, "Tomorrow, if okay?" "May I stay with you for a while?" I added. She responded, "Absolutely!" "What time do you think you'll get here?" she said. "I just got up after a long sleep from about ten this morning, after being up from about 2 a.m. 'till then." With that said, I added, "Do you work tomorrow?" Sara said, "Yes, and I'll get off about 6 p.m." "Okay," I said, "I'll be there to greet you when you get off."

I was hungry and had some version of "Jet Lag," it seemed. Should I have breakfast, lunch or dinner? I decided to go to a very nice little Italian restaurant on Duval, within walking distance called "Antonia's." A nice little stroll, always wondering if all tourists act like the ones in Key West. They're mostly drunk, ignore all traffic lights and etiquette, are somewhat arrogant and rude and never tip enough or at all to some of the hardworking locals. Oh well, "It is."

I arrived, sat down, ordered a nice Brunello and looked over the menu. I always order veal and usually Veal Marsala, but this time would be different. A seafood medley of shrimp, scallops, calamari and clams, called "Frutti Du Mare," caught my eye. I ordered as I had another sip of Brunello. The atmosphere was nice, and again there was a table of inebriated visitors to the Conch Republic. They did lighten up the night's repast, as homemade Italian bread and balsamic and virgin olive oil, with a nice wine made a super combo.

The big bowl of seafood and linguine looked awesome. As I took a bite it really tasted awesome, as well. What a good decision to come here, and the people at the tourist table were having a ball, at this point.

I finished with a nice Taylor Fladgate 18 and a Crème Brûleé. I left a nice tip, signed the check and left the building. I thought, another stroll might lighten the meal and started north on Duval. There was a divergent mix of shops along the way. As I mentioned before, they ranged from "Top of the Line," Art Galleries and Coach shops to T-shirts. The T-shirt shops were disproportionately numerous, but attractions nonetheless.

Strolling and stopping. I thought, "One more drink as a nightcap may be in order, so I stepped up to the bar at Fogarty's. A nice bartender, maybe Hawaiian, asked, "What would you like, sir?" I said, "You!" I was joking, but an unmistakable eye glance made it not funny at all. She came back after preparing and handing me my

Hennessy shot and said, "Well, maybe later." I was joking, but she evidently liked what she saw and what I said.

It was esteem building to have this kind of response from such an attractive young lady, but my thoughts turned to Sara Sonata. I said, after downing my shot, "Maybe next time, beautiful!"

Took my time walking past the topless and bottomless teaser lounges, the T-shirt shops the smoke shops, the ice cream shops, the sandwich shops (even Denny's); all interesting on the walk back to the Conch House.

Got back, had had enough to drink, still feeling it after the long walk. Headed for bed, took off my clothes, set my super cellphone alarm for 10 a.m.; if I slept that long. I wanted to be there when Sara got off work at 6 p.m., so I'd start around 10 a.m. to give extra time to arrange a flight to Havana and drive across Cuba. Good night world, "As it is," before altered Coffee rules!

Got up at 8 a.m. anyway. Made my coffee (there it is again) and sat down to wake up. I wondered what the hell Jack and the FBI, CIA and others were coming up with? Got a second cup and called Jack. "Jack Warner," he said. I said, "Paul, calling to find out where we are?" Jack said, "We have corroboration on five of the sites at this point. Various methods and all means are deployed, or in process, to the locations extracted from El Patron. Photography, thermal and otherwise has been invaluable, as have been the drones. One drone uses super-quiet engines and rotors with oil-covered Titanium bearings to reduce the abominable high-pitched whir from conventional drones. Some locations have been ground surveyed and all so far have coffee fields. Some access has been through innocent looking tourista or salespeople. All in all, great progress, but none would be fast enough, given the impending threat." He added, "I can't thank you enough, Paul, for your detection and involvement." "No problem," I said, "I live on this planet as well, and would do all possible to prevent the Coffee Cartel from utter domination of it." I added, "Anything else I can do now?" Jack said, "No, I don't think so." I said, "Okay Jack, I'm planning on going on the other side of the island to be with my new girlfriend." "What's her name?" Jack said. "Sara Sonata," I replied. "Good luck, have fun, will advise; carry your super phone," Jack said. "I will," I said, and hung up.

A ball's out effort had been made, it sounded like. I was gratified that Armando and I had been so successful extracting valid information out of Padron and Patron. Got fully dressed and walked down to a Cuban breakfast shop and had a grilled and smashed, sausage, egg and cheese sandwich on Cuban bread. Super good! I had a leisurely walk back to the hacienda and called Carl. One ringy dinghy, two ringy dinghy, three ringy dinghy's and no answer? I wondered what was going on. He was supposed to be watching the BFB and enjoying life; well, I'll bet he and Lupita, his latest, were just fine. I'll call later, I said to myself. I'd known Carl for about twenty years and he was really the best and most diligent, honest and persistent person that I ever knew. (Sober!) True enough, I thought. I finally got back to the Conch House and sat down to gather my thoughts. I was thinking about where the hell Carl was when the phone rang. I answered, "Hello." The voice on the other phone said, "Paul?" I said, "Yes." The voice seemed somewhat familiar when I first heard it, but I didn't say anything. The voice said, "Paul, this is Associate Deputy Director, Harvey Hyde and I was instructed to call you. We don't know how it happened, but El Patron's deputies are trying to break Patron out." They're at it now, Paul!" Harvey said, "You're to get there ASAP, with weapon." "Roger," said I.

I didn't have a weapon, so I called Harvey back and asked for a weapon to be at NAS gate. I ran to the front porch and to the carpool Chevy. I sped up and got up to 80 once on A1A to the NAS. I quickly showed my credentials to the guard, and he tossed me an AK-47. I went through to the street adjacent to the Holding Building, so that I wouldn't be detected. I heard rifle fire from the building housing El Patron!

I crept along the adjacent building's green space, ever so slowly, until I could see men shooting at a guard inside a doorway. I thought, how in the hell did El Patron's people determine where he was? We had swept him away by helicopter and no destination transmitted anywhere?

I crept closer still and sighted the visible shooter on my AK. Bang, he went down! Another ran over and started shooting in my direction, but wildly missed. I found him in my sight and let him have it. Down he went as well. How many of these sons of bitches were there? It appeared that their efforts were all focused on the main entrance. I waited and waited; here came another from behind me. Thank God, he made a little noise, so

I turned and waited. From behind the building's side planter he peeked; not enough to get a shot! Patience is paramount in a situation like this.

Where were the guard force on the base? This had been going on for some time. At least a half hour, based on my call from Harvey and the fast ride here.

Waiting, waiting? My enemy peeked out and moved his gun around the planter, just enough to get a head shot. Bang, I got him, and down he went. Okay, what now? Refocusing to the main entrance, I didn't see anyone, except I noted several bodies heretofore unseen on the ground. Focusing more, I felt that those on the ground must have been Air Station guards. A shot was fired from a window near the entrance, but I couldn't see where it was aimed. A guard inside the window must have seen someone in the yard. I crept again around the planter, getting on the ground and shimmying along the ground holding my AK in my left hand; slowly, quietly, until the end of the plants stopped. I peeked around and there was another of El Patron's cohorts! I eased just past the bushes and with my gun at the ready, sighted that SOB in! Finger pressure, easy – bang – got him! I then saw someone come to the front entrance with a rifle and he opened the front door, looking around.

Four or five minutes passed as this guard or guy (whatever) looked and cautiously moved out away from the Holding Building.

I carefully yelled, "Friendly!" He said, "Paul?" I said, "Yes." He said, as he moved to me, "We heard you would come, Thank God! I think you took four or five out." I said, "Yes, did they get El Patron?" He said, "No, but it was close. They surprised us with a helicopter landing on the lawn!" "A dozen came out loaded and firing," he went on. "We normally had four guarding his cell but lost three of them to their fire," he went on. "I'm the last one and we got all twelve." "I went slow as I came out, just to count the bodies," he added. "I wonder how in the hell they knew where we took him?" I said. He said, "No fucking idea." "I guess it's over and if they knew, others do too, so staff up my friend!" I said. "I'll notify Harvey and see what's up with Jack Warner of the FBI, who's been involved from the first." I asked him his name and he said "Isaac." I said, "Well, Isaac, you did well." I walked toward the Chevy and got in. Driving away, I thought it strange that an outright helicopter assault in broad daylight was tried? And, it almost worked, as who guards the airspace around a Naval Air Station in the middle of the day on an island filled with sightseeing helicopters and small planes. We stopped them though!

I called Jack, but no answer. I then called Harvey Hyde on my super phone and he didn't answer either. Nobody else to call except Carl or Sara. Carl was probably with Lupita and I really didn't need to share anything with Carl. Sara, on the other hand, was the one I wanted to call.

"Hola," she said. I said, "Pablito!" "Ha, Ha, Ha, I thought you were coming to meet me at 6 p.m.?" she said. I responded, "I told you that I had to be available 24/7." "They called me after breakfast and I urgently went to the local NAS and was in a gunfight," I said. She said,

"Oh, Oh my God. Are you alright?" I said, "Yes, I'm fine, but I didn't come to meet you, my ebony angel." "Oh my God, Pablo, I'm just glad you're okay!" Sara said. "I wish I could say just when I can see you again," I said, "As soon as you can, mi amour," she said. That was the first time that love was offered in either direction, I thought. Well, that first time was from her! Maybe I need to be shot at more often. It was wonderful, however, that she said it.

"Pablo, are you there?" she exclaimed. "Yes, my love," I said, "My mind was just wandering." "I just had to let you know, because this thing I'm involved in is colossal, to say the least, and dangerous, but I can tell you it's a must for me to do!" I added. "I will keep you posted," I said, and hung up.

I was hungry as hell again and again went on to Antonia's on Duval. I got there and said sternly that I had had reservations at 6:30 p.m. for one. The Maître d' said, "I'm sorry sir, we can't find you." I said, "That's your problem, buster," and slipped him $20. He looked at his computer roster and said, "Oh yes Sir, I see it now, right this way." He sat me down at a table for two, and I wished Sara was here with me.

I ordered a Ruffino Gold Chianti and Veal Marsala, with a small House Italian Dressing, and caught my breath. The adrenaline had pumped and the testosterone flowed as I confronted those Patron fighters, just four hours ago. We had won the battle and thank God that Harvey had called me, since the guards at NAS were done in by the jailbreakers from Costa Rica. I felt proud that I'd been able to stop the assault on our holding cell for El Patron. The wine was a bit tart to start, but all-in-all, a good choice with Marsala.

The breadsticks, butter, olive oil and balsamic made the salad, and were great. After the salad the veal melted in my mouth and was paired well with the Gold Label. I slowly consumed everything, savoring each bite and sip.

Since I could walk back to the Conch House, I thought a Bailey's, on ice, would be a nice finish.

I tipped twenty-five percent, because everything was outstanding and left. I walked back the shortest way, through an alley between buildings, and then on to an open street. A drunken couple struggled to help each other, when appearances indicated that they couldn't help themselves! She kneeled down and threw up. This is Key West, I thought, and crossed the street to avoid contact or odor.

Walked up the stairs to the front porch and went to my room. Undressed, nightly meds and to bed.

I didn't wake up until 9:30 a.m. the next morning and made coffee. One cup down and thoughts wandered to the FBI, the Coffee Cartel and of course, Sara. The status of the Cartel was paramount, so I called Jack. "Jack Warner," he answered. I said, "Jack, what's going on? This Harvey Hyde called me, when I was expecting you." Jack responded, "Yes, I was out two days due to my wife's illness; she has multiple sclerosis and sometimes can't hardly walk. This episode was the worst yet, but her mother came to help. So, I'm back to help eliminate the Coffee Cartel threat! I've secured confirmation on three more sites, although the one in Suriname was very hidden and difficult to confirm. That makes eight to eliminate. Two have been neutralized already; the two in Guatemala were relatively easy. 'Pretend Guards' were killed or disarmed."

"I heard from Harvey that you're a hero," Jack said. "We were fortunate to have you in Key West and your response stopped the breakout of El Patron. We still can't figure out how Patron's henchmen knew where he was held?" "Thanks," I said. "Do you anticipate anything for me to help with at this point?" "Nothing right now," he said. "I may try again to see Sara but will be out of pocket about six to eight hours from here," I said. "Do you know the status of Pascal Padron's operation near Trinidad?" I added. "We sent twenty Seals in the middle of the night and took the security guards out and captured all that were alive. Yes, the Trinidad operation with your sister ship docked out back has been neutralized. Maybe we can confiscate or impound that Hatteras and arrange for you to get the boat that everyone thought you wanted to buy," Jack summarized and speculated. Amazing that the picture taken from the nighttime intruder in my cockpit has led to all of this; incredible is a better word. "Alright, Jack, I think I'll head over to Trinidad myself," if I can get a flight from EYW to HAV?

I still wondered what Carl was up to. I gave him a call and this time he answered. "Hola," he said. I said, "Hola Hell! What in the hell is going on?" Carl said, "It's all good, the BFB is fine, 'Loopee' is fantastic and I'm just hanging around here waiting for you." I said, "I called you yesterday, but no answer." He said, "I saw that you had called, but missed it. 'Loopee' (his nickname for Lupita) and I are doing very well. I found out that she's a stripper down the road. Ironically, she is very religious and quite moral. Maybe ironically is too strong, but she is in a business non-conducive to religion or morals," he said. "She treats this as a profession; using high heels, skimpy attire and tits as tools of the trade!" Carl said. I said, "Sounds good, Carl. I've had my hands full, as Patron's men tried to break him out of jail at NAS, and I was called to help stop them. We stopped the bastards, but never could figure out how they knew El Patron was there." I then added, "Padron's complex at Trinidad has also been neutralized. Big progress has been made on the other twelve operations as well." "But, do you know about all of the operations, maybe there's twelve more?" Carl asked. "We think, based on El Patron's interrogation, that there were thirteen total," I said. "I'll be going back to Trinidad to be with Sara," I said. "Roger that, Captain, I'll be right here on the "Big Fuckin Boat, and with Loopee as much as I can," Carl concluded.

I called Sara. "Hola, En qué te puedo ayudar?" her voice said. "Si Señorita te Quiera," I replied. "Pablito," she said, "Cómo está." "I'm good and I'd be better if I could see you tonight," I said. "Well, do!" she said. "Okay, it looks like I can come pretty soon if I can catch a plane to Havana and be there by 6 p.m., if alright?" I said. "Ci, Ci!" she said. I had time to pack some, shit, shower and shave, get something to eat for lunch, and get to the airport.

Got everything ready, got in the Chevy, got to the airport and waited for the flight. The flight was only a half hour and uneventful to Trinidad in the rental car. At least I'd gotten there without the phone ringing, this time. It was 5:30 p.m. and I'd gone to the shopping center to catch her getting off work. I sat there in the parking lot, wondering how the fight against the Coffee Cartel was going. The damn phone rang, it was Jack. "Update, Paul. Several cases of severe addiction withdrawals discovered in Key Largo, Florida. It's very possible that a shipment or two of tainted coffee was made prior to your discovery and the "Café Negro," your sister ship, may have made it. Key Largo is some 150 miles from Trinidad. The withdrawals were caused by laced coffee. Another force was dispatched to Key Largo earlier today to discover where the coffee was purchased and stop sales." "We were afraid of that," I said. "Yes, hopefully we won't find other partial, premature deliveries," Jack added. "Talk later, you are on the super phone, aren't you?" he said. I said, "Yes, Jack."

Jack was OCD about the nitty gritty, every detail clearly stated. He was like he was!

Sara just came out from the Mall and looked around, spying my obviously new airport rented KIA in the parking lot. She jogged over and said, "Get out and give me a hug, at least." "Yes!" I followed, getting out of the car. "Oh, it's good to see you Pablo!" she said. "I know, I know," I said, giving a very tight hug. I could feel those D-cupped girls on my chest. Felt so good! "What's the agenda?" I said. "Do you want a nice, dress-up dinner or an average, go as is, dinner?" Sara said. I responded, "Go as is, Chinese." "Okay, follow me," she said. I followed her to the 'Happy Family' restaurant in Trinidad. It was just like every other Chinese restaurant around the world and decorated in green, red and gold, just like all the others.

Beef and broccoli and Kung Pau Chicken, with Pork Fried Rice was ordered. Sara said, "I've missed you." "Same here," I said. "I'm so glad you came through the NAS assault okay," she said. "It was intense and I had to shoot four of El Patron's people. But I really want to talk about something else," I said. "Of course," she said. "Where would you want to go on a vacation?" I said. "The Bahamas," and she quickly added, "I've never been and have heard so much; cleaner water, cleaner beaches, tropical breezes, fresher conch, better fishing, better hospitality, to name a few."

"You know Sara, I could take the BFB from Hemingway Marina to Key West (90 miles), to Marathon (90 miles), Marathon to Miami Beach (70 miles), and Miami Beach to Bimini (50 miles). So, a 300-mile, four-day trip would get us there with the convenience of living on the BFB," I said. "Okay," I went on, "We could fly from Havana to Bimini or Nassau, or wherever – AND – I'd love to take you!"

Our meal came and was good, not great, but good. As we ate, "I'd love to go with you Pablo," she said.

I followed her to her place, parked and sauntered up to her porch, saying, "I think you and I have something unique!" "Si, Pablo," she replied. We went in, she got me a drink, turned on some music and we snuggled on her couch. I took a drink of scotch and remarked to myself, it's nice to be warm inside and out. One snug led to another, so to bed we went. A climactic event to say the least. Good dinner, better drink, best sex! The rule of the day: "Good, Better, Best, never let it rest. 'Til your good is better and your better is best!

We drifted off, and I felt absolutely fulfilled as we did so, at least I did, and I felt she felt fulfilled as well.

I woke to the smell of bacon. I didn't even ask last night if Sara was working today. In fact, I didn't even know what day of the week it was. Her presence in the kitchen said "Yes," she was off. "Buenos dias, Pablo," Sara said, as I walked into the kitchen. "I didn't think to tell you that I'm off today," she added. "Great news to me," I said. "Breakfast is almost ready," Sara said. "Super; bacon, eggs, fried potatoes, toast and butter, can't get much better," I said. "How long will this threat exist, Pablo?" she said. "I don't know; we'll have to destroy all producers of the tainted coffee and develop a new detection scenario for consumption phenomenon like this. It is a very scary concept, adding a highly addictive component to a highly consumed product. Coffee was ideal because of the addictive caffeine inherent in the beans. Although improbable, world domination is possible; which adds a political and dictatorial component to the threat. To answer your question less verbose . . . as soon as all traces of production are destroyed! Total destruction could take weeks but this would probably not involve me, Sara," I said. "I'm involved now only because I'm ex-FBI, a mercenary of sorts, and stumbled on the threat myself. I'm hoping I'm involved only a short time, but it all depends on the success of various Task and Special Forces," I added.

"But changing the subject, what would you like to do after breakfast?" I asked. "Take a ride and a picnic lunch to a beach I know of nearby, "The Playa Ancon," she said. "Sounds good to me," I said. We washed the breakfast dishes, put away food and got out lunch stuff. Chorizo bologna was new to me, but cheese crackers and wine rounded out chorizo sandwiches. We talked about our childhoods, while packing our picnic lunch. She had been abused by her uncle at 14 years old; just blooming into a beautiful body and spirit. So, she moved out on her own a year later; rough, but it taught her to be tough, and she had toughened into a survivor. She cleaned, washed, and babysat until she got a job as a stock boy (although by now there would be no mistaking her for a boy) and she has been at the Galleria Commercial Universo ever since. It was good to get to know her better. She then asked, "So what was your childhood like?" "I guess that I've always been blessed," I said. "My first job was cutting grass, this moved on to delivering newspapers (the only source of news in those days; no competitors, most had no television, and radio was very commercial, but I digress). I got interested in magic by seeing a movie with Tony Curtis, about Harry Houdini. I mastered cards and small hand tricks in my bedroom at home until I got pretty good. I then offered to perform at local Senior Citizen Old Age Homes and pretty soon got offers to do shows for pay at birthday parties, etc. I enjoyed doing my passion and getting paid pretty well for it. I wasn't very good in school, not because I was dumb but because I didn't apply myself. At least I tell myself that. I saved enough money to buy a car and was "Hot Shit" in my senior year in High School. I went to a land grant college in the same city and studied problem solving and criminal law. Graduated Salutatorian and was offered a job at the FBI. Clerical stuff to begin with, then field work fighting crime and corruption. That's about it; fell in love with fishing along the way and ended up with the BFB."

"Wow," Sara said, "Now we know both of our backgrounds and I do love you." "I do love you too, Sara Sonata!" I said. "How in the hell did two pirates in the Straits of Florida attacking my boat lead to a romance turned into love and devotion?" I said.

"God works in mysterious ways," Sara said.

"Are you ready to go to the Playa Ancon?" she suggested, changing the subject. I said, "Yes, let's do this." I took the lunch bag and towels and Sara took the wine and a small cooler, and we went to my car since it was an expensed rental.

We drove to the beach and it was almost deserted due to overcast skies, probably? Parked, got out, grabbed our lunch stuff and walked down about ten yards from the surf and sat down on towels. Beautiful! The ocean is a majestic, magnificent thing; both gentle and powerful, and much of the earth. We enjoyed the serenity, looked, laughed and loved. "Te guiero," she said. "Te quiero, mas," I said. "Right here?" I said. She said, "Why not?" Alrighty then; we gently removed each other's shirts and swimsuits and proceeded to magnify the majesty existing in this place, at this time. Who cared about the four other people some four hundred yards away; they didn't even notice our carnal conjugation on the white sands of Playa Ancon.

We lie there, hearing the surf, staring at the clouds in the sky, trying to make faces or objects out of the cloud's formations and Sara said, "Thank you, Pablo." I said, "No, thank you, and do you think we should put our suits back on?" We put our bathing attire back on and continued to lie on our backs, enraptured.

Nearly lunch time, so I broke out the vino and poured two glasses of Chardonnay (with ice in the glass).

PART THREE

Suriname

My super, son of a bitch, cellphone rang and my heart sank. Okay, what now? "Jack Warner, here," the voice said. "Just an update Paul, just an update." "Okay," I said. "We've successfully shut down two more Cartel operations. But the last one in Suriname, that one has been a hard nut to crack, but we do know that it has a lab, several storage facilities and is surrounded by coffee fields and heavy forest as well. The Suriname complex was also larger than the other operations. We surmised that it was because it was geared up to cover Brazil, a very large country. Numerous ports were on the periphery of this country and easily accessed by boats with hulls full of modified coffee. Suriname is 1900 miles from you, Paul. Just think about it, we may want you to head an assault on the Suriname facility." "I plan to contact Armando Ortega and Andy Pellerito to put on standby with you," Jack added. "Okay, Jack, advise of any changes. Should I just hold on here or go back to Key West?" I said. "I think you should probably go back to Key West because it's close to NAS, and they can accommodate a large C-17," Jack said. "Will do, keep me posted," I said as I clicked off my phone.

"Well," I told Sara, "That was Jack Warner and he has put me on standby for a probable mission to Suriname in Brazil."

"There were thirteen major operations in the Coffee Cartel and Suriname appears to be the largest and most invasive," I said. "Could you come with me?" I added. "Well, I'm supposed to work tomorrow. I don't get much time off, since I run the Mall," she said. But added, "Maybe I can work something out." "I probably need to get on the road, it's 1 p.m. and I can get back to the Havana Airport by 6 p.m. There's a 7 p.m. flight to Key West," I said. She said, "It's okay, we had a beautiful time here on the beach and last night, which will hold me for a while."

"Okay, honey," I said as I started picking up towels and picnic basket. We packed up and headed for my rental KIA. We drove, not speaking a word, until we reached her place. I let her with all the beach paraphernalia out. Sara set the things down and came over to the driver's side. I rolled the window down and said, "Okay, I'm getting out." We hugged, kissed and she said, "I love you Pablo. Please be careful if you get this mission, and it sounds like a dangerous one."

I Said, "I will, my love." I got in and drove off. The road to Havana was scenic and all, but this is ridiculous . . . Cienfuegos, Güines, LA Catalina, Guanabacoa, the Santa

Fe suburb. I knew them all by heart now, having made so many trips. The trip always seemed much longer coming back from Trinidad. I guess because that's where Sara is.

Got there in time after taking in the Kia, ticket purchase and security check. Thank God that many more flights are available since Obama reduced restrictions. I sat at the gate wondering what was going to transpire if I was called to Brazil. They called boarding and I got on.

It was 7:36 p.m. when they landed and I was exhausted. I thought I'd better get rest and exercise, if possible, to get in shape for a takeover in Suriname. Found the Chevy and headed to the Conch House and to bed.

Got up at 8 a.m. after over eleven hours of good sleep; only had to get up once. Got coffee downstairs and tried to wake up. A second cup would be required, after the whirlwind trip to Trinidad and back. I'll do some exercises in my room, I thought; pushups, sit-ups, knee bends, all the things you can do without benefit of weights or a gym. Really just as good a workout if done right. After my room workout, I thought I'd just jog down Truman Street to Denny's and get breakfast. The workout and jog were refreshing, and a big breakfast didn't hurt either. Ironically; Healthy and unhealthy combined in the morning.

I anticipated a call soon, especially since Jack wanted me back in Key West and the fact that squashing the Coffee Cartel completely was so urgent. I walked further down to Duval and turned towards LaTeDa and remembered that I jogged to breakfast without my super cellphone and turned around, walking back past CVS, the laundry and the "Better Than Sex" dessert restaurant.

Walking more briskly, I felt I had gotten a call. I got back to the room and checked my phone; no calls! "Lucked out on that faux pas!" I thought. I just remembered that I hadn't let Sara know that I'd gotten here. I texted her, "Arrived last night and went to bed, all is good."

Turned on the TV and the Key Largo outbreak was on. It was apparent that the newscasters didn't know the cause of the sickness. I felt that the FBI had probably influenced the news to create a virus and not cause panic with the real threat. It was not a virus as it was portrayed, it was withdrawal from altered cocaine-tainted coffee. If Jack had not updated me, I too would have wondered what kind of virus Key Largo was stricken with?

Sara texted me back, "Glad you made it, please keep me posted, Love Sara." Wow, not only did I discover one of the biggest threats ever known to our planet but found the best woman for me on this same planet! God is good, and he not only used me to help avert the threat but rewarded me with a satisfying and fulfilling love.

Got the call. "Paul?" it said. "Yes," I said. "Get to NAS by 6 p.m. for a six and half hour flight to the Cartel location near Suriname, Brazil. About thirty Seals and Special Forces will accompany you, Armando and Andy. There will be Nomex jumpsuits and boots for everyone in the hanger building next to the airfield. The C-17 will fly over and you will all parachute out into the adjacent coffee field. I'll text you a map showing the main building and laboratory. You should enter the NW corner of the main building (which usually has four guards – two on the back side of the door). There are normally two more guards on top of each building, which are assumed to be snipers. There is also a helicopter in the middle of the main roof. There are over a dozen souls inside the main building and a half dozen in the lab. We assume most of them are armed, due to their positioning or the thermal imaging; i.e., two inside the lab door, almost always stationary. We'll have a fighter flyby just after you parachute out and land, to take out those snipers and helicopter on the roof, so don't worry about them; you'll be ground assault all the way. I suggest you send ten of the Special Forces and Seals around to the lab and the remainder will simultaneously attack the main building."

"Sounds like a plan," I said, "Ammo?" Jack said, "Yes, you will have four grenades each (two colored smoke and two new fragmentation, all with five second delays). Each of you will also have fully automatic AO-38 assault rifles with two additional clips each. Each will have a set of Sightmark Ghost Hunter night vision goggles, since the fighter will take out the power supply to the complex prior to firing on the snipers and helicopter." Each will also have a Gerber Serrated Knife. Each allotment will be on the C-17's bulkhead along both sides. Each Seal grabs their allotment in flight," he said. "Anything else," I said. "God Speed," he said.

It was noon and I sat on the couch trying to revisit each element of what Jack had just spelled out. Timing and surprise would be everything, I thought. The jet flyover and take out of the copter and snipers should be just as we attack the four guards outside the main door. The departure time of 7 p.m. from NAS would put us parachuting out about 2 a.m. in the dark of night and all but posted sentries would be asleep.

I could go over the plan with the troops slowly and methodically during the long flight, with ample time for refinement and questions and answers. Armando and I would head the assault with backup from the rest. Andy would lead the lab attack simultaneously with our main building assault.

After reflecting on the plan, I became more and more confident that it would be successful and maybe the last attack on the Coffee Cartel? I just hoped that there were only thirteen sites and that this would be the last to fall.

I ordered an Italian BMT from the Subway sandwich shop a block away, and they deliver! I studied the photo and map that Jack had texted me. I would use a marker on a large, unpainted canvas taken from the artist's room of the B&B and duplicate the map, as close as possible.

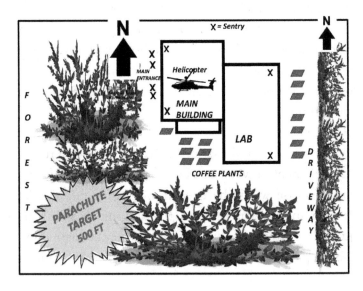

Okay, I said to myself, what else do I need to do to assure success? I must outwardly display complete confidence and composure. The weather forecast was 20% chance of rain, with SW wind of about 6 KTS. The forecast would be great for the assault, I thought, even if it did rain. Our A0-38 night vision goggles and grenades were all water proof.

It was now about 3 p.m., so I thought I had time to go over the plan from start to finish and expose any flaws. Group assembly in the hanger where the jumpsuits are. Addressing the group and assertion of the complete agenda would be dealt with on the six and half hour flight to Suriname. The element of surprise and timing were paramount, as noted earlier.

My thoughts shifted to Sara. I'd better call her as I said I would to keep her notified. I called on my encrypted phone. "Hola," she said, truncating her normal greeting? "Hola, En qué te puedo ayudar?" I said, "Pablo here." She said, "Thank God, I was worried about you!" I said, "I've been busy planning an attack on the last Coffee Cartel operation in Suriname. We're scheduled to leave NAS at 7 p.m. this evening." I added, "It will be a 2 a.m. assault with me and about thirty-two others. The others are super-trained Seals and Special Ops warriors, so I'm confident the mission will be successful."

Sara said, "I'll be praying for you Pablo." "Thanks, my love," I said. "It will be a while before I'll be able to talk to you, but I'll be fine," I added. "I love you Pablo," she said. "Love you too," I said, and hung up.

What else did I need to do before heading to NAS? I guess a redundant mental recap of the assault procedure would be in order. Da to Da, Ta Da, Te Da, Te Da, . . . as I mentally recalled each step.

I thought I would leave about 5 p.m., since there wasn't anything to do here. I took my credentials and canvas sketch and got in my blue, carpool Chevy and drove off. It was a short fifteen-mile drive to NAS. Over and over I reviewed the assault scenario.

The gate guard knew me by now and waived me through.

I thought I knew where to go and looked for the large C-17, found at the nearby hanger. I found several airmen separating our weaponry and taking it to the C-17, just in time. It was a noteworthy effort to get all those supplies to the plane before the 7 p.m. departure time, since the plan was only generated this morning, per Jack.

I felt confident that we were ready. I went to the cubby-holes housing our jumpsuits, boots, goggles and change of clothes. A busload of Special Ops and Seals drove up and unloaded. They too donned their jumpsuits. I greeted each with a confident "Hello, bless you." They deliberately put on their suits and reported on the ready.

After they were all assembled, I announced, "My name is Pilot, Paul Pilot and I'll be your commander on this mission. All aspects of this assault will be given on the way to Suriname." "Bless you all, we are on the right hand of God and country on this one," I added. Everyone pulled down the bulkhead flight chairs and sat down, preparing for departure. Solemn facial expressions were the norm. No one said a word. The C-17's main engine revved up; a powerful sound. Six and a half hours of calm engine noise would be followed by a few minutes of terror. As we reached an altitude of nearly horizontal flight, I got up to start my pre-attack submission to the troops. I said, "You may or may not be aware that this mission will help stop a threat of world domination. I know that is mind boggling, but that's the way it is. A Cartel was formed, we think in Costa Rica, by a man called El Patron and his subordinates. The Cartel's laboratories were led by a genius, biochemical master who developed a transformed version of the cocaine molecule that defied detection. It was even more addictive than cocaine in its purest form. The Cartel experimented with consumer goods and came up with tainted coffee. Coffee is consumed worldwide and when the altered cocaine saturated the coffee beans, the resultant coffee was so addictive that the user had to get more.

This Coffee Cartel raised crops of coffee all over the southern latitudes and began shipments via medium-sized vessels with an innocent exterior that appeared to observers to be fishing or cruising yachts. We believe only a few shipments were made before the Cartel's motives were discovered. Key Largo, Florida, for example, was one of the original target markets, and those that consumed are currently going through horrible withdrawals.

This Coffee Cartel has been seriously incapacitated, as our special forces have destroyed or neutralized ten coffee operations to date. We believe the Suriname

Operation to be the last of them and we are charged with its destruction.

You will find behind each seat a stash of weapons; four grenades, two smoke (yellow paint) and two frag (blue paint). Your rifles are fully automatic AO-38's with two additional clips above the one in the gun. You also have a serrated knife as backup.

I pulled out the rolled-up canvas showing an aerial plan view of the Suriname installation and asked the group to come in closer.

Our plan is to parachute out and all land as close as possible in a coffee field southwest of the main buildings. The lab is on the southeast side and connected to the main building. Andy Pellerito is leading the lab assault team; I pointed to Andy and an accumulated ten soldiers to be on the lab team under Andy. Thermal reconnaissance revealed that two sentries are normally on each side of the lab door. There are thought to be an additional five or six potential guards inside the lab. Andy will talk to his ten separately.

The remaining twenty of you will be following Armando and I; I pointed to Arm (Armando). There are snipers on the roof of the main building, along with a helicopter. Those snipers and copter will be taken out by fighters as soon as we've landed in the coffee field. There are four guards normally positioned at the NW corner of the main building (pointing to my sketch). There are another dozen guards inside the main building. Our early morning assault will be initiated by the fighter flyover to take out the copter and snipers. We will separate in the field into two groups; the lab ten and the main building twenty. Each group runs to and disables the outside guards with rifle fire. Then each group enters and eliminates any hostiles!

"Any questions?" I asked. "Why the two types of grenades?" someone asked. "It is thought that the fragmentation grenades, the ones painted blue, will be thrown in the main rooms prior to entry, followed by the smoke grenades, painted yellow." I said.

"All this orientation is a suggested approach . . . you are all well-trained soldiers. Use your intuition and guts to kill these criminals. The Coffee Cartel must be stopped," I said. "We'll have another meeting one hour prior to the assault, in case you have further concerns," I added.

Storm clouds and thermals over water at about four hours into the flight caused some turbulence and rough riding for a while, but it passed. Small talk prevailed among the troops; some talking about their families and others boasting about their female quests. All of this talk most assuredly caused by the anticipation and fear involved in this kind of raid. We all knew the sentries, guards and henchmen were all armed and protecting their livelihood; albeit corrupt, illegal, immoral and devastating to innocent coffee consumers.

Armando came over and said, "We've come a long way in stopping this threat, but something keeps bugging me?" I said, "What's that, my friend?" "Well, you know when we questioned Pascal Padron, I had no doubt that he had told us all he knew, but El Patron's disclosure was somewhat different?" he said, and went on, "El Patron was hurt, lost a finger and all that, but I can't get rid of the feeling he didn't give up everything." He added, "I know that everything he gave us checked out, it's just gnawing at me that there's more? Maybe I'm crazy, but intuition in interrogation is a requirement, isn't it?" I said, "Armando you may be right, even though El Patron seemed distraught, there might have been some deception there as well." "Maybe we should go back and see if we can get more after this Suriname operation is terminated?"

We'd been in the air for over five hours, so I got the attention of the troops and reminded them that I said there would be another session about an hour ahead of our assault. "Your parachutes are located in the high bulkhead locker behind you. They are the MC1-1C series and have been double- checked for proper rigging. They should help us all land in the small area of the coffee field, shown here near the SW corner of the complex." I pointed to the area again on the canvas I'd taken from the Conch House. "Any questions?" I said. "We'll split up in groups of ten and twenty, as I alluded to earlier, and take these SOB's down! Any weaponry questions or concerns?" I said. SILENCE. "Okay, God be with us," I said. "Henry, the pilot, will advise ten minutes prior to our jump!" I concluded.

The ten-minute warning came sooner than expected, due to a tailwind of 15-Knots. "Okay everyone, crunch time in nine minutes, parachutes on and stand ready with weapons in-hand!" I said.

"Four minutes." "Three minutes." "Two minutes." "open jump door, attach carabiners!"

"Go, Go, Go!"

One-by-one we all jumped, one immediately after the other. And with some string guidance on the chutes, we landed in a fairly tight formation. A minute or so after we all landed the fighters roared over, hopefully taking out the snipers on top of the main building and lab. The copter exploded in a ball of flames, so we advanced and the group split, running to our respectful targets.

Armando, myself and the Seals got within range of the sentries who were normally at the NW corner of the main building. But they were far from stationary. They were running around shouting in a very strange language, as a result of the fire and explosion on top of their building. Moving targets, though they were, we all unloaded on them and they all went down; not one or two, all went down! We moved closer and closer until shots were being fired from two or three windows. I motioned for two Seals each to fire in each window continuously until the rest of us could enter. I snuck under a window and tossed in a frag grenade. It went well and no more shots came out of that window.

We went in the door one-by-one, darting behind pillars and furniture to avoid fire. There were plenty of shots being fired. I motioned to a half dozen to get out smoke grenades and throw them toward the flashes of gunfire. Onward we pushed. The grenades seemed to stop most of their firepower but some persisted, which our Seals made silent very quickly. Another room, another gun to face, I thought in a flash. Someone behind me saw the shooter that I'd missed, and shot him! "Thanks," I yelled, not knowing who exactly I was thanking. Onward! We quickly cleared the entire building; several bodies lay behind, but who was in charge (he must be in the building)? Where was he? Main bedroom would be my first choice, so I walked to the main bedroom to see if the Chief was there? Yes, almost under the Super King-sized bed was a nicely robed man in his fifties! I looked around for identification, but nothing. We'd been told to "neutralize and get out!" by the Sector Chief prior to the Suriname mission.

Okay, I told myself, I don't need to dwell over a potential Chief, just go out to where the CH-53K Stallion Helicopters would be (just west of the main building's main entrance). I was one of the last to arrive in the yard and Stallions were landing in succession.

I learned, en-route, that Andy and the lab team had been equally successful and the entire Suriname operation was destroyed! We had only lost one of our troops, but ironically that was still a great success! Sadly, as Commander of this mission, I would have to be the conveyor of horrible news to his spouse.

The Stallion took us to the Johan Pengel International Airport to change back to the Troop Carrier C-170 that would take us back to NAS, Key West. I'm sure that Jack Warner or someone will arrange for the deceased's spouse to be at NAS when the troops return. I dreaded the encounter, but really it was an honor! We, including her husband, may have stopped one of the biggest threats mankind has known. It would be over six hours before we'd get back, and I and the others quickly closed our eyes and dropped off. A lot of calorie energy was expended from all of us in that takeover, I thought. No wonder we all collapsed in our fold-down chairs! We all seemed to gain consciousness about the same time; about three hours into the flight. Now, it was the opposite vibe than it was when we were on our way to Suriname. An air of accomplishment was pervasive in the large hull of this airship.

I too, felt the sense of accomplishment, but Armando's reservation had me thinking that the destruction of this Suriname complex may not be the last? The sense of achievement was dampened by Armando's reservations. I kept reflecting on El Patron's interrogation. He certainly appeared tortured and submissive, but we must question him again as soon as we can arrange it upon our return. I went to Armando and asked again if he agreed to re-question El Patron. He said, "Of course, Paul." "It would just continue to haunt me if we didn't interrogate and satisfy our minds; either Suriname was the last of the Cartel's operations or not?" he added. I would call Jack after arriving back in Key West and catching some sleep! I'm sure everyone in this mission felt the same. A lost night's sleep was a small price to pay when the mission was as important as ours, especially since I was not injured or killed, which could have been so easy! I sat there in the huge belly of that plane praying to God and thanking him for allowing me to keep fighting for what I truly believed was his will. This Coffee Cartel could possibly have controlled coffee consumers worldwide! I looked around and about half the troops were sound asleep; I too, drifted off again.

A distinct slowing of the engines and a slight downward inclination caused me and several others to awaken. Yes, it appeared we were on a downward decent. It had been a hell of a trip, I thought. The Co-captain came back and told us, "We should land in about ten minutes. There will be several spouses, the Commander of NAS, the Deputy Director of the FBI (Harvey Hyde), Special Agent Jack Warner and others in a reception party. I know, I know; but they are a very grateful and congratulatory group, don't fight it. Thank God that they're there.

We landed, the aft hatch opened, and we started to depart leaving our weapons, etc. behind. It was a crowd, it was very bright, about noon Key West time and we slowly stepped down the stairway to the tarmac. Hell, there was Jack, Harvey, and I don't know who all? I shook Jack's hand, while he said, "Welcome Paul!" I said, "Thanks Jack!" He said, "We have Isaac's wife here." Issac was the Seal who lost his life in the assault. What a shame, after such a successful mission, but as I thought before, an honor. Jack pulled her off to the side and I told her that I was truly sorry, but Isaac didn't make it. She collapsed, screaming, "No, No, No!" I tried to console her, but it was a feeble attempt at best.

Two NAS counselors escorted Mrs. Robinson (Isaac's wife) away and all I could do was look on as she departed. Another mission! I went back to Jack and told him that Armando and I had reservations about El Patron's interrogation. Jack said, "What? Reservations? Everything that he told us was verified!" "I know, I know," I said. "Everything El Patron told us was corroborated, I understand, but Armando and I doubt that he told us everything!" I said. "There was just a hint of nondisclosure felt by Armando, and when I reflected back on the entire scenario, I too shared Armando's concern," I added. "What the hell, Paul? I thought we'd squelched the Coffee Cartel with this last Suriname raid; but you say no!" Jack said. "I didn't say no, I said maybe and what the hell can it hurt to go at El Patron again. He's a ruthless bastard anyway!" I said.

As the reception party disbursed and the couples left, Armando and I walked with Jack to the nearest hangar office. "Okay guys," Jack said after we got in and closed the door. "When do you want to do this thing? I must tell you, if there are more, it's urgent. But, I didn't need to tell you that did I?"

"We're exhausted Jack, and wouldn't be on top of our game; we would not be able to do a re-interrogation of a tough cookie justice!" I said. He agreed. "Where are you staying Arm?" I said. "Nowhere," he said, "I just flew in to make the Suriname raid." "Okay, Jack, Armando and I will go to my place and get back here about 9 p.m. tonight to question our beloved El Patron," I posited. Jack said, "Okay, I'll be here as well. I need peace of mind also."

Armando and I walked to where I'd left the blue carpool Chevy, and got in. "Armando, are you hungry?"

I said. "Famished," he said. So I thought we'd go to Goldman's Deli and get a real breakfast. It was only a little out of the way to the Conch House. We pulled up in the Winn-Dixie parking lot where Goldman's was located. We walked in and looked at the menu, and simultaneously chose the Lumberjack's Breakfast: 3 eggs, bagel and cream cheese; three pieces of French toast, sausage and ham; with apple butter and syrup on the side. We both ate the whole damn thing and drove back to my place for some sleep. Armando was happy with the couch at this point and I set the alarm for 8 p.m. It was 1:15 p.m.; a decent sleep period, I thought. My mind was racing around and around; the attack adrenalin should have been dissipated and absorbed by now. So, I guest it was just anxiety, but I finally dropped off.

The alarm sounded like Old Ben and it took a moment to grip reality and turn it off. I made some untainted coffee and had to shake my old friend Armando. He was in REM big time, and grabbed me when I shook him. I said, "Java is pending, my friend." "Okay!" he said. "Wow, we died, didn't we Pablo," he added. We sat for a minute, drinking our coffee. "I hope you're wrong Armando, but I have a gnawing feeling that you're right," I said. "Well, for sure we'll find out the whole story tonight. I'll start with Agua and see where we go from there," Armando said. I was thinking how lucky we were to have Armando. He was a relentless and knowledgeable interrogator and soldier. I'd go into battle with him anywhere, and the fact that he spoke three dialects, Spanish, Portuguese and English, made him invaluable when questioning a Cuban like El Patron. He could detect a nuance of deception in verbal Spanish responses.

I made a cup of coffee to go in a Styrofoam cup for each of us, and we put on our clothes. "Okay buddy, let's talk to the Son of a Bitch," I said, as we walked to the Chevy. It would only take ten to fifteen minutes to get to NAS and we were ready.

We pulled up to the building housing El Patron. The doors were more heavily guarded after the jail breaking attempt day before yesterday by Patron's cohorts. We showed our credentials and entered. Jack greeted us and said, "Good Luck guys, this may be the most important interrogation ever performed, anywhere." That seemed to register with both of us, as if we didn't know already how serious it was! The guards took El Patron to the interrogation room that we'd used to find the coffee operations we had learned of. Armando prepared his water procedure. El Patron said, "Que demorrios esta pasando?" which Armando said was, "What the hell is going on?" Armando said, "Nos dijeste everything antes?" "Ci," Patron responded. "No," said Armando, as he turned on a stream of water from a jury-rigged hose above him. We made El Patron disrobe and, with help from the two guards with us, made him kneel on his feet and hands with the water stream impinging on the L5 vertebrae of his back. Armando had said on the way to NAS that this particular backbone causes extreme pain if the water stream is incessant. He said it depended on the individual, but thirty minutes usually did it, even in extreme cases. El Patron was immobile in his crouching position due to the chair he rested his stomach on, as the guards held him. No response after ten minutes, so Armando put a siren on the loudspeaker to annoy him. The guards, Armando and I had earplugs, so I proceeded to get candy bars from the machine in the galley and made some coffee for us. Twenty minutes into it and Armando got out his finger scissors, while El Patron eyed him showing horror in his eyes and expression. El Patron exclaimed, "No, No se nada mas!" "Nada mas," he said again. The water must have felt like a jackhammer by now, but he was saying, "I know no more, no more." Twenty-five minutes and he started crying, screaming and saying, "No mas, No mas!"

Armando cut off another finger on the same hand that hadn't healed yet, and said, "Tell us about the entire operation in Spanish." El Patron, in extreme agony, shouted, "Okay, Okay, Okay, hay una seccion Africana!" "What the hell was that?" I said. Armando said, "There was more, another operation in Africa!" "African?" I said. "Yes, he said, African," Armando retorted. "Oh my God!" I said, as Jack came in the room. "It looks like your intuition was correct," Jack announced. "I was very doubtful after all that El Patron went through before, but you were right," Jack added. "Ask him where and who is in charge there?" Jack said, urgently. Armando asked him without stopping the water (the siren only was silenced when we addressed El Patron), "A Donde esta el Operation?" Silence! "Okay," Armando said, getting his finger shears again, "A Donde esta Operation?" Armando severed another finger (only a thumb and forefinger left on this appendage). "AHE," El Patron screamed, "Okay, Okay." "El Gran Jefe me matara!" Armando offered; it means that the big chief will kill him! "El Gran Jefe me matara," El Patron said again. Armando went for the finger shears again and cut off El Patron's right forefinger, an essential digit to say the least! El Patron, almost collapsing, said, "Okay, Okay," and fainted.

PART FOUR

Isiolo, Kenya

"Smelling Salts," Arm asked of the guards. The guard immediately went to a wall cabinet and retrieved smelling salts for Arm. Arm broke one capsule and El Patron jumped to awareness. "Okay, Okay," he said. "Que pregutaste?" Armando immediately said, "A Donde esta el Operacion?" El Patron said, "Kenya." "Kenya," I said out loud, "Kenya?" "Holy Shit!" I said. "That's a different continent! They and we are facing the same damn threat." "Shit," Arm said, "Africa is a big coffee consumer, although tea is big there also; it is a substantial producer of coffee, although few knew. Kenya produces 150,000 metric tons of coffee a year, and the notorious Ivory Coast is very close!" Arm never ceased to amaze me with his knowledge. "Donde en Kenya," he asked. "Isiolo!" El Patron screamed. "Quun dirige everything?" Which meant, "who runs everything?" Armando replied. "El Gran Jefe en Isiolo,

Kenya," El Patron quickly responded. Jack, intently listening to every Word, said, "Jesus, there's a Gran Jefe in friggin' Africa!" Armando, not satisfied, asked, "Como se llama?". El Patron said, "No se?" Which even I knew meant, I don't know. "Estas Seguro," Armando added. El Patron said, "Ci, Ci Senor!" Armando said, "I think we have all we're going to get." Jack agreed, so we stopped the water and had El Patron taken to his cell, crying and moaning.

Wow, what a revelation, I thought. The earth had two Coffee Cartel operations on opposite sides of the globe! We hoped we got all of the Central American and Cuban operations, but only hoped! Now we had a real threat, maybe bigger, in Isiolo, Kenya. Isiolo was centrally located in Kenya and GMO coffee plants thrive in the central Kenyan high-altitude environment. The FBI and Jack had more surveillance and investigation to do, for sure!

I caught Arm, after Jack had left and El Patron was taken back to his cell after they tended to his lost fingers, and said, "Armando, you are a fantastic interrogator and your intuition about El Patron holding something back during the first interrogation was right on! It's obvious now, that Patron's strong reluctance was the fear of death at the hands of El Gran Jefe!"

His fear was offset by Armando's persistence and mind-bending tactics. "Thanks again," I said. "Por nada," he said, "Esta Gratis."

It was 2 a.m. and we were both tired again, so I said, "Are you ready to go back to my place and get some shuteye?" Armando said, "Yes, absolutely." The guards helped us close up shop and we went to my Chevy. As we departed NAS, I thought of how strategic it was for the Coffee Cartel to be in two main areas and, from there, be able to cover the globe. It seemed as though the Cartel might have been started in Kenya rather than Costa Rica, as originally thought. The big chief of it all was not El Patron, but El Gran Jefe, and he was in Kenya of all places.

We got back to the Conch House and went straight to bed; no small talk, no nothing.

As I drifted off, I thought I hadn't talked to Sara for over two days. If she only knew what I'd been through?

It was 2 p.m. before I awoke and glanced at my Rolex (the best investment ever! A Pepsi Rolex that I'd acquired through a jeweler in Tucson who imported it through Nogales, Mexico and I paid $750.00 for it. It was now worth $17,000!). Oh well, need coffee! As soon as I became somewhat coherent, I called Sara. It was the same time in Trinidad, so she would be at the Mall. She again answered, "Hola, Como puedo Ayudarte?" I said, "Hola, Angel." She said, "Oh Pablo, I've been worried sick about you!" "I'm fine," I said. "We had a successful raid of the Suriname operation and have uncovered another coffee organization in Kenya, Africa." "Wow," she said, "So the threat persists?" "Yes," I said, "We just found out about the Kenyan Operation last night, so there's still a lot of unknowns." "Evidently, there was a bigger chief than El Patron in Africa. El Patron called him El Gran Jefe." "The big chief," she said. "Stay safe my love, and when can I see you?" she added. "I have no idea, Sara. This Kenyan discovery opens a new can of worms," I said. "I'll just call when I can," I concluded. "Okay," she said.

Armando was up and looking for coffee. I thought, I'd better call Carl and see if the BFB is still afloat. I called Carl's cell, but no answer. Why was I not surprised?

Armando said, "I feel like I've been hit by a train." "I know, I know," I said. "I can only imagine what Jack Warner's going through; calling, re-energizing surveillance, drone, plane and helicopter flights, Special Forces (which now includes charade teams posing as realtors, insurance salesmen, etc.)." "This is certainly a departure from the norm; Isiolo, Kenya was certainly an unexpected and unusual target. I looked on the net and it has about 80,000 residents. I doubt that El Gran Jefe lives in town; he probably has an estate similar to El Patron's outside of the city," I said. "You know, Armando, El Patron said that the Big Chief (El Gran Jefe) was the other complex or another complex? It could well be the head of a network of enterprises, just like El Patron's. Patron had thirteen in total, we think? What if any network does the Big Chief have? Are they in their infancy or did they start long before the Central America and Cuban operations? One hell of a lot of unanswered questions, at this point," I thought out loud.

Armando said, "God only knows?" "But with all the agencies, special forces and state of the art surveillance technology at its disposal, well soon get answers to these questions," he added.

I thought, maybe this is a lull in activity until enough is known to act on, and I could find out about my boat, Carl and see Sara? Yes, it would be some time, although accelerated as fast as the FBI could to find actionable info! It was 3 p.m. now and if I was to charge off, find a flight, rent a car and go like hell, it would probably be around midnight before I could get to Sara and again tired. So I thought I should call Jack and tell him of my plans.

I dialed Jack; the phone was busy, so I left a message. He'd call when he got a break from finding out about the Coffee Cartel in Kenya and El Gran Jefe! I looked and found an early departure from EYW to Havana at 7 a.m. on Spirit. They had six open seats, so I wanted to book one, but still waited for Jack. Armando was enjoying leisure for a change and said he'd walk down to Duval and check the tourists out. I had probably called too much when Sara was at work; but hell, she was the boss! But then I said to myself, it was only an hour ago that I had filled her in on the Suriname affair, so I would wait until I had Jack's blessing and her agreement before booking the flight. Just keep your pants on Pablo, I thought.

I didn't want to get too far away, but I too wanted to be leisurely, so I decided to take a drive to Oceanside Marina and see if one of my old captain friends was still running out of there. Oceanside Marina was only about ten minutes away. I pulled up to the parking lot, parked and walked down to the slips. Bubba's boat wasn't there, but another boat's mate said, "Bubba's out right now on a full-day charter." "When do you think he may get back?" I said. "Usually five, but sometimes later," he said. "Okay, tell him Paul Pilot came to see him," I said, as I walked off. Got back to the car and drove off. I wouldn't think of anyone or anything else to go see, so I drove back via the old College Road, past the Lower Keys Medical Center (I had a nurse friend there a couple of years back), but I drove on and around to Roosevelt, and to the Conch House.

Arm was still walking or crawling Duval. Just as I was thinking I'd join Armando in a stroll, the phone rang. The voice said, "answer Paul," a flawed code for "really answer!" I said, "This is Paul." Jack said, "Paul, I've got some news, as preliminary as it is!" "What Jack?" I said. Jack said, "We've zeroed in on El Gran Jefe in Isiolo, Kenya!" I said, "What?" Jack said, "It appears that the Gran Jefe is a big business man in minerals and agriculture. It has been accepted that he is "The Big Chief!" around a very large central portion of Kenya. The Big Chief or Kubwa Mkuu is respected only because of his tyrannical demeaner, including threats and murder. The local merchants agree that "No one fucks with The Big Chief." His real name is "Wongari Kamau," and Kamau Farms is an Arabica coffee dynasty. Kamau Farms cultivates, grows and distributes Arabica coffee throughout Africa. We don't know much more at this point, except thermal imaging and drone flights show a sizeable number of sentinels and workers in a complex similar to El Patron's."

I said, "It doesn't look good, does it?" Jack responded, "No, it doesn't Paul." "There's a lot more to learn, but local rumors are that some of his coffee is making people sick in Mogadishu, Addis Ababa and Madagascar," he added.

I only hope it isn't what I think it is that ails these areas," he added. "It's not a stretch to think that," I said. "Look Jack, I would like to go check on the BFB and see Sara in Cuba for a while. Is that okay?" I asked. "Sure Paul, it will take some time to develop a takedown strategy, but this threat seems to be growing exponentially," Jack replied.

Alright then, call the airlines and make reservations for tomorrow morning. Computer apps are great for some things, like making flight reservations. It took one minute to get the 7:10 a.m. out of EYW to Havana. I then reserved a compact car (no use taking advantage of Uncle Sam) and poured myself a Macallan 18!

Wow! The Big Chief! Ironically, the Kenyans called him that and the Spanish speaking countries called him: El Gran Jefe! All the same thing; the head of the entire Coffee Cartel in, of all places, Kenya, Africa. The world is full of ironies and this one is horrific, I thought. Live, Laugh and Love, I thought; it will be wonderful to see Sara again! Those three "L's" continue to guide me, especially when being involved with anti-drug lord actions, like the Suriname raid. Live on, three L's, Live on, I thought.

Time for dinner and nothing to cook, and nothing to cook on, led to the conclusion to walk down to Duval and Antonio's. I didn't change attire or even take a shower, just walked off the front porch and started down Truman Avenue; walked past DJ's Clam Shack and Margaritaville to Antonia's. I had a thing for Italian food, in spite of a little reflux sometimes. I was seated and ordered my Ruffino Gold, as I sat. I couldn't resist the "Frutti de Mare" in white wine sauce. The combo of shrimp, scallops, clams and calamari in fettucine is superb.

My dinner came and it was as anticipated. I savored the last bite and ordered a Taylor Fladgate 20 to top things off, along with Tiramisu.

Walked back to the Conch House and Arm was still out on a well-deserved Holiday. I hit the sack, while setting my alarm for 5:30 a.m.

BAM! Rat-a-Tat, Tat, Tat, Tat; my alarm was the sound of an AR-15 shooting, so I got up. Untainted coffee was first on any day. I was eager to go back to Sara and got a shower, shaved, Pasha aftershave, teeth brushed, underarm deodorant; the whole nine yards. My best duds, levies and a Cuban vertically-striped white shirt, white loafers and a straw Panama. Packed enough for three days, but that might be too much in view of Jack's latest information. Another raid seemed imminent.

Went to the Chevy and drove to South Roosevelt and the airport. Went through security in a flash and was waiting in the holding area at 6:40 a.m. Loading Momentarily. I was Zone 2, so I patiently waited with my overnight bag.

Gave my boarding pass to the agent and walked out to the Saab 340B plane on the tarmac. Sat in Seat 15A and all is well.

Only 37 minutes later we set down in Havana, and it was forever before I could get off; some lady pulled her luggage from the overhead and couldn't hold on. It hit a little girl on the head and nothing but apologies and crying followed. They finally departed and so did I. The car rental was quick and easy, so I walked to the Nova I'd reserved.

I knew the highway to the Hemingway Marina and drove there. While driving to the marina, I called Arm's cell; he answered. I told him a synopsis of what Jack told me and told him to enjoy the Conch House and Key West, but be on standby per Jack Warner. I parked and walked to the BFB. I opened the plated Salon door (having been plated with Starboard after I'd blown a hole in it, that fateful night afloat!) and entered. No Carl! I stepped down the stairs to the Guest Suite and no one there, or the main suite. "No one home," I said out loud. I surveyed the interior and went to the engine room to check it out. A-OK. Bilges working, charger charging, no thru-hull leaks, no shaft leaks; all apparently shipshape. But where the hell was Carl? I called his cell and after two tries, he answered. "Carl O'Clancy, here." I said, "Carl, where are you?" He said, "Right here, Paul, right here." "Right where?" I said. "Loopee's Lair, my friend," he retorted. "Where the hell are you?" "I'm on the BFB, my bud," I said. "Alrighty then, hope you found her shipshape," he said. "I did, I did. Are you having a good time?" I said. "Never better, I'm in love," Carl confessed. "Hell, I guess we both are, my friend. I guess we both are! I'm going to run over to Trinidad to see my love and will keep in touch. This Coffee Cartel business is not over," I said. "Okay, keep me posted. Say, Paul, I wanted to take Loopee and some friends fishing, is that okay?" he said. "Sure," I said. "Tight lines," and I hung up.

I turned up the A/C and locked the salon door (old habits are hard to break). Went to the Nova and started on my familiar A1 Highway back to the other side of the island. I drove slowly, as there was no need to hurry; Sara wouldn't get off until six, but she told me where her key was so I could get in and freshen up.

I drove up (about 3 p.m.) to her hacienda, parked, took my bag, found the key, unlocked the door and laid on her couch. I set the cell alarm for 4:30 p.m., in case I went to sleep. I did.

Rat-a-Tat, Tat, Tat, Tat, and it was 4:30 p.m. Enough time to freshen up and get ready for my ebony angel. I showered and spritzed my face and neck with her favorite scent, Pasha by Cartier. Combed my mop, and put on the clothes I wore here. I turned on the TV, but couldn't understand a word, only bits and pieces of the news made sense. But I got a flash of the outbreak in Key Largo, and it appeared that it was now being called an altered virus! An altered coffee bean was more like it, I thought. A thorough autopsy of one of the victims, by an accomplished post mortem expert might reveal the real reason for their death. A thorough and detailed necropsy should show organs suffering from deprivation of a chemical and this chemical could be discovered to be a modified cocaine molecule, with unbelievable dependence properties.

Sara came in and we hugged for the longest time. "I missed you terribly," she said. "I missed you more!" I emphatically responded. "Thank God you made it through that Suriname ordeal," she said. "Yes, I'm blessed, but it isn't over," I said. "I never dreamed I would become a mercenary, but I guess I am," I added. I thought to myself, I'll bet Jack will follow through and give me the papers for the "Café Negro" Hatteras seized from El Patron a week ago.

"So, what's your pleasure my angel?" I said. "Why don't we go get dinner and come back here to find out more about one another?" she said. "We could, but if you have spaghetti or taco ingredients, I'll make you dinner while we get to know more!" I said. "No," she said, "I appreciate and will take you up on that offer, but let someone else cook." "Okay," I said, and she went to her bedroom to get ready. She returned in ten and she said, "Do you want to go back to the restaurant we met?" "Only if you do," I said. "We could also go to a new place." "I know of a nice, cozy upscale place called Sol Anoda that you should like," Sara said. "Yes," I said, "Sounds great."

I opened the front door for her and we left. We got in my rented Nova and drove off. She said, "It's on Real Del Jigüe." "Say What?" I muttered. "Just give me directions," I said. "Go about two miles and turn left," she said. 'Now, left," she said, "Then it will be on your right in about three miles." The building appeared old, but as we walked in I was pleasantly surprised. There was a very large room with tables of four to eight sitting all around. The waiter took us to a table for two on the side, facing each other, beside a window. The table was set well, with hand-crocheted doilies, linen napkins and a hand-stitched placemat with charger plates and old Stainless utensils. "This place also is known for their 'Bone-in Ribeye and sides," she said.

"Decision made," I offered. I ordered a nice Nichols Cab (surprised to see this here, but it is what it is) and a Lobster Bisque for both of us for starters. Sara said, "Well, have you had lovers before?" "Oh my, you cut to the chase, don't you," I said. "Yes, but it depends on how you define lover, I guess," I said. "I've made love to several, but only had three that went on for more than a night or two and one of those was my wife of twelve years." "And you?" I said. Sara paused, "I've never been married because I couldn't find someone who wanted the real me, not just my body." "I've had lovers to mutually satisfy needs, but nothing truly serious," she added. "Sometimes they seemed serious, but time exposed the superficial reality," she went on. "What happened with your wife?" she said. "Well, she smoked heavily before and after we were married and they and God took her about four years ago," I said.

Our dinner came and looked amazing. A sprig of Rosemary stuck out of the garlic potatoes, and white, smoked Gouda and macaroni and cheese balanced out the plates. We'd drunk three quarters of the bottle, so I ordered another. We stopped talking as much and enjoyed the meal. Sara said, "I'm glad that we've both had lovers, so that we can now appreciate what we have more!" "I never would have thought about it that way, but you're absolutely right, my dear," I responded. "Oh my God, that was good!" she said. "Yes, any more room?" I asked. "No mas, por favor," she responded. "Alright then," I said.

The waiter came back for dessert, but no takers around here. I waved him off and motioned for the check, which he acknowledged. She was just staring at me and said, "Pablito, Pablito!" I saw the admiration in her eyes and didn't say a word. We just sat looking admiringly at each other until Jorge, the waiter, brought the check. I gave him my travel rewards card, which the FBI had issued me, and he left momentarily. I added an additional ten percent to the bill, which had fifteen percent gratuity already in it (I hated the audacity of a restaurant that did this, but it was a wonderful meal and a beautiful evening there, so I made it twenty-five percent total).

We left after consuming one and three quarters bottles (about 1300 ml) of nice red wine and she asked if I could drive. I said, "I think so, can you?" She said, "I'm not sure, me amore?" So I opened the door for her and she said, "Such a gentleman, Pablo." I closed her door and got in the driver's side. "I think I know the way back, but help me, please," I stated. I aimed the Nova back the way we'd come and remembered it was about three miles before a right turn. As we approached what I thought was the right turn, she said, "Turn right my love." Her place should be a couple of miles away on the right. Sure enough it was, but she was out cold. I parked and went around to her side, opened the door and tried to wake her. Shake, Shake; "Pablito," she said. "Let's go into your home, Sara," I replied. "Okay," she whimpered. We walked arm-in-arm up to her home. I found her key in her purse, as I was hanging on to her; unlocked and opened the door, took her in to bed, laid her down, pulled her feet up onto the bed, and exhaled. We've all been there, I thought. The only thing about love, it's not sex, it's mutual respect, and I had it. I went into her living room and thought, what a lucky guy I am. I too, after a moments reflection, went into the bedroom, shed my clothes, and gently lay down next to her, so as not to disturb her.

I awoke with the sun shining brightly in her window, got up and closed the curtains and laid back down, next to "Sleeping Beauty." Eyes wide open, after about 5 minutes, I got up and went into her kitchen to make some coffee. Making coffee made me think of all the people around the world making coffee to start their day and how the Coffee Cartel could surreptitiously alter their coffee and cause widespread addiction around the world. I only hoped that the Kenyan Operation was in its infancy, like the Cuban and South American groups were. Just one bag or can of coffee could be enough for 25 cups of coffee and that would cause catastrophic withdrawals, if they didn't consume the same tainted brand. I wondered what the FBI was finding? Both Jack and Harvey were convinced of the Cartel's menace to say the least.

Sara awoke to the scent of brewing coffee and said, "I'll take mine with two creams and honey, my dear!" I found the honey by the coffee maker and took her a cup. "May I make you breakfast?" I said. She said, "No, come sit down." She moved to the center of the bed to give me room to sit. "Wow, too tired and too much vino, I guess," she whispered. "I know, I was out too, but what a great evening we had." I whispered back. "Si", she said.

"What would you like to do today? You don't have to work, right?" I said. "No work, just you, Pablo," as she grabbed my arm and pulled me to her. She kissed my arm and pulled me closer still. I could feel the blood rushing as the heart increased it's rhythm. I moved onto the bed and moved my body next to hers. She draped her arm over my waist and pulled my midsection closer. An erection started pulsating, and I kissed her voluptuous, full, Negroid lips. Tongues started thrashing in our mouths and there was no mistaking the following movements. I ascended and she repositioned to accept me. She lent a slight assist and . . . Oh My God! Numerous thrusts ended with both of us screaming and we collapsed, side-by-side. She said, "Pablo, you're amazing!" We both closed our eyes to enjoy the fulfillment that our creator instilled in all procreating species.

We awoke again and I rolled out of bed, content, satisfied and hungry. I went to the kitchen, found eggs, sausages, bread, cheese, onion, bell pepper, mushrooms and cheese ; all I would need for a nice omelet for two. Her frying pan was still in the dishwasher, but I finally found it. I looked again in the fridge for butter and milk. I heated the pan and broke five eggs in a pool of bubbling butter. Stirring with a wooden spoon, I added a little milk and cheese; stirring more, I added a sprinkle of chives, onion, pepper, mushrooms and cilantro. I hand-separated the sausage into little balls and added them after simmering them to golden brown in a separate frying pan. A little more cheese, stirring all the time, and I pushed the toaster lever down to start time completion for omelet and toast together. Perfecta mundo, it was ready! I plated her portion, buttered her toast, found a cookie pan and presented her breakfast in bed.

I made more coffee and enjoyed my half of the omelet and toast.

What a beautiful morning, sexual fulfillment, affection, sunlight, a nice breakfast; life was good and I thanked God for it!

Sara said that she loved the omelet, as I took her another cup of coffee. She had barely touched the first cup, before she seduced me!

"Let's take a drive around with no specific destination, just improvisation," she said. "Sounds good to me," I responded, as I went for another cup of Café Bustello.

We took our sweet time showering independently and getting ready for a casual, non-targeted drive around the area. We looked like touristas in our short pants and shirt and departed her hacienda for my rental Nova.

My temptation got the best of me and I asked if she would mind if we drove by the Patron Plantation to see what was going on? She said, "No, that's fine." I said, "I think it's on the road, right?" "Ci," she responded. Only a few miles and nothing apparent from outside the gate. The gate where Carl and I asked about buying the "Café

Negro," a while back. Chances are, I thought, I might get that boat for nothing now! There was no sign of life, no guards, no activity at all; so we drove on. I told Sara that Jack had hinted that an FBI confiscated boat might be coming my way. She said, "Great, but didn't you say it was full of this bad coffee?" "Yes," I said, "It would certainly be a fixer-upper; but free would be worth a fix-up. The rest of it looked pristine and the engines had to be in good shape being in this drug delivery service.

We drove on to Playa Ancon and pulled over, parked and got out for a stroll down to the water. Azure and turquoise water broke milky white and gray foam, as it approached the beach. A picnicker had spread out near the grass on top of the beach, much like the grass that was covering the deflated craft that Carl and I used to uncover this whole "Coffee Cartel" mess.

Sara and I walked along picking up an occasional shell, bone or shark's tooth. Sara, still slightly hungover, suggested we go back to her place for a nap. Sounded good to me too. So, we walked to the car and started back to her place. We arrived, went in, took our clothes off and dropped in bed.

A nice nap abruptly ended when my super cellphone rang. It was Jack again. Jack said, "Paul?" I said, "Yes." "We've found out more about Wongari Kamau, El Gran Jefe or Kubwa Mkuu, as he is known locally. He is big in local quartz mining around Mt. Kenya and it was found the quartz was only a side mineral now; although his mining interests all started with quartz as the objective. Quartz was a viable commodity because of its use in glass manufacturing, but gold veins are sometimes created with heat when it is present in the minerology. To make a long story short, gold veins as big as your arm were found in one of Kamau's mines and that started financing this entire Coffee Cartel's horrible mission! He hired and/or forced renowned chemists to find a highly addictive form of cocaine and they did it here, not in Costa Rica as first thought. Kamau hired El Patron, Pascal Padron and all the others to grow, modify, transport and sell the "Killer Coffee" to wholesalers and ultimately, consumers. We also found, as Jack went on, that his African markets had been active consumers for some time; hence, the misdiagnosed virus outbreaks in Mogadishu, Addis Ababa and Madagascar, that we had heard about! We will only find out more, we think, if we take over his Isiolo operation and again, raid and interrogate. That's where you and Armando come in again." I said, "We can be ready, but please give me eight hours to get back to NAS or wherever you want us." "Roger, Paul, will advise," Jack concluded.

Sara was up and listening to my side of the conversation, and said, "It's not good, is it?" "Not good," I replied. I told her I had to call Armando. She understood. I called Armando's cellphone (he had the same encrypted super phone that I did), and he answered, "Armando here." I said, "Armando, I just talked to Jack and we're on standby for a possible raid and subsequent interrogation of El Gran Jefe; Wongari Kamau, in Kenya. The complex is outside of Isiolo and specific strategies are being developed as we speak, post drone and other surveillance activity. Nonetheless, we'll be activated shortly to head up another raid." "I'm so grateful that you are with me, Arm. Enjoy Key West while you can and see if you can get ahold of Andy Pellerito, he's a valuable mercenary and fighter. Advise if you can't, and I'll have Jack get him. Goodbye for now, I'm still with Sara in Trinidad."

I told Sara, "The FBI is compensating me very well for these missions, but after the last raid I doubt if it's enough. I just hope I get out alive and we can stop this Coffee Cartel in its tracks before the planet is addicted." "I do love you and want to spend the rest of my life with you, somehow?" I added. "Would you consider marrying me, soon, before I'm called for this next raid? At least that way, if I'm killed, you would get what I have coming to me.", I implored. She said, "Yes, Pablo, I love you too and I'd love to be married to you for what you are, not what I'd get. You've made it through the last assaults just fine." "Have faith in God, he knows you're on a mission for mankind (his children) and for good!" she added. "Thanks for that," I said. "I don't have a ring, but I give my heart and life to you," I said. "Me too, and we'll get rings later," she said. "Me Padre in the Church of the Holy trinity, here in Trinidad might marry us," she added. "Should I give him a call?" "Yes," I said.

Sara called Father Cisneros and he immediately said yes. "When?" she said. "When do you need me and what arrangements?" Father asked. "No arrangements, no audience, just as soon as you can, my Father!" Sara said. "Okay," he said, "How about 10 a.m., here at the church,

me officina." Sara said, "Thank you Father, so much."
"See you then, my child," he added.

"God is with us, Pablo," Sara said to me. "I know,
I know," I said. "We need to get dressed and ready," I
added. We both took showers, got dressed in the best
we had and sat down for reflection. Sara came out in a
beautiful white dress, not a wedding dress, but a full-
length evening gown with lace around her neckline.
Gorgeous, I thought. "Gorgeous," I said. "Thank you,
sweetheart," she said. "I know we're doing the right
thing and I give myself to you, till we die," she said.
"Indeed!" I answered.

It was 9:30 a.m., so we walked to my Nova, I opened
the door, closed it and walked to my side, got in, started
it and asked Sara for directions. It's just off of Calle Cristo
in North Side of Trinidad. We can go right from here to
Calle Buen Retera and then to Calle Cristo. I drove to
the Church, parked and went to open her door. She was
beautiful and although I didn't have appropriate attire, I
felt like a king, marrying a queen.

We walked in the front door of the cathedral-like
setting, with beautiful stained glass windows glowing
in the sunlight. Father Cisneros greeted us at the alter
and said we can perform the ritual here or in my office. I
immediately said, "Here, please." Sara shook her head in
agreement, so in front of the alter in the Church of the
Holy Trinity in Trinidad, Cuba, we were to be married.
"Do you Paul Pilot take Sara Sonata to be your lawfully
wedded wife? To have, to hold, from this day forward,
for better, for worse, for richer, for poorer, in sickness

and in health, to love and to cherish, till death do you part?" "I Do," I said. "Do you Sara Sonata take Paul Pilot to be your wedded husband? To have, to hold, from this day forward, for better, for worse, for richer, for poorer, in sickness and in health, to love and to cherish, till death do you part?" "Yes, I do!" she said. "Then by the power vested in me by Almighty God, I pronounce you, husband and wife," Father Cisneros concluded and I kissed Sara in a long and meaningful manner.

We both cried and Father Cisneros consoled us as we walked down the aisle to the front door. I departed the Church with new meaning to life and a feeling of jubilance.

We got in the car and drove away, not caring where we were going. I just drove and drove. We finally, after a few unintentional side trips, got back to her place and I said, "Well, we're all dressed up, married, in love and no place to go." "Ha, ha," she said. "We could go to lunch if you want?" "I know a cozy little restaurant on Calle Alameda that you might like," she said. "Great," I said. "This will be our first lunch as a married couple," she said. I found Calle Alameda and drove to Guitarra Mia.

I parked, and we went in. A cozy, nice and appropriate setting for lunch. We sat, ordered Huevos Rancheros for two and dos Cafés Negro. A beautiful lunch enjoyed, I thought, and how lucky I've been. Called back by the FBI to serve as a Mercenary, based on my unblemished and outstanding performance over twenty-three years, and now I'm married to a beautiful Ebony Angel. Thank you, GOD,!!!

We finished, paid, walked to the car and left. Driving back to Sara's place or my place? I guess now, what I have is hers and what she has is mine; go figure! I couldn't quite remember where to turn, so I asked my wife (HA!) for directions. She gave them and we arrived, for yet another nice afternoon nap. Walked up the walkway, unlocked and opened the door, went to her bedroom, disrobed and lay down; all without uttering a word.

Rat-a-Tat, Tat, Tat, Tat, Tat, the phone rang. I said, "Hello." "Jack here," the voice said. "Paul here," I said. "Okay Paul, more intel," he said. "The complex is four miles to the south of Isiolo, in again a walled-in plantation-like setting. There are two main gates; one for general traffic and one for large trucks and vans. The complex is surrounded by coffee fields, much like Trinidad and Suriname but larger and covering everything. Another dual residence, and a large laboratory building joined to a ground residence. Guards show up everywhere 24/7, per drone and thermal imaging, and our attack plan almost duplicates Suriname, if you concur? I did get in touch with of Andy Pellerito and he will join Armando and you to head up the assault. An early morning surprise raid with sixty troops, and a powerful pint-sized armored tank called the M-30 Stryker. The Stryker has a missile launcher and a 30 mm automatic cannon that will parachute out the aft ramp prior to troop deployment. The C-17 that you'll be flying in is ample for the payload of tank, sixty troops (Seals and Special Forces, as before) and crew. The tank should easily take out the bunker-type fortress preceding the main entrance. The lab has a similar barricade. This El Gran Jefe or The Big Chief seems prepared for almost any assault, but he won't be ready for this one! The C-17 will fuel up at NAS, Key West and fly all the way to Isiolo, Kenya by being refueled three times during the flight. The flight will be sixteen hours and cots will allow sleep and a galley forward will have ample meals.

It's 8000 miles from Key West to Isiolo, so refueling is a must. The plane will land and refuel again in Nairobi, after deploying your team. There will be transport vehicles on the ready to take you and your brigade south to Nairobi, only 125 miles away, after your mission; the C-17 will then take you all back to Key West." "Any questions," he asked. "I'm just trying to digest all of that, Jack," I said. "Is the lab complex more fortified than the main building or what?" I added. "Surveillance indicates more manpower and weaponry at the main building, say thirty percent more, so I'd suggest thirty-five Seals to the main building under your command, along with Armando and twenty-five Seals to the lab under Andy's command," Jack offered. "The Stryker would take out the main building's added fortification and then advance to the lab. "All weapons, Brownell, NV67 night vision goggles, smoke and frag grenades, will be at the ready in the bulkhead lockers, just like Suriname," Jack added. "Sounds like a plan, Jack," I said. "I'll get back to you if I have any other concerns." "By the way, I assume that you will advise all concerned!" I said. "Yes, I'll call Armando, Andy and Admiral Reichert for the troops. All implements are being readied as we speak." "Okay, one last thing. When will this happen, Jack?" I asked. "Departure from NAS at 10 a.m. EST tomorrow morning. That will put you parachuting to the coffee field, north of the complex, at 2 a.m. their time," Jack added. "Alrighty then," I said, and hung up. "Oh my GOD," I said to Sara, still lying in bed. I laid back down on the bed with my new wife. I was very happy that we'd been married this morning. I rolled over and wrapped my arms around her and gently squeezed her. My mind was racing to assimilate the information Jack had given me, along with arousal caused by body-to-body contact with my lady. An erection shifted priority from assault tactics to passion. My penis was gently throbbing and pulsing against her thigh, and she felt it! Bump, bump, bump. Three bumps and you're in, I thought. Yes, she rolled over to accept me and insertion ensued. Simple sex is definitely much more gratifying when combined with genuine love and an impending circumstance (like the upcoming raid) that could mean the end of your life!!

"Wow," I said, "That was the best I've ever experienced." "Oh my God!," she said. "I love you Pablo," she added.

"Well," I said, "It looks like I'll have to leave soon, in order to get back to Key West and ready for a 10 a.m. departure tomorrow.

I called Jack back, "Jack Warner, here," he said. "Jack," I said, "Text me an aerial plan view of El Gran Jefe's complex so I can inform the troops of our assault tactic prior to arrival in Kenya." "Sure, Paul, anything else?" he said. "Not now," and hung up.

I got dressed, packed my overnight bag and called the airport for a Silver flight to Key West, EYW. They had a 7 p.m. flight, which I reserved, and I'd have to get moving to make it. I told Sara, "I'll be back and let you know, but I'll be in flight for nearly two days, separated by our all-out raid on El Gran Jefe's complex in Kenya. But, I shall return. God is on my side, as I mentioned before. "I know, Pablo, I know," she said.

I gave her a long loving hug and a gentle kiss and walked to her front door, giving a thumbs-up as I left. I got in the Nova and drove to the closest petrol station, filled up and got on my familiar road to Havana. My familiarity of the road helped me negotiate the winding the winding, non-US standard highway. I exceeded the speed limit almost all the way and made it to the airport at 6:05, a record! Perfect timing for security and a snack before leaving.

We landed in Key West at 7:36 p.m. and since my bag was with me, I went directly to the carpool Chevy NAS had loaned me before. I got out on Roosevelt and headed down to the Conch House. Armando was there making notes on the dinette. I said, "Hello, my friend!" "Another raid, I'm afraid!" he said. "Yes, Jack called earlier and it sounds like they've found out what El Gran Jefe has and what we need to overtake it. Did Jack tell you about the bunker fortifications and the Stryker tank?" "Yes," he said. "You and I will lead the main building assault and Andy, who will be at NAS tomorrow morning, will head up the lab assault," I said. "Jack gave all the rundown, and I'm pumped," Arm added. "If we can essentially duplicate the Suriname raid, we'll be fine, and we have the added advantage of the Stryker and a practice run with almost all of the same personnel we had at Suriname," I said.

"Have you eaten?" Armando said. "I had a sandwich at the Havana Airport," I said, "But I could eat something." Armando said, "I ordered a pizza from Papa John's and what's left is in the fridge." "Alrighty then, I'll get a slice or two and a Corona to go with it," I said. "Perfecta mundo, Armando!" I added. I inhaled the pizza and drank two Coronas, while Armando sketched the aerial that Jack had sent both of us. This time we would land to the north of the main building, with flat land for the Stryker to traverse to the bunker fortress preceding the main entrance. "The Javelin missiles and 30 mm cannon should make mincemeat out of that barrier," we agreed.

"As soon as the main fortress is neutralized, the Stryker will head for the lab barrier; similar but smaller, with fewer sentries," I said. "Andy has been brought up to speed, per Jack's last telecon," I said. "What do you think?" Armando said, as he showed me his sketch. I looked and said, "Super, I'd like to use that for the inflight orientation. There may be an app for a screen projection. I'll call Jack and see," I said.

I called Jack, "Me again." "Is there a way to project an image from my cellphone's photo album to a large screen?" Jack said, "Yes, and I'll have the projector there prior to your flight." "You didn't mention rifles and clips before?" "Sorry Paul. Yes, each Seal will have the same suits and rifles as before with eight clips, and each has four grenades, and the MC1-1C parachutes as before.

Henry will again be your C-17 pilot." Jack said, "I think all bases have been covered, but don't hesitate to call me Paul. This is still the biggest threat we have ever faced, short of the asteroid that wiped out the dinosaurs," Jack concluded, and hung up.

I think it's time to hit the hay Arm" I said. "Jack said he had a projector for your sketch, the parachutes, rifles, clips, grenades and everything else covered; including most of the same guys we were with in Suriname, and Henry the C-17 pilot!"

Armando agreed and said, "Goodnight Paul." "Oh, Arm, I didn't tell you that I got married in Trinidad to Sara this morning!" "Bless you, Paul," he said, as he went to his bedroom.

I texted Sara to say that I'd made it to Key West and that I loved her.

Rat-a-Tat, Tat, Tat, Tat; my ringtone and alarm had the same AR-15 sound and it let me know it was on. Make coffee (a reminder of our threat every time I made a cup), take a shower and get ready. I yelled, "Arm!" to get my mate up.

We took showers without shame and got off to the Chevy. We would be early, but needed to be to assess all the gear and projection capabilities. We pulled up to the NAS gate and the guard waived us through. The C-17 was parked adjacent to the building we interrogated Pascal Padron in, eons ago, it seemed. As we approached, we saw Jack, who must have flown in from DC earlier, and Henry, Andy and several other familiar and friendly Seal forces; as well as a BFT (Big Fucking Tank, the Stryker), sitting in the back of the open rear cavity of the C-17. What a sight! The cannon and Javelin missile system appeared equally impressive. We needed all the edge we could have taking down what has been confirmed to be the genesis of all this "Coffee Cartel" organization, I thought.

Jack pulled me aside and said, "Intelligence has verified that Wongari Kamau, El Gran Jefe, is in the Isiolo complex now and, hopefully, will still be there in the morning. We are constantly monitoring the complex to assure that he doesn't allude us. Remember, his interrogation, or rather your interrogation of him, will be the best and maybe the only way to determine the extent of the African continent of this Cartel. Approach carefully, please Paul, so we can interrogate him." "I'll be careful, but shit happens on a raid like this, Jack," I said, "I realize how important this is."

Those that were involved with the assault got on the plane. We all looked over the tank, checked out our weapons and chutes. We got fairly situated before liftoff.

I waited to get everyone's attention until leveling off. Henry's co-pilot will advise when the theoretical "Seat Belt Sign" goes off. So, we just sat on our fold-downs and relaxed.

We leveled off and shortly the co-pilot gave me the high sign. I got up, walked to the center of the huge belly of the plane, and asked for everyone's attention. "Attention please, Attention; we've all been selected to help stop a serious threat. Several of you were on the Suriname raid and we were successful in putting them out of business. This African contingent really started it all and they too must be stopped. I'll be your commander on this mission, along with Armando and Andy here (pointed to each one). The Stryker tank will be deployed first and will be our first line of offense. We'll parachute down and take over the entire operation. I'll show you more about an hour before we get there. We have fifteen hours to go, so pull down the cots from high on the bulkhead and try and get some rest. I'll get your attention again in about fourteen hours. God is with us in this mission, so take solace in that, and bless you all!"

I went back to my position, pulled down my cot and laid down. I thought, what a plane; we had sixty-six people, a small tank and weaponry for all, cots spread all over the huge cavity and still had room!

Again, the low-pitched hum of the plane's four engines was mixed with a higher-pitched hum of our troops voices; talking about their friends, families and future plans in the face of the impending raid.

I got up and made my way to the front of the plane. I talked to the co-pilot about the projector for my orientation and he said it was all set up on a forward bulkhead and that he would assist me for the presentation. I thanked him and made my way back to my cot.

It was hard to sleep, but I finally managed to fall off. I dreamt about my Sara and how blessed I was to have become involved in this Coffee Cartel opposition and was guided to Trinidad and the Restaurant San Jose, where we met. I also thought about my fishing partner, Carl, and how he was caught up in this mess. He was, however, enjoying his time at Marina Hemingway and his new squeeze, "Loopee." I hoped he had taken her fishing, as the fishing is good offshore of Havana and northern Cuba. I just hoped that we would be as successful with this raid as we were with the Trinidad and Suriname raids and hopefully squash the last of the Coffee Cartel's operations.

The hum of the C-17's engines was uninterrupted and continuous; the hum of voices had stopped, however, and it was only the engine hum that was audible. My body was resting, even if I couldn't sleep very long at a time.

I was surprised when Henry, the pilot, came back to my cot and talked seriously. He said, "Paul, I consider myself privileged to be a part of this assault. Jack Warner has explained all that I need to know, and I wanted to personally thank you for your leadership and success in Suriname. And you will be equally successful in Kenya, I've been praying on it!" "Thank you, Henry, that means a lot and yes, I'm determined to stop this Cartel's threat!" I said. Henry walked back to his cockpit. I felt great and had a fleeting thought that Sara would be pleased with Henry's comments. I also thought of Jack, back at NAS or maybe DC, wondering just how our raid would go; as was, I'm sure the FBI, our President and all others with knowledge of the Coffee Cartel's life-threatening operations.

I again drifted off until Ralph, the co-captain, came to advise one hour 'till chutes hooked. He then showed me up forward how the projector worked, as he pulled down a large white canvas from above the forward lockers.

I put up Armando's sketch and plan view of El Gran Jefe's Isiolo complex. It was quite different from the others, in that the buildings were irregular-shaped and covered with foliage to disguise them and blend into surrounding vegetation and topography. Coffee plants ran right up to the sides of the building, to blend in and with the bushes on top of the buildings. It's appearance from a satellite or aerial vantage point just looked like any other of El Gran Jefe's farming sites.

"Can I get everyone's attention! My name is Paul Pilot; for those that don't know, and I'm your Commander for this mission. Many of us were on a similar raid on a Suriname operation. The raid was very successful and I'm sure this one will be also, because we now have more tactical advantages, equipment and most importantly you (pointing to them)! We now have a Stryker tank with 30 mm cannon and Javelin Missiles, superior Night-Vision goggles, and God is on our side! We fight for mankind, not against it!!

I'd like you all to look at this aerial plan view of the complex we're hitting this morning! Note that the buildings are camouflaged with living vegetation and it all looks like a farm from above. As I mentioned, the buildings are irregular, and the adjacent laboratory is egg shaped. There is a camouflaged parking lot to the West of the buildings. The 8 foot cement wall almost totally surrounds the complex.

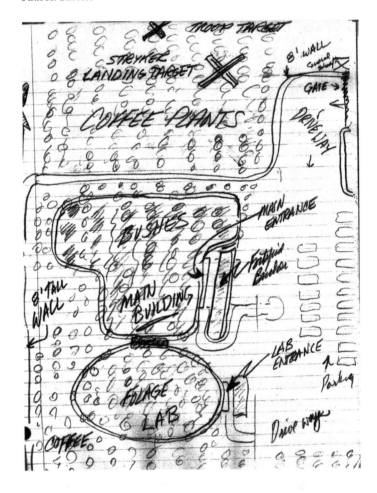

Coffee plants surround and run up to the building in places. The main building is where we believe El Gran Jefe will be; asleep in his quarters. May I remind you all that El Gran Jefe must be taken with care, and alive. But, getting back to the map; yes, a main building and a laboratory building in the shape of an oval or an egg. Our objective is to land the tank in the coffee field north of the buildings. We want to hit the "X" as shown above (pointing to the X). Henry, our pilot already has the coordinates. We will all land behind and to the north of the Stryker.

We intend the Stryker to take out the wall near the driveway entrance. We will follow in two separate groups; Group 1, led by Armando here (pointing to Armando), will be the thirty-five having white stars on your lapel (troops looking). Group 1 will proceed to take out the main building. Stryker will follow with fire power. The main building usually has eight guards at the main entrance door and four on the roof. Other guards will be inside the main building, at every room!

Group 2 will be led by Andy here (pointing to Andy). Group 2 is without lapel stars. You twenty-five will report to Andy Pellerito here! Group 2 will raid the lab building. We do want hostages if possible, from both buildings, both groups. A smaller bunker is just east of the lab's entrance, but the Stryker will blow it away for you!

That concludes my show. "Any questions?" I said. "Yes," a voice from the group of Seals. "How in the hell do you expect that damn tank to hit the "X" on your sketch?" he went on loudly. "Well," I said, "I'm glad you asked. We fortunately have Harold Robbins with us, who is the world-famous Sky Parachute Jumper from Texas! He will ride on top of the Stryker, with parachute guidelines and I'm positive that Harold will hit his "X"!

Any other questions? "Yes," another Seal said. "How many damn guards are there for the entire complex?" "We believe from twenty-five to thirty and, of course, that varies. "Surveillance indicated the count goes way down, to as few as twelve at night; including the number we hit in 25 minutes," I said.

"Anything further?" (5-second silence) "Okay then, GOD BLESS YOU ALL," I said.

We went back to our cot areas or stayed talking. I sat down, hoping that everything had been covered.

"Ten-minute warning," came over the loud speaker. The Ten-minute warning was to make sure that you have ready all your equipment, arms, weapons and chutes. In a few, "Five-minute warning," came over the speaker. The Five-minute warning was to line up in descending order of deployment and be on the ready. In a couple more minutes the troops attached their carabiners to the chute cable.

"ONE MINUTE WARNING," which meant, you had better have been READY!

A red light lit up our cavern hull, which meant the tank was to be deployed. It went, with Harold on top of it! Then, one-by-one we went. I was third and I would land ahead of the troops. I hit a coffee plant, which threw me for a loop. I got up and was with Andy and the lab team, Group 2. I looked over and the Stryker was close to its target, and Harold was fine. I looked for Armando or Andy, who jumped before me. I finally saw Andy and went to him. I looked back and most of our force had landed. The Stryker shot one missile and wiped out the eight-foot wall, which I'm sure woke up everyone at the complex.

I followed Andy through the wall opening and past the first building. I looked into the main building's bunker. We advanced, with retaliatory fire just beginning, and got down in the prone position. The tank was using its automatic 30 mm cannon to take out any fire coming from the main building, while advancing south with us. Andy took a shot to his leg and the Stryker stopped in its tracks and opened fire, with a missile to the lab's bunker. We got up and fired at what remained of the lab's entrance. No response, as we neared the lab. Then, two sentries from inside opened fire. We took them out quickly and advanced some more. A roof sniper's rifle flash caught my upper peripheral vision and I opened fire on him. His firing ceased, so I must have gotten him. We advanced to the main door's jagged opening, Andy limping all the way.

We advanced, all twenty-three that were left, one-by-one into the lab. More fire, and Andy threw in a frag grenade. Silence! We advanced to the next room; again, shots fired.

The next room had three or four guards that fired on us; several of us opened fire at once, and the shots stopped and the guards fell. This was the large laboratory where I imagined the first of the modified cocaine molecule was created. There was a large cylindrical vessel mid-room that appeared to be a hyperbolic chamber, like those used with the bends for divers. Maybe the new molecule required extreme pressure regulation; who knew?

It appeared that we had taken the lab, as more Seals shouted, "Clear." My thoughts turned to Armando and Group 1. I looked at Andy's leg, and the shot was below the knee in the left calf muscle. Painful but not too serious, we agreed. I told Andy, "I'm going to the main building to see how Armando and Group 1 is doing capturing El Gran Jefe."

I got to the main building, and no firing; they too had taken the building. I advanced, but no Armando. I finally found him in a large bedroom looking at the floor. There was a square opening with a lid that conformed exactly with the floor's rug design. Armando said, "El Gran Jefe must have gone down this way!" He and I got in cautiously, and the tunnel that led from the opening was lit. No one was in the tunnel, so we advanced. It led to a ladder and an exit hatch. We opened the hatch to hear the whir of a camouflaged, small helicopter going skyward. It must have been covered and not noticed from surveillance, but this most assuredly was a helicopter carrying El Gran Jefe. We couldn't shoot for fear of killing him, so we just watched the ascending craft.

I called Jack on my cellphone, not knowing what the hell else to do, and thank God he answered. I said, "Jack, the raid went well, but El Gran Jefe just flew away in a small Robinson-like helicopter, and I'm at a loss for what to do." "Look Paul, I'll call Henry who just landed at Jomo Kenyatta Airport, he may be able to track or intercept the copter," he said. "Standby!"

Transport trucks rolled up just east of the complex and the troops assembled next to them. I congratulated them all and took a count. We had lost four to fire and fifty-six remained. Some were injured, like Andy, but not seriously. We all loaded up in the two transport trucks and started on our 125-mile trip down to the Nairobi Jomo Kenyatta Airport. About ten minutes later Jack called back. "Paul, I contacted Henry at the airport and he contacted the airport's General Manager, who alerted traffic control and radar tracking of the rogue Robinson-type copter. He also managed a Nairobi Police Airbus helicopter (H125M) to be released to Henry by the Chief of Police. Henry had flown about everything and the Airbus Police Copter would be easy," Jack said. "Henry is airborne now and being guided by Jomo Kenyatta's air traffic control," he added. "Will advise," he concluded.

The ride to Nairobi was quiet and small talk among the Seals was refreshing. Another successful raid, but the primary objective had eluded us, I thought.

Wongari Kamau, El Gran Jefe, had managed to escape the raid, but at least he was still alive and not killed in the takeover.

Unbeknownst to me, the skilled radar techs at the Nairobi Airport had managed to just detect the small helicopter blip. They tracked it as it headed south toward Nairobi. Henry was on his way north toward Isiolo when traffic control gave him the blip's coordinates. The blip stopped its horizontal vector and seemed to hover near Embu. There was no airfield there, but it appeared that Jefe's copter was landing anyway.

Henry approached the small copter with caution and landed near to it in a field. There was only Kamau and his pilot. No gunfire came from Kamau's copter, so Henry and two Nairobi SWAT team members jumped out of his

Airbus Copter and ran to them. They ran and Henry and his two policemen gained and tackled the two. One of the policemen knocked out Kamau's pilot, while Henry and the other policeman put handcuffs on Kamau.

We arrived at the Jomo Kenyatta Airport and reassembled near the C-17 that had brought us to Kenya. Not knowing what was going on with Henry was almost unbearable. About ten minutes later my super cellphone rang and it was Jack. "Paul, your Gran Jefe has been captured by Henry and two Nairobi policemen!" he said. "Thank God Jack, I thought we'd lost him," I said. "We'll bring him to you and transport him with you, Armando, Andy, Henry and your troops back to NAS, Key West for troop dissemination and Kamau's interrogation," Jack said. A lunch wagon pulled up to the group and gave out coffee (hopefully untainted), drinks and sandwiches to the troops. The sun was up and it appeared to be another great day, especially since the raid was successful and, although questionable for a time, El Gran Jefe had been secured.

It was another few minutes before Henry and Kamau showed up. The two policemen grabbed and escorted Kamau to the rear of the C-17. Our troops took over Kamau and tied him up in the plane. I thanked the two Nairobi policemen that had taken Kamau with Henry. I also thanked Henry for his unorthodox and heroic actions to seize Kamau. He said, "You're welcome Paul; I thought I was just going to fly you and the troops to Kenya, not capture this bastard!" "God and country thank you, Henry, my hero!" I said.

We all got settled in the huge cavity of this mammoth aircraft. The aft loading door closed and we waited for liftoff. Kamau, the Big Chief, didn't look very big now, as he was cuffed behind his back and tied to the starboard bulkhead. His face was angry and distraught at the same time.

The cots were still there, so I and the others used them. Hell, we'd been up for at least twenty-two hours on this mission alone, not to mention those that traveled to NAS for the mission. I lay there thanking God for our mission's success and my safety! Henry was not flying back to NAS, as his relief was an Airforce Captain flown in as backup.

Most of us collapsed on our cots and went to sleep quickly. The hum of the engines was soothing, as compared to the roar and rattle of gunfire. Most of the plane was in deep sleep for much of the sixteen-hour trip back to Key West. We were all exhausted.

I awoke after some nine hours, as some others had. I looked at our guest, Wongari Kamau, who was asleep in spite of being fastened by his handcuffs and tied to the bulkhead. Wow, I thought, we almost missed him due to his hidden escape route to a hidden helicopter. Thanks goes to Henry and Jack for outsmarting the terrorist. A surreptitious terrorist, but a terrorist none-the-less. He was bringing the terror and the horror of withdrawal to all who consume and become addicted to his modified cocaine coffee, and then don't get it. All this horror in exchange for money and subsequent coffee costs that would go up and up until no one could afford it.

Hopefully, one more interrogation would give us enough information to stop all of the Coffee Cartel's worldwide operations. I hoped that Armando had gotten some shuteye, as we were most likely going right into interrogation mode as soon as we get to NAS. I got up and walked over to Andy Pellerito who had taken a slug in his left calf muscle. A Seal EMT had tended to his wound as he did others on this return trip. Andy was in good spirits and thanked me for having his back during the lab raid. Comraderies were strong and apparent throughout the plane.

I walked on up to the cockpit and asked the pilot what ETA we had. He said, "Thirty minutes, my friend, we're over Cat Cay in the Bahamas now." He added, "There will be a welcoming party at NAS when we land." Then, I thought, OMG! The spouses of the four Seals that lost their lives will be there waiting for their men and I, as Commander, again must tell them of their loss. This was the most dreaded part of my obligations but, as I've said before, it was also a profound honor as well.

Ten minutes out and the plane was bustling with jubilation and active voices. The hum of the engines was nearly equaled by the hum of voices. We came in over Old Town, Key west and lined up with the East-West runway at NAS. An extremely soft landing gave rise to movement and jostling among the troops. We taxied up to the same hangars and buildings, as before, and stopped. It seemed like an hour before the rear ramp opened up to let us depart.

We jostled for position and gradually we departed. The greeting party was there; I saw Jack, Commander NAS, Harvey Hyde (Assistant Director, FBI), many spouses and Sara? How in the hell did Sara get here and through the gate of a Naval Air Station? How did she even come to the U.S? She was a Cuban citizen? Well, she was here and I was glad; that was all that really mattered! Last to de-plane was El Gran Jefe, still cuffed and escorted by two Seals to the holding building where El Patron was held before him.

I stepped down the stairs and ran over to hug Sara. We kissed and squeezed until she said, "OW!" "Thanks for coming," I said. "I love you and was worried," she said. I shook Jack and Harvey's hands and asked Jack how was I to handle the deceased spouses?

He said, "Let things settle down and couples depart." "Okay," I said. As couples departed it became obvious who was missing, and Harvey and Jack compassionately pulled them off to the side and confirmed their identity. Ultimately, all four were standing together and I excused myself from Sara and walked over. "I'm Paul Pilot, Commander of this raid. Unfortunately, although the raid was successful, we lost four brave and gallant soldiers! Your husbands did not make it. (Pause) My heart goes out to you and may God bless you." Tears by all and one collapse followed. All three of us consoled and gently touched the ladies mourning. Jack and Harvey slowly and courteously escorted them off, while one was taken by gurney to the hangar's sickbay.

I went back to Sara, explaining how this was the worst part of my duties as Commander. The instant facial expressions of agony, prompted by my words, are almost unbearable, I thought.

We walked to the Chevy, where it was parked and Armando (who had no one waiting) came up to us. "Well, you're Sara!" he said. "Yes, I am," she said. "Or should I say, Mrs. Pilot?" he said. "Yes, that too!" she responded.

"Let me go catch Jack," I said, "and see what's up now." I walked over where Jack was helping a spouse get in a car and waited. Jack saw that I was waiting and came over. "I see your new bride made it," he said. "Yes, thanks," I said. "Paul, I understand you're tired and that you have your new bride, but we must move forward. Take her to your temporary home, get situated, and come back with Armando at 10 p.m. prepared to interrogate this Kamau character!"

I walked back to the blue Chevy and told Armando and Sara the plan. We all got into the car and I drove off. I couldn't wait to ask Sara how she pulled off coming to greet me? "How did you manage coming to greet me, my love?" I said. She said, "I was worried and couldn't do anything about it but then I thought, I want to meet him when he gets back. I remembered you talking about Jack Warner and I called him. It wasn't easy, but finally they transferred me through and I told him that I wanted to meet you. He said that as your wife I had every right to travel to the US, and he made the necessary arrangements." "He even met me at Key West International and brought me here," she added. "I should call Jack and thank him," I said. "But I'll see him when we come back at 10 p.m. and plan on telling him then.

We drove to the Conch House, parked, got out, and Sara and I walked behind Armando, who led the way to my apartment. I showed her our room and the kitchen. I said, "Are you hungry?" She said, "No, I'm really tired." "Okay, you make yourself at home and Armando and I will get a bite to eat and go back to the Air Station. I should be back by morning, but I'm not sure? At least Armando and I got some rest on the way back from Kenya," I said. Sara and I went into my bedroom; I helped her get undressed, had a fleeting moment of arousal, and then laid her down on the bed. I said, "Sweet dreams, my angel," and left the room, closing the door behind me. Armando was sitting on the couch and said, "You hungry?" I said, "Yes, let's go!"

I remembered that there was a 24-hour Denny's down on Duval, so we got in the Chevy and I drove there. We got two sausage and egg croissants and coffee, sat down for a minute and discussed our situation. "This Big Chief, Mother Fucker will tell us about everything!" Armando said. "I'm tired of all this bullshit; we must stop this Cartel in its tracks," he said. "I agree, my friend," I said. "I have more tricks up my sleeve," he said. "Well, let's do this thing," I said. We got up, walked around the building to the parking lot, and got in the Chevy.

We drove to NAS and parked outside the building and walked in. We told the guards to bring Kamau to the interrogation room. We walked in and all of Armando's paraphernalia was on a table next to the chair in front of a large bright lamp. Jack was watching behind a mirrored window, in a room adjacent to our interrogation room. The guards brought a hobbled and cuffed El Gran Jefe in and sat him down in the big chair. I asked him, "How many coffee operations do you have?" Nothing, silence. Armando got a syringe filled with the enhanced sodium pentothal that he used on Pascal Padron. Armando found a vein in Kamau's left arm and squeezed the syringe. No reaction! Kamau's facial expression changed from defiant to calm. I asked again, "How many coffee operations do you have?" Silence! Immediately, Armando got his finger shears. Kamau's eyes showed concern, but he said nothing. Armando, without hesitation, cut off Kamau's little finger. Kamau cringed and grimaced, but said nothing. I asked again, "How many coffee operations do you have?" Visibly distraught, Kamau only muttered, "Several!" "How many and where?" I said. "East Africa," he said. "How many and where?" I said again. Armando was obviously pissed that results were poor. He asked the guards to take him out of the chair and put his thighs on the chair with his chest and head hanging down on the other side of the chair and his knees on the other edge and his legs from the knees down either out vertically or up in a 30° angle above the chair. This was an uncomfortable, blood rushing to the head position. I asked again, "How many operations and where?" "Many in East Africa," he answered. "But how many and exactly where?" I said. Armando grabbed a scalpel and cut through his pants from the bottom of Kamau's right buttock cheek to halfway down the back of his leg toward the "armpit" of his knee. Armando, more precisely, made a deeper cut in the same area. Armando said, "A little deeper in this area and I'll hit his sciatic nerve. The largest and most sensitive nerve in our body." Kamau obviously understood and said, "Okay, there are farms and labs in East Africa, Cuba and South America!" "We know all of that already! We need specifics!" I said. Arm touched the partially exposed sciatic nerve on the back of Kamau's leg. "AAAHH!.," an agonized scream came out of Kamau's contorted mouth. "Okay, okay," he said. "I have five operations in East Africa and a dozen in Cuba and South America!" he shouted. I said, "Again, specifics." "There's one at my home in Isiolo, Mt. Kenya and another near the Meru National Park, southeast of Isiolo; another near Meru, the city, south of Isiolo." Silence! "Okay, that's three; you said two more in Africa, right?" I said, emphatically. Armando had a bottle of Muriatic Acid for just such an occasion and dripped some in the gash on the back of Kamau's leg, while the guards held him down over the chair and the big fucking Chief screamed bloody murder. "AAAHH!" "NO MORE!" "AAAHH!" "There's one in . . . silence!" "AAAHH!" "There's one near Mombasa!" he managed to say. I said, "How can you grow coffee near Mombasa, when Isiolo is at such a high elevation?" He said, "I grow Robusto near Mombasa, it's Arabica in Isiolo, you bastard!" "Okay, one more," I said. Kamau said, "There is one near Degeli Bur in Ethiopia to give me a northern complex. I looked in the mirror and told Armando and the two guards to excuse me for a minute. I stepped next door and Jack was already calling someone at the FBI. Jack told them all of the East African farms that he'd written down as Kamau had divulged them. Once he finished, I asked, "Okay Jack, he said five farms in East Africa, but he said a dozen farms in Cuba and South America, not 13 like we thought." "I caught that," he said. "Was it a mistake, or a statement of truth?" he said. "I've got agents assigning surveillance activities to the East African complexes now, but you need to go back now while he's in agony and get more specifics about Cuban or South American complexes." I couldn't believe that El Patron had withheld a location! He had appeared to be a classic case of full disclosure, prompted by the cascading water, siren, finger loss and everything Armando had administered in this very room!

I went back in with Armando, El Gran Jefe and the two guards. I told Armando about the missing South American operation and he said, "Yes, he did say a dozen, didn't he." I asked Kamau, "Okay, you said you had a dozen operations in Cuba and South America; I want specifics! Name each one! Now!" Silence! Armando got his jug of Muriatic Acid and made a motion to pour more on his exposed sciatic nerve, but the very motion caused Kamau to say, "Cuba, near Trinidad, was where my friend Pascal Padron had his operation. Also in Cuba at Las Tunis, run by Orlando Rojas. One in Nicaragua, near Masaya and close to Lake Nicaragua, run by Concetto Vasili; another in Columbia near Cartagena, run by Jose' Yasuni; there are two in Costa Rica near Jaco, run by El Patron, my second in command and in charge of all

South American and Cuban operations. There are two in Venezuela; one in Barinas, run by Oscar Alveda and one in Cumana, run by Dida Cortez. There are smaller complexes in Ecuador and Panama and a very large one in Suriname near Paramaribo, run by Hector Arroy; and two very small but growing complexes in Guatemala, giving a total of thirteen in those South American countries," he said. All of these complexes given between moans and groans due to the exposed sciatic nerve in his leg.

Along with the five in Africa, that totaled eighteen complexes in all of the Coffee Cartel's worldwide operation. Wow, how it had grown from one in Cuba to thirteen in Cuba and South America to five on the other side of the world in Africa.

"Is that the extent of it, or are you still holding out?" Armando said. "No more," Kamau uttered. Armando took his Muriatic acid jug and poured more on Kamau's exposed nerve. "AHA! AHA! MUNGO, NAPENDA!" Kamau yelled. I asked one of the guards to look up on the net translator just what the hell that meant? The guard said, "God, please stop!" Kamau was in agony, so more smelling salts. He then said, "Brazil, Brazil, we have a last one; the last holdout in Teresina, Brazil," Kamau said, as he passed out completely.

Armando and I wondered what the hell was so special about Teresina? Even under severe torture, losing digits, etc. neither Padron or Patron divulged the Teresina Operation. Did they both know about Teresina or just one? El Patron almost certainly knew about Teresina!

We already knew that Brazil was a very large consumer of coffee and maybe it was just another farm and lab to satisfy that demand. But, why omit Teresina after divulging thirteen others? It just didn't make any sense to me and Armando agreed. I again excused myself, went in the next room and called Jack and told him about Teresina, and he didn't believe it! I assured him that it was legitimate, and he couldn't believe that both Pascal Padron and El Patron held out while they were enduring such acts of torture. "There's no way!" Jack said, emphatically. "I know Jack, but you must check it out," I said. "We will Paul, but don't count on success! El Gran Jefe might be handing you a diversion or a decoy for some unknown reason," Jack concluded, and said, "I will notify you of what surveillance shows us!"

I went back to the interrogation room with Kamau and guards. Kamau had passed out from the pain, and Armando was just waiting. "What did Jack say?" he asked. "He didn't believe it either, but said his surveillance team will check out Teresina." "What about this Little Chief Jefe motherfucker?" he said. "I don't know what more we could get even if he does come to?" Armando offered. "I'll give him some more smelling salts and call the base doctor and nurses to stich him up," Armando added. Smelling salts brought Kamau back to life and he started whimpering, so I called the base hospital for assistance and wrapped things up. It was refreshing to know that we had gotten everything pertinent from Kamau and that we were on the right side of human and moral laws.

Armando and I left the room, walked outside exhausted, and got in the Chevy to head home. It was morning and the sunrise was gorgeous, reminding me of God's unparalleled creations and how blessed I was. There were only a few cars on the road, but traffic came to a halt near the Boca Chica bridge. As we got closer we could see an SUV smashed into a truck with a boat trailer. All three were wedged up against the concrete siderails of the bridge. The police were alternatively letting one open lane of traffic go by; first easterly, then westerly. We got our turn and I prayed for the occupants. Some poor bastard was going to Key West to fish and never made it, I thought.

We finally got back to the Conch House and Sara was up and standing on the porch outside the bedroom. I walked out onto the porch and gave her a big hug. "I love you," I said. "Me too, you," she said. Armando said, "Do you guys want breakfast?" We both said in unison, "Si." We all walked downstairs to get their famous and well-thought-out breakfast; including fresh fruit, cereal, omelets, bacon, home fries, and the whole nine yards.

"How did it go?" Sara said. I said, "Well, we not only found out about his African operations, but also a very important one that had eluded us, in Brazil." "Good," she said. "Does that mean all of this Coffee Cartel business is over?" she added. "No!" I said. "There's surveillance, verification, more raids to destroy their labs and distribution capability and, most importantly, verify that all operations are destroyed. But we can't do that until Jack and designated diplomats make arrangements with the various governments. Those arrangements must include our ability to raid the complexes involved. There are also many innocent coffee consumers, suffering from the addiction brought on with the tainted Cartel's Coffee, that need to be treated. The CDC was working on a Methadone-like cure for the addiction by analyzing the remaining beans from the "Café Negro" that I'd sent to Jack. Methadone, or something like it, may be able to help those addicted to the Coffee Cartel's coffee!" "Thank God, Sara, the outbreaks of withdrawal seem to be limited to northeastern Africa, Madagascar and Key Largo, although Brazil is suspected but they're very private about their ordeals," I added.

"Maybe we can have some time together for a while?" Sara noted. "I think so, my love, I think so. It will take time to assess, and get governmental cooperation, on the sites that Wongari Kamau told us about, but I'll not be involved with the CDC or medical teams dealing with the withdrawal cases.

"Maybe we can have some rest and relaxation together," I said. "Sara, I've never asked you, have I, about whether you liked fishing or not?" I said. "You may have but, yes, I like fishing. My father took me fishing as a child, and those trips were the best and closest to my father as I've ever been," she said.

"Carl is back at the BFB and I'll bet he took his girlfriend Loopee fishing, while I'm fighting Cartel strongholds," I said. "But that's okay, that's what I wanted him to do, and using a boat is better than having it sit. We could go back to Cuba and fish out of the Hemingway

Marina, or we could take a cruise to the Caribbean, or stay here and enjoy Key West, or go to Vegas, or whatever you want to do (subject to a call from Jack Warner)," I said. Sara said, "How long did it take the FBI to assess the Cuban operation in Trinidad or those others?" "Only two days, my angel," I said. "Then, let's just stay here until we find out and put this Cartel/FBI involvement behind us," Sara said.

Armando said, "Look Paul, you've been a super host and I've enjoyed staying here with you and experiencing Key West, but you have your bride with you now and I have some things to check up on in Puerto Rico." Armando's home was in Puerto Rico and I was relieved that he was leaving, only because I had my Sara with me now. He didn't have much with him and so he looked up American Airlines on his phone, which he knew had flights to San Juan. He got one connecting to Miami then San Juan, leaving Key West (EYW) at 11:30 a.m., arriving San Juan at 3 p.m. Online reservations were quick and easy.

I said, "Okay Armando, we'll probably be called again in a few days, depending?" "I know, but this is the thing to do and I can get almost anywhere in a day but chances are, based on history, that will emanate from NAS here," he said. "I'll just go on to the airport and wish you guys a long, happy and loving life together. Paul is a super guy, good interrogator and soldier; but more importantly, he's a good, caring person," Armando said. I said, "Thanks, my friend. Look, you should call Jack and let him know your plans and be sure and take that super-duper fucking cellphone with you!" Armando laughed and said, "Yes, Jack, I've got this," and walked out the door.

"He seems like a hell of a nice guy," Sara said. "He is," I said. "Have you ever seen an apothecary or conservatory, or whatever they're called? They have all kinds of beautiful butterflies and are just down on Duval, within walking distance," I said. "Sounds good to me," she said. So, I freshened up a bit, washed under my arms, face and put on deodorant, combed my hair, and put on a new shirt. She did similarly, and we met on the porch overhanging Truman Street. "This is a nice, homey Bed & Breakfast, isn't it?" Sara said. "Yes, it is but better yet it's owned by a friend of mine," I responded. "You ready?" I said. "Yes," she said. We walked downstairs and said hello to fellow roomers. The Conch House featured antique furniture, and a hutch near the entrance caught Sara's eye. "Beautiful piece of furniture, No, Pablo?" she said. "Si," I said, chuckling. We walked out on Truman and west toward Duval. We passed Denny's, Panini Schamini, and many other tourist traps as we casually strolled south on Duval. I pointed out the Banana Café, which features pseudo-French cuisine and is very good. "We must go there sometime," I said. Another couple of blocks and we were at the Butterfly Conservatory. We paid, they stamped our hand and we went in. What an amazing place and so many species of beautiful butterflies of all colors and symmetric configurations. She too was amazed at God's beautiful flying creations. It wasn't a very large room but if you looked carefully, every crevice and tree had a butterfly. They had bananas and fruit dishes set around the large room for the butterflies to dine on.

How they could co-habitat was amazing. "This is great and well worth the walk, thanks Pablo," she said. "Yes, it's a welcome diversion from my mercenary life and much safer!" I said.

We walked north on Duval, retracing our route down. We walked past "La Te Da," a restaurant and showplace for female impersonation and catered to the gay crowd. "I've seen pictures and advertisements for La Te Da and some of them are impressive," I said. It was lunchtime and I asked if Sara was hungry. She said yes, so we walked to Panini Schamini and got a great wrap with veggies. We sat outside the place, with a rooster begging for a bite. Sara was beautiful and she was my wife, I thought. Thank you, God, I said to myself. I looked on my phone and saw that "Caffeine Carl" was playing at the Smokin' Tuna and asked Sara if she wanted to go tonight? She said, "Sure, but what else is happening in Key West?" "There are lots of bars with bands, there are lots of great restaurants, some shows, and Jimmy Buffett owns and comes to Margaritaville sometimes. There's a showplace or theater at the Community College on Stock Island, but shows are mainly in the winter when the snowbirds are here. There's always something going on in Key West. There's even topless and bottomless bars!" "I'm not into strip clubs," she said, "But I would like to see a salsa band, where we could dance."

We continued to walk down Duval and noted lots of tourists. Sara said, "Are there always this many tourists in town?" I said, "No, only when there are cruise ships at dock." It so happened that we could see the tops of two cruise ships above the rooftops. We walked back up Truman Street to the Conch House, opened our door and sat down on the couch. "Those butterflies were beautiful, thank you for that Pablo," she said. We moved closer and snuggled. What a great feeling, I thought. Again, I was glad that the two nighttime invaders that boarded us in the Straits of Florida, long ago, were the catalyst that led me to Sara in Trinidad, Cuba.

We laid back and stretched out on the couch, loving the feel of the other's body against ours. It doesn't get any better than this, she thought, without my knowledge. Loving another of opposite sex seemed to be the way God intended things; otherwise, why would God have put a penis on men and a vagina on women? I couldn't get past that truth. I also thought that there were many same sex couples that were happy and in love but sadly, could never experience copulation the way that the creator intended. Live and let live! I thought. We both closed our eyes while touching along the entire length of our bodies.

We fell asleep glowing with affection.

I woke up sometime later, but Sara had surreptitiously un-snuggled and slipped off the couch. I got up and looked here and there, in every room and on the porch, and Sara was nowhere to be found? I even looked for a note, but none was found. I put on my clothes and went downstairs onto the front porch at ground level; no Sara. I asked one of the B & B guests and she said, "There was a pretty woman at the pool a minute ago." I walked out the back door and sure enough, there by the pool on a lounge chair was my angel.

"Hi there," she said, as I walked toward her. "This is a nice pool isn't it?" she added. "Yes," I said. "We need to go shopping and buy you a swimsuit," I said. "Yes, I'm ready," she said. So, we walked back up to the room, got my keys, money clip and wallet and locked our door behind us. We walked down to the blue Chevy and got in. We drove to a Sears store in a shopping center on Roosevelt, since the stores on Duval always doubled their prices for tourists. We parked and went in the Sears store. I looked at shirts, while Sara went to the women's section. I found a couple of shirts, a swimsuit, and a pair of casual slip-on shoes by Sketcher. I walked over and Sara had gone to the changing room. I sat down on a display and waited. Sara emerged wearing a nice summer dress. She asked, "Like it?" "Yes," I said. She went back in the changing room and in a few minutes came out again. "I think I've got it Pablo," she said. We went to the cashier and paid, walked out to the car and drove back to the Conch House. We went in, up the stairs, and in our room. Sara immediately went to the bedroom, closed the door and came out in five minutes looking like a bathing beauty in her two-piece bathing suit. "Wow," I said. She grabbed a towel from the bathroom and said, "I'm going back to the pool, join me?" "I'll be down in a minute," I said. I walked in the bedroom with my bag of shirts, shoes and swimsuit. I took off my clothes and put on my new suit and a new shirt and went down. She was swimming and I shed my shirt, laid down my keys and cellphone, and jumped in. She was swimming on her back, so I did as well. What a great time, and refreshing; it was over 90° today and the cool water felt good. We swam around for a while, then got out and laid on side-by-side lounge chairs. A beautiful day. We lounged and swam, and loved and swam, and had a beer and lounged.

Sara said, "I've had enough sun and although you might not know it, I can sunburn the same as you. You'd think that dark skin would not be adversely affected, but I can burn and I think I am." She covered herself with a towel and went back upstairs. I followed.

She took a shower and did her thing in the bathroom; I waited, turned on some Reggae, and relaxed with a book called, "The Power of Now," by Ekhart Tolle. One thing is for sure, the past is gone, so don't reflect or regret what's passed because there is nothing you can do or say that will change it. Live now and only now, I say, and Tolle did too. An interesting read.

It was getting close to a time to think about dinner. I shouted to Sara, "I'm thinking about dinner and have an Italian, French or Steak place for you to choose." "Italian," she said. "Alright, about seven?" I said. "What time is it now?" she said. "5:30," I responded. "Fine," she said, so I called Le Trattoria on Duval and made reservations for 7 p.m. The "Tratt," as I called them, had two locations but the Duval restaurant was the original and seemed to have an ambiance that few in the world have. There was a second Tratt on South Roosevelt Street that was great, as well, but with a different environment.

Sara had a beautiful tight-fitting dress on that only someone with her body could wear. It was blue, with small white snowflake-like spots. Her hair was short, natural and cap-like. I thought, there is no way that this woman is mine!! I went and quickly showered, shaved, shit, shined, combed, brushed, and put on my best Nat Nast Shirt, Tommy Bahama slacks and Topsider shoes.

"We've got time to walk, would you like that?" I said. "Yes," she said. Again, I locked our doors and we walked west on Truman, then north on Duval. A proud walk it was, for me. We saw tourists and visitors from all over the country, and even the world.

A nice stroll and we crossed Duval to get to the restaurant. They had our reservations and sat us in a booth for two. We ordered my favorite Chianti, Ruffino Gold Label and an antipasto of Melon and Prosciutto. "We'll order later," I said. We toasted to our future together. Another newlywed couple was in the corner of the room and we both felt a kinship, so I went over and said, "Hello, I too am a new husband, we got married just three days ago in Cuba." The woman said, "God bless you!" I shook their hands and went back to my booth.

I told Sara that they were lucky, but I'm luckier. I told the waiter (they have waiters, not waitresses, for some reason) I would pay for the newlywed couple's wine and dinner. "Okay," he said. We ordered lamb chops in a rosemary classic Italian sauce, which would pair with the Chianti perfectly. We sipped and enjoyed the antipasto leisurely and talked about where we go from here. "If you get right down to the "nitty gritty," she said, "It won't matter where we live, as long as I can live with you." "I feel that way too," I said.

Our meal came and looked awesome. We ate, drank and enjoyed. The newlywed couple came over to our booth and said, "Thank you, very much!" I said, "May you live, laugh and love one another forever!" They said, "Thank you and you as well." They left and we felt good about them and us.

We finished and I ordered Tiramisu for two and two Tia Marias. We felt good, and satisfied; at least I did.

I signed the check, gave our water twenty-five percent on top of both bills and proud of it. We left the restaurant, and I asked Sara if she felt like walking? She said, "Sure!" We walked north, where we hadn't been before. We heard the music coming from the Smokin' Tuna and walked in. It was Caffeine Carl's group and we enjoyed the Bluesy Jazz they were putting down. We ordered two Limoncello's and listened. They played a slower Blues tune and they did have a small dancing area, so I asked her, "Would you care to dance?" She shook her head in the affirmative and got up. We danced our first dance and I felt good because I was never a good dancer, although my drumming background helped me feel the beat of a slow Blues. She smiled and we glided around the floor.

We sat back down, listened to two more tunes, finished our drinks, paid and left. We automatically turned south to head back to our temporary abode. The tourists were out in full force and the different languages we heard verified that visitors from all over the world visit Key West.

A drunk woman was bent over to regurgitate on the side of the street. Her man, who appeared in a little better shape, held her waist and was consoling her. A while later a panhandler, with a dog with sunglasses on, wanted us to buy a hat made out of palm leaves. I said, "No thanks," and walked on. As we approached Truman, there was a couple (two men) kissing on the corner. I told Sara, "This is Key West!" "Yes, I know," she said.

We got back to the Conch House and slowly walked up the stairs to our room. I unlocked and opened our door and said, "How do you feel, my dear?" "Satisfied, happy and a bit tired," she said. I responded, "That's exactly how I feel, as well." "Let's go to bed," I said. "Yes," she said as she went to her side of the bed and disrobed. I took my clothes off as well and got in. I slid over to hold her beautiful body next to mine. "Skin-to-Skin," how exceptional and magnificent, I thought. That was fulfillment enough, so we drifted off in a twilight zone of satisfaction.

The sun's light came like laser streams past the window's curtain, as I opened my eyes. I glanced over at my Sara's face, relaxed, eye's closed, serene in sleep. I carefully and gently got out of bed and put on my robe to go get untainted coffee downstairs. As always, coffee was ready downstairs and I filled two large Styrofoam cups with Columbian. I thought about others in the world, probably northeastern Africa, that were pouring their tainted coffee not knowing about the molecules of altered cocaine that would almost instantly cause addiction. As I was informed, if they didn't get more coffee in about twenty-four hours, there would be withdrawal, relatively mild, symptoms; perspiration, anxiety and a headache. More coffee would most certainly cause more severe withdrawal symptoms, unless more coffee was again consumed.

The B & B coffee was great, however. I asked the attendant what kind it was and she said Dunkin Donut's Colombian. It was great and by the time I got back upstairs, Sara was awake and I took her the other coffee. "Thank you, my angel," she said. "No, you're my angel, let's get that straight!" I said in my Humphrey Bogart voice. She laughed.

"What's on your agenda today, Pablo?" she said. I said, "First, I serve you breakfast in bed!" I left and went back downstairs to get Sara a plate of fresh fruit, blueberry muffin and a bagel with cream cheese. I took it back to our bedroom and found a large art book on the coffee table to serve as her tray. "I'll get more if you like, angel," I said.

I left to go downstairs and get my breakfast. I didn't have the figure that Sara did, and I was a mercenary for the FBI, I thought; justifying my breakfast of toast, bacon, omelet and home fries. I took it back up and pulled up a chair, then another large book for a tray sitting on the edge of the bed next to her.

We finished our breakfasts and I asked if I could get her anything else? She said, "Just you!" I leaned over to give her a kiss and she grabbed my back and pulled me down. "I love you, Pablito!" she said. I was instantly aroused and threw my robe off and got under the covers. A breathtaking few minutes followed with both of us rolling over in near exhaustion. We both passed out, as if we'd imbibed for the preceding four hours.

I awoke again about an hour later and Sara had already gotten up. I said, "Good morning, again." Sara said, "Okay, no breakfast this time and I know now why you didn't tell me what was next on the agenda!" "What do you mean, Jelly Bean?" I said. She said, "Love making, was next on your agenda." I said, "You're the one! You pulled me down to you, two times!"

"No, really, what I had on the agenda was kayaking," I said. "Have you ever done any kayaking?" She said, "No, but I'm game." "You just have this one-man kayak and a big oar with paddles on both ends, and you row through the mangroves," I added. She said, "Sounds fun!" "Alright then, and we put on our best semblance of kayaking attire. She said, "I'm ready if you are." "Okay," I said.

We walked to the parked Chevy and got in. It was only a short drive to the Boca Chica bridge and a quaint place called "Hurricane Hole" rented kayaks. We walked up to the outside bar and rented two. I also rented a pair of life preservers, just in case. A girl accompanied us down to the water's edge, gave us succinct and almost robotic instructions and asked if we had any questions. I looked at Sara and she shook her head in the negative.

We got in our kayaks, not too gracefully either, and the girl pushed us off. I got my oar and tried to get out of Sara's way. We both started south, away from the bridge and next to some mangroves. An iguana jumped off a nearby mangrove bush into the water and Sara said, "Did you see that, what the hell?" I said, "It was just a vegetarian iguana." We paddled and paddled, enjoying, laughing, loving. It reminded me again of my three "L's;" Live, Laugh and Love. We certainly were doing them today, Praise the Lord, I thought. She intentionally rammed her kayak into me and laughed like hell. I, in turn, paddled away, turned around and rammed into her, nearly overturning her. She said, "Okay, okay, I give up!" I said, "I'm sorry Sara, just trying to have a little fun, like you." "I am having a great time; this was a super idea Pablo!" she said.

We started paddling back to the Hurricane Hole but this time the tide was with us, making it a bit easier to paddle. We pulled up and I got out first but slipped and fell under the damn kayak. Soaked, I stood up and said emphatically, "That's the way you're suppose to get out of a kayak Sara!" She, in turn, got out of hers gracefully. Then she added, "I didn't realize that you were an expert kayaker, Pablo!" "Smart ass!" I said. We laughed and walked up to the bar and got two Corona's with a lime wedge. We sat down by the water and she said, "Okay Pablo, what's next on your expert agenda (laughing)?"

"We're still dressed for about anything in Key West, except I'm soaked," I said. I had laid out my money and wallet on the table to dry, but they too were still wet. Sara laughed and said, "So, what's on your agenda?" I asked, "Have you ever seen the Mel Fisher Museum (I know the answer, but asked anyway)." She said, "No.

Who's Mel Fisher?" I said, "He was a treasure hunter and a very successful one." "What kind of treasure?" she asked. "Underwater ship wrecks," I said. "He and his crew found a Spanish Ship called the Atocha and it was carrying a treasure of coins, gold bars and all kinds of necklaces, rings, and gold jewelry."

"Mel fought Spain and the US, and with legal help from a Key West lawyer named Horan, finally won most of it since he found it. It's an interesting place to see," I said. "Let's go," Sara said. I picked up my soggy bills and wallet, finished my beer and got up. She got up and we walked to the car.

The Mel Fisher Museum was on Green Street, right down near the Key West Museum and Mallory Square, so I started that way down Roosevelt.

We got near the museum and tried to park, but no spaces near the museum. I finally found one on a side street and parked. We walked to the museum and paid at the entrance desk. There were posters of Mel and his crew, their boats, and explanations of how it was done. Every day Mel would say, "Today's the Day," and one day it was. They found coins dating back to the 1600's and forged in Spain out of silver and gold. These were gold bars, cannon, necklaces, bracelets, Rosario tiaras, gold chains and more coins. Quite an interesting exhibit, and Sara was thrilled. A hurricane had sunk the Atocha in some fifty feet of water in 1622!

We both enjoyed the Mel Fisher Museum and even looked at the store, which was the only way out, so I felt captive and didn't even ask Sara if she wanted anything. We walked to the car and got in.

Sara said, "That was really interesting, and I'll bet there are many more galleons and shipwrecks out there." I agreed; in fact, I said, "A friend of mine used to dive for Mel and now has a charter boat for fishing out of Key West. Yes, there are crews looking for wrecks all the time and at one time Key West was home to numerous salvagers who made their living that way."

We arrived at the Conch House and Sara said, laughingly, "So, Pablo, what's on the agenda now?" I said, "We need to shower and dress for dinner, and where we have it is a surprise." I'd called and made reservations, while Sara was getting ready this morning, at Sunset Key's Latitudes Restaurant. We would have to get a move on because our reservation was for the 7:30 departure of the launch from Mallory Square.

"Sara," I said, "We'll really have to move fast; I'm sorry. I made reservations on an island west of Key West and the boat that takes us there leaves at 7:30 sharp from Mallory Square, near where we were at the Mel Fisher Museum." "Okay," she said. I changed clothes in the bedroom, while she got ready in the bathroom. We both made it to a state of readiness at 6:50 p.m.

We left rapidly, walking fast to the "Blue Bomb" and got in. Traffic was hectic, but we got on Duval and headed north. We moved over to Whitehead and there was less traffic. Got to the Mel Fisher Museum and I remembered a parking lot in the building next to what is now the Margaritaville Hotel and pulled in, took the ticket and found a place. We walked down the stairs out to the pier and we were on time. It was only five minutes until our launch started its engines and untied. The captain backed out of the slip slowly. The sun was setting and was absolutely gorgeous. There were still two cruise ships in port and three sailboats in the channel. One sailboat was right out of the 1600's, like the Atocha, a three-masted schooner.

The ride over to Sunset Key was nice. Sara and I sat inside on a leather covered seat and held hands, like teenagers. The captain docked the boat with ease and an attendant tied her up. There was a covered walkway from the launch to the island and the building that housed the restaurant. They had my reservation, but since we wanted to sit on the outside beach area, we had to wait at the bar. We got our drinks and chatted with our barstool neighbors. We'd just finished most of our drink, when they called us and led us to a perfect table outside. Tropical torches lit up the area and added to the ambiance.

I ordered a Cakebread Cellars Chardonnay after asking Sara what she felt like. "Seafood," she said. I ordered Deep Sea Scallops on Risotto, while Sara got Chilean Sea Bass. I told the waiter to hold off for a while so we could have a glass of Chardonnay and talk.

I asked Sara again, where she would like to live after my FBI assignment fighting the Coffee Cartel is over? "As I said before, wherever you are Pablo," she said. "Well, I live on the BFB now, but I know its not that big," I answered. "We could get a place near the water and a place to dock my boat and live at both when we wanted," I offered. "That sounds fine with me," she said. I said, "I went to Costa Rica a while back and real estate is reasonable there and it's a tropical paradise." "Let's just look around, visit and decide when you're finished with this assignment," Sara said. "Okay," I said and our dinner came. It was wonderful and we savored every bite. No dessert for us, we were again content.

I signed the check and we left our table. "Do you want to investigate the Island or just go back?" I said. "When does the boat leave again?" she said. "I asked the waiter and he said, "they run every half hour till 11:30 p.m." It was 9:10 p.m., so Sara said, "Let's just go back."

We walked to the covered slip and the launch was there. We boarded and sat in the same seats as we did on the trip over. A nice trip back, but entirely different in the dark this time.

We landed at Mallory Square, they tied us up, and we offloaded. We walked up to the stairs of the parking lot, found the Blue Chevy, and I opened her door and let her in. She said, "You don't need to do that." I said, "My mother told me I do!" She laughed, "Love you, Pablo."

We got back to the Conch House, and OMG, I'd forgot and left my super-duper phone on the night stand because we were in such a hurry to catch the boat to Sunset Key. There was a message from Jack: "Update Paul, call ASAP." Shit, it was 10:30 p.m., but I know I should call anyway. I told Sara, and she said, "I'll just go on to bed, good luck with him."

PART FIVE

Terasina, Brazil

I went into the entrance room and called Jack. "Jack Warner here," he said. "Sorry, I'm just getting back to you, so late!" I said. "We have surveillance reports on Kamau's African operation, but not Teresina, Brazil. We found and verified all of El Gran Jefe's African operations, but the Brazil holdout has not been verified. The Isiolo operation you, Armando and Andy took out. The one by Meru National Park, bordered the park but was on Kamau's property. Since no further interrogation is required, I've sent a Seal contingent into the Meru Park complex, which will be hit in the morning. The Meru City complex looked just like his Isiolo complex and coffee fields, except smaller and no camouflaged, irregular buildings, and will be hit tomorrow morning as well. Again, no interrogation required. The Mombasa operation is still being analyzed and will be hot when analysis is complete. The Degeli Bur operation in

Ethiopia appears to be the direct cause of the supposed viral outbreaks in Addis Ababa and non-Eritrea. As you know, they weren't viral but tainted coffee withdrawal symptoms undiagnosed by local doctors. The Degeli Bur complex is also close to Asib, which is on the Red Sea a short boat ride to Yemen. We're still analyzing all of that, plus shipments to Yemen from either Asib or Ras Doumeira? We just can't figure out what was up with that Teresina operation? It's centrally located, not on the coast, and has only a few miles in any direction to highly populated areas. There is river access for boats to ship coffee via the Rio Poti and Parnaiba Rivers. Drone surveillance and conventional means, all show nothing. That's where you may come in. You, Armando and others may have to go to Teresina and help figure out what's going on there, then ultimately shut it down if one exists. I know there are a lot of unanswered questions, but you will probably be called shortly to go to Teresina, Brazil. I've advised Armando as well. I'm not sure at this point if surveillance is needed there, but we do know, because of its being hidden by Padron and El Patron and held out by El Gran Jefe, that we want our best soldiers, invaders and people on this one if we can find the Damn Place??" "We do know it's hidden and different from all the others," he added. "I'll be standing by and on the ready," I said. He hung up. Sara appeared to be sleeping, so I didn't wake her; I'll tell her about all this tomorrow morning and I pulled off my clothes and gently crawled in bed.

I woke about 8 a.m. with glints of sunlight shining through the curtains and noticed that Sara was gone.

She heard me getting up and came through the door holding a cup of coffee and said, "What's good for the gander, is good for the goose; or something like that." "You were supposed to get your coffee in bed like you gave me yesterday," she added. I said, "Thank you, my dear, but let me come tell you about my conversation with Jack last night."

We went back to the dinette table and sat down. "They're making progress on all of the Coffee Cartel's operations, but one. The one in Teresina, Brazil was held out by both Padron and El Patron and almost by El Gran Jefe, and they haven't found anything by several kinds of surveillance. Jack thinks that I and Armando and others will be required to go to Teresina and find out what the hell El Gran Jefe was talking about when he finally admitted that he had another operation in Teresina, Brazil. I'll likely be called today or tomorrow, and I'll need to be on standby 'til then."

"Thanks for the coffee," I said. "You're very welcome," Sara said, and offered to go bring up breakfast. "That would be super," I said, as I stepped into the restroom. I washed my face and came out to the dinette again. Sara returned with a nice breakfast for both of us and we ate, looking admiringly at the other between bites. We finished breakfast and Sara asked, "Okay, Pablo, I know you'll have to go on this mission, but know that I'll be waiting and praying for you. You know that we'll have to go back to Trinidad for a while to either rent or sell my place there. I'm officially on vacation from the Mall now, but will resign when I get back. I should have a pension built up also. Do you have things hanging like I do?" I said, "I have a fifty-acre property in central Florida that I invested in year's ago. It's in Dade County and now has orange trees on it. Last year the oranges paid for upkeep and taxes, but I'm expecting a profitable crop soon. I have my Hatteras, and it sounded like Jack was trying to arrange for me to get the "Café Negro," the 55' Hatteras that Pascal Padron had for transporting coffee. Nothing other than that." "Me neither," Sara said, "It's just good for us to know so we can consolidate and share our life together." "Yes, I agree," I said.

My phone rang. "Paul, this is Jack," the voice said. "Okay, this is Paul," I said. "Harvey and I want you to go to Teresina right away, but not using a NAS plane. I want you to meet Armando, whom I've notified, at Key West International at 2 p.m.; your flight is American Airlines Flight 1304 at 3 p.m. You and Armando will pass as contractors with a firm called "Brown and Shoot" out of Texas. The Vice President in Teresina is Clyde Alverey and he knows you're coming. Armando has your passport, driver's license, etc. and your name is Paul Bennett; his is Armando Chavez. Specifics are in your paperwork that Armando will have, but your mission is to find Kamau's Teresina operation, if there is one? Clyde Alverey at Brown and Shoot has your work badges and has made motel arrangements." "Got it," I said. "And you say drones or any surveillance has not detected anything there, and how far from Teresina have you covered?" I asked. Jack said, "We think we've covered a circle of fifty miles from Teresina, without anything; no coffee plants, no suspicious buildings, nothing!" "Maybe we should have got more from Wongari Kamau when we questioned him?" I said. "Maybe, but we won't try more unless you and Armando come up empty," Jack said. "Anything else?" Jack added. "I don't think so?" I said, and hung up.

I looked at Sara, who heard my half of the conversation, and said, "Well, this is it! I'm to be at EYW by 2 p.m. and meet Armando who will have paperwork, passport, etc. I'll be traveling as a contractor named Paul Bennett and report to a company called Brown and Shoot in Teresina tomorrow night. Teresina is one hour ahead of us here and the flight takes fifteen and a half hours via Miami and Brasilia, so we'll get there at 7 a.m. tomorrow. He'll give us motel and other instructions when we get there, my love!" "I'll keep in touch, if I can. Our assignment is to find the Teresina operation if we can, or if there even is one? No one knows for sure," I said.

"I understand, Pablo," Sara said. "Once this is all over we'll take a vacation, or whatever you want to do, my ebony angel," I said. "I know, I know," she said.

"Well, it's almost lunchtime," she said. "Let me quickly go and pack for my trip and we'll go to lunch," I said. "Okay," she said. I put all the clothes I had in the overnight bag with toiletries, shoes and socks. Okay, I was ready.

"Where do you want to go for lunch?" I said. "I don't know." "There's a good lunch at that breakfast place, Goldman's Deli," I said. "Great," Sara said.

We drove to the Winn Dixie parking lot and parked near the Deli. There was a little waiting line, so we patiently stood by the door. A stocky little guy came and seated us at a table for two. We ordered iced tea and both got cheeseburgers and fries, the All-American lunch! They were great. We didn't say much because both of us knew what this assignment might bring . . . tragedy! I paid the check and we left.

We got in the Chevy and I drove back to the Conch House. It was almost 2:00pm, so we went up to our room and I said, "Would you drive me to the airport and keep the Chevy for transportation?" Sara said, "Sure." I grabbed my bag and we walked back to the car, got in and drove down South Roosevelt to the airport. She pulled up to the curb for departing flights and we got out.

"I've had a wonderful time with you these past two days," she said. "Me too!" I said. We gave a big hug and I walked in the ticket area. Armando was sitting on a bench. "Hola, me compadre," he said. "Hello to you too," I said. "Here we go again!"

"Here's your credentials and stuff, Paul Bennett!" he said. I laughed, as we walked down the hall. I excused myself to the restroom to open my package and get my new license, passport and paperwork out to read on the way to Brazil. Armando waited and we walked to the kiosk, got boarding passes, then to the security checkpoint. We both went through without incident. We walked to the waiting room and waited; boarding commenced as soon as we sat down. This flight went to Miami, where we switched planes for Brasilia, then another to Teresina (fifteen and a half hours total time, certainly a long haul for sure!). Our zone was called and we pulled out our boarding passes and gave them to the checker person. All good and we walked to the boarding ladder and boarded. We weren't sitting together, so I motioned . . . I'm here. Armando walked back to his seat.

The flight was good and only took forty minutes. We got off, got a water and waited for the flight to Brazil.

We were called, showed our passes and got on the plane. A long flight, had to take my shoes off due to swollen feet and stretched three times. Another plane switch awaited in Brasilia.

The flight to Teresina was uneventful, save a little turbulence on the descent. We met in the airport and rented a car.

We got a map at the rental place and the address of the Brown and Shoot offices. It was 7 a.m., so we got breakfast before we left the airport. We finished, got into our rental, and drove to the B & R office. We parked and walked into the waiting room; the secretary said, "Mr. Alverey is expecting you." I said, "Thank you!" Clyde Alverey came out of his office and motioned for us to walk with him back into his office. We went in and sat down. Clyde said, "Jack has given me the rundown on your visit, and I'll do everything to respect your situation. You are construction engineers bidding on an apartment complex on the south side of Teresina, as far as anyone knows, including my employees. I've been compensated and wish you success. Your hotel reservations are at the Alfa on Rio Poti." "If you need anything, call me," he said. I said, "Will we work out of here or our hotel now?" Clyde said, "We have a temporary office for you here," as we walked to it, "But you will also work out of your room at the Alfa." "I think we'll just drive around the area and get our orientation. Do you know of any unorthodox construction in the area?" I said. "No, but there are other construction projects by other companies that you will, in your capacity, have access to and interest in," he said. Perfect; it looks like Jack had thought this disguise façade through, I thought. "Okay," I said, and Armando and I left our office and the building.

I told Arm, "I think we might find out something by talking to workers to see if they might know of a place that might have been built by Wongari Kamau." Armando agreed.

We drove around and noted the rivers running through Teresina. We drove and drove. The Parnaiba River was fairly large, large enough for my 55' Hatteras to navigate, having a five-foot draft. The river ran northeast all the way to Parnaiba on the coast of the South Atlantic. What, if any, was the connection to Kamau's Teresina complex? Again, if there was one? Question after question, I thought.

We drove out of town on Highway P1-112 and went for several miles; a nice country road, but nothing out of the ordinary. We drove back into town and decided to go to the Alfa Hotel and check in; we were beat from the trip from Key West. The Alfa Hotel was on Avenida Rio Poti, 959 per Clyde Alverey. Armando put the address in his cellphone and we were off. Parking was behind the hotel and it looked okay from outside: it was better inside. We got a room on the second floor and it was nice. We both looked at each other and said, "I'm done!" and went to our separate beds.

I woke up and made some coffee in the room coffeemaker; not good, but coffee. Armando was still out, so I walked down to the lobby and got much better coffee. Sitting in the lobby having coffee, I thought, if there was a building or two involved it must be on land held by Kamau or a shell company, and it must have been built by workers from the Teresina area. Those two assertions, I felt, would lead us to the complex if it did exist. I got a phonebook from a booth and took it and another coffee back up to the room. Armando was up drinking his room coffee when I got back. I said, "Armando, I've been thinking." He said, "Beware, Paul thinks!" "Seriously, if there is a Kamau complex around here, it was likely built by workers in this area and the land it's on is probably owned by Kamau, directly or indirectly!" Armando said, "Yes, you're right. Your thinking is good this morning. Aerial surveillance, or all the other means, wouldn't show any of what you're talking about. Great idea!"

"We could look up construction companies and you, Armando, better than a gringo, would pose as a worker and find out where it was built and how." "On-the-other-hand, I could go to the courthouse or where they have deeds and property taxes and find out if there are any property links to El Gran Jefe." "Sounds like a plan, my man," Armando said.

"I'll try to find property records, while you try and talk to construction workers; Brown and Shoot would be a good starting place, no?" I said. Armando shook his head in agreement. "You take the rental car, I'll catch a cab."

We got breakfast at a local place next door to the Alfa and went our separate ways; Armando to change into worker's clothes and be a construction worker and me going to the Courthouse to look for property records. The Courthouse had a hell of a name, but I finally got help and they said that the "Ordsem dos Advogados do Brasil Seção Piauí" had property records. It wasn't far from the Alfa Hotel, just across the Rio Poti River and south. I got a cab and went to the Courthouse. I asked the attendant for properties purchased in the past decade, since complexes like we've seen run by the Coffee Cartel have taken three or four years to construct. I was surprised that properties were not computerized or indexed. I looked and cross-referenced and finally, after one and a half hours, found a plot of land 20-acres in total purchased by Kamau Industries six year's ago. I got a copy of the survey and couldn't believe I was so lucky. There must a complex here and the question was, why didn't surveillance pick up on it?

I walked out of the Courthouse, anxious to share my find. I caught a taxi and went back to the Alfa. I got to our room and Armando was gone on his quest.

I called Jack, "Jack Warner, here," he said. "Jack, I found a 20-acre plot purchased by Kamau Industries six year's ago," I said. "How in the hell?" he said. I went to the Teresina Courthouse and in under two hours, found it." "Great work Paul," Jack said. "How far from Teresina is it? Do you have coordinates?" "Yes," I said. "The Kamau plot is 21 miles west of Teresina, near a country road. The coordinates are 5° 10' 30" S, 43° 12' 06" W," I continued. "Let me know what you see from drones and things!"

I just couldn't believe that after Jack had all the departments of the FBI at his disposal, that I'd found the complex in less than two hours. Sometimes, "Boots on the ground" are more productive than all the high-tech equipment in the world, I thought.

It was lunchtime, so I thought I'd see if another restaurant would be good for lunch. I wondered where and how Armando was doing with the construction workers.

I walked out the lobby door and walked east on Rio Poti Avenue. About four blocks from the hotel was a McDonald's. I got a Big Mac and fries and sat down at a table. Portuguese is a unique language, with only minor similarities to Spanish. A few words were close, but inflexion and dialect made it difficult to understand. I listened to the locals and didn't have a clue what they were saying.

I left McDonald's and walked down the street. Interesting that buildings, roads, lights and infrastructure is essentially the same all over the world. How, then, did we learn that all of these things got invented in the United States? Puzzling, huh! Department stores, jewelry stores, all very much like any city in the US, but I digress.

I had a mission, so I thought I'd give Armando a call. "Hello," he said. "This is Pablo," I said. "Sara's rubbing off on you Pablo!" he said.

"I found out where El Gran Jefe's complex is and gave the coordinates to Jack!" I said. "How in the hell?" he said. "Well, I finally found a record of his purchase in the Courthouse. Amazingly, at that time he didn't try to hide who he was and the twenty acres he bought was by Kamau Industries, six year's ago. The 20 acres is about 21 miles west of Teresina. Do you want to take a ride out there?" I said. "Sure, let's do that!" Armando said. "Where are you?" I said, "I'm on Rio Poti Avenue and will be walking west to the hotel. 'Okay," he said, and added, "I'll leave B & S and head to the hotel and pick you up in front of the lobby.

I made it to the Alfa Hotel and went into the lobby, just so I could cool off and still see when Armando got there. He pulled up to the curb and I got in. I said, "I'm anxious to see what kind of a complex he's got without coffee plants, like all the others." Armando said, "I'm sure Jack and all his people are checking the aerials of the area you found. You said that you have coordinates, right?" I said, "Yes, their 5° 10' 30" S and 43° 12' 06" W." Armando tried and then I, as the passenger, tried but the rental car's GPS only took addresses! I said, "Okay, I think I've got a Navionics App that will take coordinates." Yes, as I entered the numbers in degrees, minutes and seconds. "Okay," I said, "Turn left here and get on BR316." "What does BR stand for?" said Armando. "Back Road," I said, but I really didn't know. "You go through Timon, Teresina's sister city and I'll tell you then," I said. "Did you find out anything from the B&S construction workers?" I said. Armando said, "A little, but no one at B & S know anything. They said they didn't know of any big developments or buildings being built away from the city." "Get on 226 here," I injected. "They did give me a lead, however, and said that there was only one large equipment and crane dealer in the area and if a large operation had been constructed, that they would have supplied the cranes, etc," Armando said. "What's its name?" I said. He said, "Castro Crane Company." "We'll see what we can find at the location and probably not need to follow-up with Castro Crane!" I said. It only took thirty minutes to get close. We looked at the coordinates and we were on BR226, and at the coordinates!" Nothing! There was a fence and what looked like pasture land. No big buildings, no small buildings, only a few grown up bushes.

"Something's all fucked up!" Armando offered. "I agree! El Gran Jefe very reluctantly told us about this Teresina operation and then after losing a finger and enduring the pain of the sciatic nerve, up close and personal!" I said. "This doesn't make any sense, at all. All we can do is wait for Jack to tell us what his people find. We can get out and walk a bit on the property, after all, it is 20 acres!" I added. "Okay," he said.

We got out, crawled under the fence, and started walking across the pasture-like property. We walked; there were some small tree stumps, bushes, weeds and grass everywhere. Nothing else; no sign of buildings, huts, shelters, or even life?? We kept walking and I said, "Armando, there's nothing here!" He shook his head in agreement. We turned around and headed back to the car, when a small helicopter whirred above and to the south of us. "Where did he come from?" Armando said. "Out of nowhere!" I said. The copter just hovered over the empty field, edging toward us, it seemed and as we continued to the road, he stayed about 200 yards away from us. We continued walking to the car and the copter seemed to drop some and was gone. We stopped in our tracks and I said, "Okay, Armando, that wasn't a coincidence was it?" "That helicopter, although it kept its distance, only appeared as we got deep in the field," I said. "Want to go back in?" Armando said. "Yes, but not now," I retorted. "I'd feel better telling Jack what just happened and knowing what Jack finds. That could have just been a sightseeing helicopter; there were some near the airfield in Teresina, I remember," I said. "It didn't threaten us and stayed its distance; why didn't we see it or hear it coming?" Armando said.

We got back in the car and drove along the road edging Kamau's property. I said, "Look, Armando, there has to be something. Why would an African millionaire purchase a 20-acre plot of land outside of Teresina, Brazil unless there was an ulterior motive; we know he had other operations in South America, Cuba and Africa." "There is nothing but an empty field," Armando said. "There has to be something," I said. We continued along BR226, found a place to turn around and backtracked to where we had parked and looked again toward where we saw the helicopter, but there wasn't a thing in the sky or on the ground!"

Puzzled, we headed back to Teresina. Armando said, "The helicopter was the clincher for me; there must be something there!" "I agree," I said. "There must be something underground."

We got back to the Alfa Hotel and parked in back, as always. We got out and walked through the hotel lobby to their bar. We sat down and ordered a drink. "I'm getting sick and tired of this Coffee Cartel bull and now we're down to an empty field," Armando said. "I feel the same, my friend," I said. "Well, where do we go from here?" Armando added. "I guess we wait for Jack's analysis, but I want to tell him about our trip to the coordinates and the Copter encounter. Then maybe look at the construction workers and the Castro Crane Company," I said. "I'm having a drink and not worrying about it anymore today!" Armando said. "Salut!" I said. We ordered another.

We had still another and decided we were hungry, so we walked with a slight wobble to a restaurant a couple of blocks away called Baiao De Does and had Mahi Mahi over seasoned Risotto; very good. We finished and walked back to the Alfa.

We just get back to the room and Jack called. "Paul," he said. "Yes," I replied. "You won't believe this Paul!" he said. "What, I won't believe what?" I said, "There are no buildings or structures on that 20-acres!" he said. "Well, I know that now too because Armando and I drove out there this afternoon. We even walked across a fence from

225

the road, and there was nothing!" I said. I continued, "There was something, Jack. A damn helicopter came from nowhere and appeared somewhat threatening." "What kind of helicopter?" Jack asked. "A small Bell-type, like those used for tourists. It stayed a couple hundred yards away and never really threatened us, but it was very strange and a little unnerving, so we left!" I responded. Jack answered, "We had appropriate divisions look at this property. They turned up nothing except numerous, faint, thermographic images that they first mistook for false image feedback, which happens sometimes with thermal imaging. Another enhanced, scrutinized look showed what could be shielded, underground images of lots of workers!" "How could that be; there was nothing above ground except bushes, weeds and grass?" I asked. "It is possible, Paul. There are shields, magnetic and electronic, there are massive hydraulic lifting devices, etc." Jack retorted. "Okay, Jack, Okay!" I answered. Arm and I will go back to really search," I said. "Yes," Jack said, "But because of Kamau's other locations and the threat to the world, we will be sending you a contingent of personnel to have a thorough search of this property." I said, "Good news! Thank you. Armando and I will go tomorrow, and don't forget the helicopter!" Jack hung up.

I looked at Armando and said, "Un-fucking believable! "There is something there! That copter was just giving a "you're too close' warning!" Armando said. "I think you're right, buddy, and we'll go find something tomorrow!" I said and added, "You know, I would feel a hell of a lot better if we were armed." "I was thinking the same thing Paul," he said. "Let's see if we can get something in the morning; I want to see if I can get Sara on the phone." "I'm good and going to bed," Armando said. "Good night," I said.

I called Sara, as her international number was on my phone; one ringy dinghy, two ringy dinghys, "Hola, Le puedo ayudor?" the voice said. I said, "Como esta, me amore!" "Pablo, how are you? I've missed you so much!" Sara said. "Me too!" I said, "Everything is fine here in Teresina." "I hope so, I love you," she said. "What does it really look like down there in Teresina? When can I see you?" she added. "The truth! I have no idea. I love you too, my ebony angel, but I should get off the phone, it's very expensive. After I've said I love you for the third time, should I say more?" I said, and hung up.

I went to bed!

I woke up at 6:30 a.m., wide awake. Need coffee, but the need was certainly less than those already addicted to Kamau's coffee.

We needed to go back to the plot, but Armando and I both knew we couldn't go unarmed because of that ominous copter. And also because of the possible subterranean images that Jack had told me about. I looked up a local gun store called Zero1 – Armas e Municoes, which I assumed meant arms and ammunition in Portuguese. The shop was east of us on the Avenida João XXII. They opened at 8:00 a.m., so I thought I'd get Armando up and be there when they opened. I went down to the lobby to get some better coffee and got two cups. Back in the room I woke up Armando, gave him coffee and told him about the gun store.

Arm was groggy, but said, "Okay, gringo!" Arm sipped his café negro and I went to the couch and sat down. I thought about fighting fire with fire and renting our own helicopter to check out Kamau's property. That would probably be too blatant and would surely meet with opposition, I thought, now that we knew there were possibly several people under the pasture. Probably the best and safest way to find out more would be to drive, park and walk like we did yesterday.

I asked Armando, who had joined me on the couch, and he agreed. I also told him that I was going to call Jack back to see if he could give me the exact location of where his pseudo-thermal images emanated from. He said, "Perfecto, Pablo."

We got dressed and went to the restaurant downstairs to get a breakfast burrito and more coffee. I ate, excused myself and went to the lobby to call Jack. "Jack Warner, here," he said. "Jack, could you give me the precise location of those pseudo-thermals of people?" I said. He said, "I'll text them to you, ASAP. What's your plan, as the entourage of agents I told you about will arrive tonight." "Armando and I will go out to the plot and see what's up with the land at those coordinates," I said. "Be careful Paul, we know something is there," he said, and hung up.

I walked back into the restaurant and said, "You ready, Freddie?" Armando said, "Sure, whore!" We left and got in the car. "We're looking for Avenida João XXII,"

I said. Arm entered the street and said, "Turn right out of here, then left at the first stop light." I just drove and soon we were heading east on Avenida João XXII. The gun shop was on the right, so I pulled over and parked. Amazed, as we walked in, that this was just like a gun store in the U.S; handguns, assault rifles, hunting rifles, the whole schmear. We selected a Barrett REC7 and told the attendant we wanted two of those, four extra clips, and ammunition and bulletproof vests. He said, "You'll need to sign the paperwork." "Okay," I said. I filled out the paperwork and gave it back to the guy with two hundred-dollar bills. He immediately put the bills in his pocket and said, "Eu vou cuidar disso!" I looked at Armando and he said, "Muy bien, Pablo." Soon the attendant came back with two guns, four clips, ammo and vests. He said, "4000 Reals, por favor." I looked at Armando and he said, "Good, pay the man!" I tried to write a check, but the guy shook his head in the negative. "Cash, cash!" he said.

Armando said, "He wants cash only, so I guess we have to get cash?" I said, "Okay, por favor, hold, hold," and we left to find a bank. We got back on the main street and drove a little way to find a bank. We found a Bank of Brazil at 2994 João XXII just down the road, and I parked. I went in and left Armando in the car. I gave my credit card to the teller and she checked it electronically. "Okay," she said, "Cuanto?" Even I knew that meant, "How much?" "5000 Reals," I said and she handed me a strip of paper; I wrote 5000 Reals. She said, "Okay." Soon, she put the bills in a counting machine, showed me the digital total and counted out 5000 Reals. "Mucho Gracias," I said. She got the message and smiled. I stuck the wad in my pocket and left. I got in the car and told Armando, "Success." We drove back to the gun shop and gave the attendant the 4000 Reals he'd asked for. He had a large cardboard box with everything in it, as I double checked it's contents. We left and Armando got in the back seat with the box. I said, "I'll go back to the Kamau land." Armando said, "Okay," as he opened and readied the REC7's. Jack had just texted me the refined coordinates, so we were ready.

It didn't take long to get to the big pasture, a little over half an hour, and we parked like we did before beside the fence surrounding Kamau's land. We put on the vests, readied our Barrett's, and stuck two clips each in our pockets. We tried to hold the guns vertically down our legs while walking, in case we were watched. But there was nothing in sight, I thought, but grass, weeds and bushes. We got across the fence and I entered Jack's most recent coordinates. "Northwest," I said, pointing in the direction. We were quite a distance away, but kept walking. As we approached the coordinates, a helicopter appeared as if it was raised out of the ground. It started and lifted vertically and just hovered there. We had stopped when we saw it emerge. It looked as though a grass-covered platform had elevated and shifted, then another platform hydraulically lifted the small helicopter. It just hovered; it was too far away to get a shot, so we tried to conceal our gun's and moved closer. The copter seemed to advance toward us, but at this distance we couldn't see any weapons on the hovering adversary.

We were getting closer and closer; I did see two turrets under the cockpit of the craft and told Armando, "It's armed!" "I see," he said. We both advanced. Luckily, there was a bush in front of us, so I told Armando, "Go for the bush!" He gave me a thumb's up and we ran for it. Before we hit the ground, the copter fired at us; missing us, except for my stomach. I took aim, as did Armando, and we fired at the pilot. He hovered, firing all the time and coming in our direction.

He got about thirty yards away and started down, fast. One of us had hit our target and the small, lethal bastard hit the pasture. We got up, started for the coordinates again, and from the ground come a dozen or so soldier-looking guys. We looked at each other and simultaneously decided to run for the car.

We glanced back, but the sentries or guards or whomever they were, decided to hold their position and let us go. We got to the rental, threw our rifles in the back and ran for it back down Road 226! We went like hell, but weren't pursued? We took a diversionary route back to the hotel, just in case, but we're satisfied that no one had followed.

We got to our room and took a breath! "There's no doubt now, is there?" I said. "None at all," Arm said. "I guess I'd better call Jack and give him an update," I said. Arm affirmed with a headshake.

I called Jack. "Jack Warner here." "Paul Pilot, I wanted to let you know what just happened!" I said.

"What just happened?" Jack said. "Arm and I were very concerned about the helicopter that emerged on our visit yesterday, so we got rifles, clips and bulletproof jackets this morning and went out there," I said. "Yes?" Jack asked. "We parked on the adjacent road, went under the fence and walked toward the coordinates that you texted me. All was good until the helicopter emerged from the ground and started shooting at us!" I added. "What then?" Jack asked. "We started shooting back and took the copter down, then about a dozen guards/ soldiers emerged from the ground and came toward us. We retreated and ran to our vehicle; they didn't pursue. I was hit in the stomach, but my BP jacket stopped any damage, other than bruising!" I said. "This changes our approach. I will call off the agents, or redirect some of them, and get a force put together; headed probably by you, Armando and Andy Pellerito. He's recovered from his Suriname injury, and with your help we can take this operation down," Jack said. "There is no doubt that the Coffee Cartel had spread everywhere, even went underground in Brazil!" I added, "I wonder what we'll find under this pasture land?" "When do you think you'll have your next assault force put together, Jack?" I said. "ASAP," he said. "Will advise!" and hung up.

"I'm sure Jack would be gathering the powers to be and planning a raid as quickly as possible. You and I will be involved, and he mentioned Andy Pellerito as well," I told Arm. Arm said, "Does Jack have any idea what's really under that pasture?" "I don't think so Arm, he didn't really know how many thermal images we're dealing with, since there is some kind of magnetic shield?. Let alone, what they might have under there," I said. "Now that we know that El Gran Jefe really does have some kind of operation, unlike the others in Teresina, Brazil, shouldn't we re-interrogate him and find out what the hell he has before a raid?" Armando offered. "A really good point, Armando, but he had urgency in his voice and that would take time!" I responded. "You're probably right Paul, but there's a lot of unique unknowns dealing with a subterranean complex with emerging security helicopters and guards?" Armando said. "We'll just wait for direction from Jack," I said.

"I'm hungry again," Armando said. "Me too!" I answered. We rode the elevator down to the lobby and I said, "There's a McDonalds a few blocks away, how's that?" "Fine," he said. We left the hotel and walked. I thought, how many of these people could imagine a complex like we just came from only a few miles away! It was nearly noon and the streets were bustling with people. We made it to McDonalds and I asked Arm, "You want a Happy Meal?" Armando said, "Yes, I need one!"

"We sat down in a booth and ate. About halfway through, Armando said, "Paul, I felt pretty good about questioning select construction workers; I know some of them must have worked on the subterranean construction. There's that crane place you mentioned to look into, as well. I could go this afternoon, before Jack solidifies his plan, and maybe find out something." "That sounds great and we have nothing to do until advised by Jack." "Did you want to go back to Brown and Shoot?" I asked. "No, there's another big one called "Constructora Sucesso" and it's on BR 226 near the river. I'll become a construction worker and see what I can find out," he said. "Okay, I'll take you there and go back to the Alfa. Just catch a cab or call me," I said.

I dropped Armando at the construction site and went back to the hotel. I parked in the back of the Alfa and walked through the rear entrance to the elevator, then to our room. It felt like it would be a good idea to lie down after such an exhausting morning. I inspected my bruise from the bullet and it was OK, thank goodness. I was hit in a stomach muscle. I dropped off to sleep. I arose a little groggy, and my stomach hurt where I took the bullet in the bulletproof vest. I took some more Tylenol and made some of that shitty room coffee. I sat on the couch reflecting and wondering why the Coffee Cartel would have a non-coffee farm and underground complex? In about two hours, I heard someone knock on the door. It was Arm.

Armando came in the room, excited. "I've got more information and I think I'd like to share it with you and Jack simultaneously. I wanted to call Jack when I was also with you, okay?" he said. "Okay," I said. Armando called Jack on his super phone. "Jack Warner here," Jack said. "This is Armando and I've been posing as a construction worker this afternoon. I talked to a welder at Constructora Sucesso, a local contractor, and after essentially bribing him with $200 American dollars he reluctantly said that he and many others worked on the Kamau project a long time ago. He said that they were all given incentive pay and threatened to not disclose what was built there. He said, after I gave him $200, that I had to promise not to tell anyone connected to Kamau Industries, and I promised! He was visibly shaken about his disclosure, and he had a few drinks in a nearby bar before I sprung the $200 on him. To make a long story short, he said they constructed three levels or stories below the surface! The third level down was nothing but a very large tank, with a large vertical chute connecting to the surface, and covered with a sizeable platform, apparently movable via hydraulics."

"The second level housed offices and a large laboratory. The top level was the main residence, with a separate large housing area for others. A large area near the surface was constructed for helicopters to be shuttled to a launching platform and then elevated after a surface platform was hydraulically moved out of its way. It appeared to this welder that the site was almost military in nature, and that the separate housing area on the top level was for troops," Armando said, and then asked Jack if he could put him on speaker for Paul's and his ears only. Jack agreed and said, "Wow, that explains a lot and will certainly help us with the takedown raid on the complex." He went on, "This almost duplicates, except the missing coffee plants, the other complexes in South America, Cuba, and to the best of our knowledge, Africa. And it suggests, since it was extremely difficult to extract from El Gran Jefe, that it was intended to remain hidden and undetectable by anyone. Your work, Armando, will help us refine our plan of attack on this

Teresina complex. And both of you, Paul and Armando, uncovered the retaliatory nature of the complex this morning when you shot down the first helicopter and retreated. I'll get back again with you when raid strategy is finalized," and Jack hung up.

"Nice work, Arm," I said. "How in the hell did you find this guy?" "I told officials that I was looking for work, and they said people looking for work were in a holding area. I went there, but no one would talk. I got the feeling they knew about the complex's construction, and one of the guys said that there were others looking for work that hung out in a bar around the corner. I went there and ran into Ignacio, who reluctantly (even after I gave him two hundred dollar bills) told me about the construction." "I had the distinct feeling that this company, Constructora Sucesso, was a primary contractor, but they're sworn to silence and scared to death!" Armando added.

How's the tummy?" Armando added. "I'll survive, not bad," I said. "I'll bet this last stronghold of the Cartel would be able to carry on the tainted coffee business if all other facilities were gone," I added. "I think you're right, now that we see what the complex consists of," Armando added. "What the hell did we get into?" I said. "It's not what we got into, my friend, it's what you got into when two pirates boarded the BFB in the Florida Straits!" Armando said, and added, "Thank God it was your boat that they boarded, or this Coffee Cartel might have addicted millions!"

"Thanks, Arm, and you've been just as instrumental in your interrogations, fighting and interviews," I said.

"Alright, enough kissing ass; let's go eat a big steak!" Arm said.

We took separate, much needed showers, shaved, etc. and dressed up with the clothes we had. We went to the concierge, but no one was there, so we went to the hotel's reception desk and he suggested, "Churrascaria Calcada de Casa," on Avenue Walfrido Salmito! Since we were tired, would be drinking, we called a cab. I told the cabby that we wanted to go to Churrascaria Calcada de Casa." He knew of it and drove off.

We arrived and were seated, even without a reservation, and I ordered a nice Caymus Reserve Cab. The atmosphere was casual but nice, and a little rustic like a steak house should be. The waiter brought our wine and Evian water. He opened the bottle and handed me the cork, then poured a small amount in my glass. Swirl, nose, and inhaled sip; it was fabulous! A welcome taste and experience after such a tense day, I thought. The waiter was intentionally slow to return after we both had a glass of this super vino. We ordered two aged Ribeye's, medium rare with baked potato (loaded) and asparagus. The wine was so good and the experience so appreciated, I ordered another bottle of Caymus Reserve.

The steaks came and were outstanding; we ate and enjoyed. "A great idea, coming here," Armando said. "Yes," I agreed. Too full for desert, we were completely satisfied. No after dinner drink or nightcap required. I got the check, tipped 25% and we asked the waiter to please call us a cab. We walked to the front door and waited. I wondered how Sara was doing and Carl; how were he and my boat doing at Marina Hemingway? It seemed like months ago that we had docked there.

The taxi came and I told him the Alfa Hotel; he acknowledged and drove off. We were pretty high and full of the best red I'd had in a long time, and I could only think of bed and Sara; in reverse order. I remembered that Jack had said the contingent of agents would arrive soon. We got back to the hotel and crashed.

Sun glinted around the curtains and I slowly came to. As I awoke, I said to myself, I'm going to get some good coffee downstairs. I got somewhat dressed, put on a hat and quietly left the room. I got downstairs via the elevator and although the hotel coffee downstairs was a hell of a lot better than the room coffee, I decided to get some excellent coffee next door (around the corner) at Café Noir. It was so good, I got two more cups and took one back for Armando who was up and around.

"Muchos Gracias, Senior Pablo," he said. "Por nada," I answered. "Where did you get this?" he said. "Café Noir, next door," I responded. "Muy Bien, Café Negro," he said, and continued, "Isn't that the name of your new boat?" I said, "Yes, I think so, it all depends on Jack's follow through." "One thing for sure, if you get it, don't make any Café Negro out of its hull contents!" Armando said. "Ha, ha!" I laughed, and added, "I wonder how I'll get rid of all that coffee and patch that damned starboard hole near, but above, the water level?" "Ha, ha!" Armando said." You drilled the damned hole, Pablo, don't complain too much," Arm added.

"I think I'll call Sara and Carl to see how they are?" I said. I dialed Carl, no answer, but it was only 7:15 a.m. in Cuba. I'm sure he was sound asleep, either on the BFB or at Loopee's house. I decided to wait for a while before calling Sara in Key West, since she too was an hour earlier.

Armando turned on the TV. He could understand it, and I was video limited. Arm spoke in several Latin languages, but he was fluent in Spanish dialects and Portuguese.

I relaxed with my second cup of coffee and played Sudoku on my cellphone. I couldn't turn on music since Arm had the TV on and to me, Portuguese is not really as melodic as French. It didn't matter. I told Arm that I was calling Sara anyway, and excused myself. It was 8:00 a.m. Key West time anyway! "Hola," I said. "Pablo, my angel," Sara said. "I miss you terribly, and I pray I'll see you soon!" I said. "Oh Pablo, I miss you more!" she said. "Like I said the last time, do you have any idea when I will see you?" she added. "I still don't know, but I do know things are escalating, and I'm certain we will try and shut down this operation as soon as possible. Jack Warner is putting together an assault plan as we speak!" I said. "Arm and I went out there yesterday morning and shot down a helicopter that shot at us. Then we got chased by a dozen guards but made it to the car and got the hell out of there. All is good, but El Gran Jefe has a subterranean complex under his pasture. The raid will happen soon, so pray for Arm and I and Andy, and all of us that will be involved. "God, Pablo, I will pray for you and yes, all of you, but I couldn't go on now without you!" she said. "I've had more time here in Key West to think about our relationship and it's become my whole life, all that I am is yours, Pablo." "I love you equally, my ebony angel," I responded. "Please take extra care to keep yourself out of harm's way, so that we can live the rest of our lives together," Sara went on. "I will, my love," I said. "I've got to go now, Sara," I said, and hung up. God, I said to myself, I would have started crying if I hadn't hung up.

I was out on the balcony, so I went back in our room and told Arm I was just going to take a walk. Arm said, "Okay." I walked to the first floor by stairs and then out on the street's sidewalk to nowhere in particular.

What a life I've had, so blessed! I've dodged death several times, and then I stumble onto this Coffee Cartel and a Negroid Cuban named Sara who caught my love forever!

I just have to try to stay out of harm's way, as Sara said. I have to get this commitment over with and make a new life with Sara!

I must have walked four or five miles, and I was far away from the Alfa. I just kept walking, consulting my iPhone GS tracking APP once in a while, and was enjoying it. I stopped at a department store and wondered if Sara would like the dress in the window. Now that's bad, or maybe good, I wondered. Yes, it was very good to give to the one you love; give in any way possible: spiritually, mentally, physically, socially, financially, and in every way I can comprehend.

I made it back to the Alfa, went through the lobby and up to the room and believe it or not, Arm was watching the local news channel. He said, "Como Esta, Pablo." I said, "Muy Bien, Arm, me compadre." "Good walk?" Arm said. "Yes," I responded.

"How are you doing?" I asked. "Okay, just wondering what we were going to do and how to handle an underground complex like we ran into? If the damn thing opens up, we'll just have to jump or climb or whatever? Maybe we should call Jack and ask about hooks, lines, carabiners, and all the implements many of us should have for a subterranean stronghold like this. I assume they have stairs or elevators. If we can get to the top floor and access stairs or an elevator, we're home free," Arm said. "You're absolutely right, should I call him or you?" I said. "You call him," Arm said. "You sure?" I said. "Yes," he said, and I dialed.

"Jack Warner here," he said. "Paul here," I said. "Jack, Armando came up with a good idea. Our troops should all be made aware of the subterranean threat we have and he thinks that hooks, lines, carabiners and whatever climbing implements you can get should be provided to several of our group." "Okay, that sounds like a good plan, given the unknowns about access to this unique complex. Will do," Jack said, then "Anything else?" "Not now," I said. "Anymore on timing?" I added. "Could be as soon as 3 a.m. tomorrow morning. The middle of the night raids have been successful to date, why change anything. Will advise," Jack said, and hung up.

"Good idea, Arm," I said "And it looks like an early morning raid, as early as tomorrow morning!" "I know, I know," he said. "I guess we should just chill until we hear something from Jack?" Arm said. "Yes, and my gut tells me we'll hear this afternoon for a 3 a.m. raid," I said. "Roger," Arm said.

"You know Arm, Jack suggested that we would be instrumental in the raid, but all we have are vests and our Barrett REC7's. They might be able to bring and hand-off something, but I'd feel better if we had ammunition; I shot mine at the helicopter," I said. "Roger," Arm said. "Let's go get whatever we can," I said. We went downstairs through the lobby and out the back door to our rental. Arm said, "It was Zero 1 – Armas e Municoes on Avenida João XXII, right." "Yes, I think so," I said. "We'll get on that Avenue and I'm sure we'll recognize it." We drove to the gun shop easily and parked. We went in and asked for ammunition for our Barrett REC7's and looked around for other things. Lots of guns and ammunition, but little else except gun cleaners, bump stocks and cases.

We bought our replacement ammo and left the store. Arm said, "We'll have to ask Jack to have someone designated to bring us grenades, climbing line, hooks, carabiners and helmets. We can make it with our boots and clothes." "Right on Arm," I said.

It was lunchtime and we parked as close as we could to the McDonalds near the hotel and got lunch. We went back to the Alfa and decided we could both use a nap, especially if we go on a likely early morning raid.

The phone rang and woke us both up; it was Jack. "Paul, you and Armando are to silently, and without detection, go to the pasture location and park at 2:30 a.m. in the morning. Two large King Stallion helicopters will land with fifty troops each at 3:00 a.m. I know, I know, it's overkill, but the nature of this subterranean complex requires overkill in Harvey's opinion. All troops outfitted to the hilt and there are two members with red fluorescent helmets that will have your climbing gear."

"We'll just use our Barrett's that we bought here and we got more ammo earlier today, but we need grenades and helmets," I said. "Okay Paul, anything else?" "Yes, those night goggles that we used in Cuba and Suriname would sure help," Arm said, and I repeated to Jack. "Yes, will have the red helmets bring you two, as the others will have them already," Jack said, "And as soon as you hear the Stallions, advance to the area where the helicopters came from and shoot flares off. I assume you can acquire flares somewhere in Teresina this afternoon?" "We'll make it happen," I said. "Good luck. Oh, by the way, Andy Pellerito will be orienting one Stallion's troops, while a Seal named Oscar Sanchez will be orienting the other Stallion's troops. You'll both hook up with them, as possible, and they will be wearing white helmets; all others, except the two red ones with your stuff, will be camo green," Jack added. "That should do it. If you think, or we think, of anything else we'll call," I said. "God Bless us all, we're trying to eradicate an extraordinary threat to mankind!" Jack said, and hung up.

"That should do it," Arm said. "We should go look for flares," I said. "I didn't see any flares in the gun store, did you?" Arm said. "There should be some at a marine supply; our Coast Guard requires that each boat, in compliance, have flares, along with other safety and survival gear," I said. "Let's go ask someone where a marine supply is here," Arm said. "Okay," I said. We left the room and went down to the lobby and for once the concierge was there. We asked her for directions to a marine supply store. She looked in her phonebook and found one called "Moto Poupe" on Avenue Joaquin Ribeiro. We thanked her and followed her directions. We found it, and from outside it looked doubtful that they would have flares. They did have a kit with four flares, a mirror, a flag and a flare gun. I looked and the flares were outdated, but we had little choice. We took the kit and drove back to the Alfa.

Back in the room I knew I should give Sara a call and let her know what we were going to do in the morning. I called and she answered, "Hola." I said, "I love you Sara." She said, "Oh Pablo, I love you too!" "We got our orders Sara, we're going to raid what we think is the last stronghold of the Coffee Cartel," I said. "When?" she said. "About 3 a.m., our time, just an hour's difference my love," I said. "Remember what I said about harm's way," she said. "I do, and I will," I replied. "God be with you Pablo," she said. "I'd better go get something to eat and try and get some sleep before the alarm goes off at 1:30 a.m. to get us up and out of here ready to meet troops coming in helicopters," I said. She said, "I love you!" "Me too!" I said, and hung up.

"Let's order a pizza, since we have some things to get ready here," Arm said. "Okay," I said and looked up a pizza delivery place; yes, here in Teresina, Brazil! Arm, would you order the damn thing, a language problem for sure!" I said. "Okay," he said, "All the way?" "Right," I said, "Yes, all the way!" Arm dialed the pizza place and a conversation from hell took place, but I think Arm got us a pizza coming.

I went and checked out my Barrett and fill clips, flares (I'll have to get it ready), clothes, boots, vest and knife. I'm glad I thought about the flares, because I sure wouldn't want to do this during the raid! I got the kit and yes, the flare gun had that damn hard plastic, heat-shrink wrap on it. The flare did as well. There was one orange smoke flare and two flares to be shot from the flare gun. I loaded a flare into the chamber and took the gun and the other flare (orange smoke wouldn't help in this case). I put them in my raid pants and felt like I was as ready as I could get under the circumstances. I asked Arm if he was ready, he said, "Yes Pablo!" I said, "I'm going to hit the sack as soon as we get the pizza. Here's $20.00, will that cover it?" "Thanks, should be enough," Arm said.

Soon, there was a knock on the door. The young man said to Arm, "Como voce esta?" "Eu estou bein," Arm said. The young man handed the large pizza to Arm and Arm said, "Quantos?" The guy said, "34 Reals." Arm gave him the $20.00 bill and asked for $9.00 American back, giving him a tip, I guessed. Arm said, "Tchau," which, I guess, meant chow or goodbye. He handed me the nine dollars and sat the pizza on the coffee table.

One glass of wine would be nice but there wasn't any, so water and pizza were our dinner. It was a strange pizza, but good.

I set the alarm for 1:30 a.m. to give us enough time to dress, double check our gear and get to El Gran Jefe's inglorious pasture. It seemed like only moments before the damn alarm went off but in reality, we'd gotten six and a half hours sleep, although a little pizza reflux had postponed twilight for me.

We washed our faces and put on our pseudo fighting clothes, BP vests, knife, etc. We looked at each other when finished and simultaneously said, "Let's do this!" emphatically. We quietly went down to the lobby and out the back door to our rental and got in. I knew the route to the pasture by heart and carefully drove there. Even with care, a drunk driver almost broadsided us at an intersection. "Careful!" Arm emphasized, "We have to get there on time to meet the copters and troops!" "I know, I know," I said and drove to BR226. I turned my lights off as we got near and noted a glint of light from a new pre-waxing moon. A perfect phase for such an attack, I thought. I stopped the car a little further down the road than before and shut off the engine. All was quiet on the southeastern front.

I glanced at my Rolex and it was 2:00 a.m.; a little early, but it gives us some time to surreptitiously get close to the location that opened to eject the helicopter we shot down. It seemed like six month's ago, while only a couple of days.

We got our Barrett's and quietly slipped under the fence by the road. We slowly went toward the coordinates that Jack had given us for the faint thermal images picked up several days ago.

Arm took a step and "click," he stopped cold! Damn, after several visits to this pasture, it must be a pressure sensitive land mine and Arm just happened to step on it. If he released pressure on it, it would explode. I whispered, "Don't move, Arm, I'll take a look." I dug out around his left foot, which had stopped on this one. I carefully took my knife out and slid it under the sole of Arm's shoe, while asking Arm to continue steady downward pressure; but not too much, just so I could get my knife between the pressure plate and the sole of his shoe. It was a slow, deliberate and scary procedure, but I'd done it once before in Viet Nam. I finally got my knife all the way under and pushed down with one hand on the end of the blade and the other on the handle. I told Arm, "Okay, move your leg, I think I've got it." Arm said, "You think you've got it, hell; get it!" "Okay, I've got it!" I said. Arm moved off, leaving me holding downward pressure on the mine. "Okay, Arm," I said, "Dig more out around this thing so we can both get hands under it." Arm dug out around, but not under, the mine for fear that a slight cave-in would set it off. "Okay, let's grab the mine and while I'm holding the pressure plate with the knife, we'll invert it. See if you can find a big rock, I mean something like fifty to a hundred pounds, so that we can hold the pressure plate down from the bottom of the mine. I'll keep the knife pressing on the plate and set the mine and knife down on the ground, keeping pressure on it all the time. Once down, I'll keep pressure until we can set the heavy weight on it." I whispered. Arm went looking for weights, but in a couple of minutes he shook his head sideways and shrugged his shoulders in the dim light. I then told him to start digging up dirt and to pile it up on the mine, while my hands tightly held my knife against the pressure plate. He dug and dug and did find some sizeable rocks under the surface. I told him to keep digging and make a big pile of dirt over the mine and my hands, which he did with his knife. Finally, I thought the pile was big enough, about two feet high, and I told Arm to set on the pile while my hands were still firmly clasping the mine. He sat down and I gently and gradually wiggled my fingers and hands until I was free from the mine and, thank God, it hadn't gone off. "Sit tight, my friend, sit tight," I frantically told him. I finally had wiggled my hands and forearms free of the pile of dirt, and Arm had set the rocks he'd found in a pile next to us. I took off my shirt and made a sling or bag for all of the rocks and told Arm, "Okay, I'm going to hand you this sack of rocks. Just hold them while I put downward pressure under your butt, then slowly get off, putting the sack of rocks on the top of the mound by my hands," I said. "Okay," he said. He put the sack in the middle of the pile of dirt and I gingerly released pressure, turned my head and upper body as I did so. It didn't go off! "Thank God!" I exclaimed, too loudly for the place we were but so relieved, it just came out.

"I guess we're lucky that El Gran Jefe bought some old Army surplus, Betty-type landmines, or we'd both be goners!" I whispered. We light-footedly moved forward, wishing we'd known to pick up a metal detector before we left Teresina, but who knew?

We heard the whirring of rotors as we neared the disguised helicopter pod and grass covered platform, and I got out the flare gun. As soon as I caught a glimpse of the copters, I shot one straight up in the air. Once exploded, I moved back a little and shot the other at the ground in what I thought was the middle of the helicopter opening on the ground's surface. The big Stallions got the message and quickly landed nearby. About the time the tail ends of both Stallions opened, so did the pasture's helicopter launching pad cover and a helicopter (like the one we had shot down) emerged. Arm and I both started shooting at it, and it hardly got above the ground when it exploded due to a Barrett barrage at the copter, including its fuel tanks. It fell back on the pad that had elevated it and if there was another backup helicopter, it couldn't come out due to the fiery wreckage on its launching pad. There were guards emerging from an adjacent ground opening, but our troops were almost all out and Stallion spotlights were already aimed at the guards coming out of the ground like ants. The two troops with barely visible red helmets came to us with white helmets, grenades, and climbing gear. One said,

"Didn't you even have a shirt? At least you have a vest on!" I laughed and said, "No."

Our troops were mowing down El Gran Jefe's guards as soon as they emerged; no contest! Having received our gear from the red helmet guys, Arm and I made our way to the helicopter's launching pad opening and some of our troops were already ground-hooked and climbing down on their ropes with Belay devices. We could see as we got closer to the opening that there was a floor level about twenty-five feet below the ground surface. The other smaller opening that Jefe's guards were coming out of was only about four feet square and our troops were shooting them almost as they emerged; except a few carried what looked to be handheld, rocket-propelled grenades. One guard managed to get off a rocket before he was shot down, and the rocket grenade hit one of the Stallion helicopters and did major damage. We decided to use our climbing ropes to get in the larger helicopter opening to get to that top floor level. There was resistance to the troops entering on ropes, but our other troops were honed in from ground level on the guards on that top floor level below. Thank God we had as many troops as we did because, although a hundred was overkill, it was truly appreciated! I took a glancing blow to the helmet as we met up with Andy Pellerito and Oscar Sanchez at the large platform opening. We all hooked up with good cover fire, and lowered ourselves onto the top floor.

Once on solid footing we could see that the floor was quite large, with plates and eyebeams supporting the ground above. There were gunracks, and a few of those rocket-propelled grenade launchers on adjacent racks. There were office-like doors down a long hallway. We got to check out the first of a series of doors and no one was there; but it housed bunks, probably for the guards. We left and got caught by fire from down the hallway. The rooms down the hallway were not empty, as sentries or guards kept emerging. By that time, many of our troops had made it down to the top floor and were returning fire. El Gran Jefe's guards were no match for ours! One of them had a rocket launcher and aimed it at us; he got it off and the rocket ignited a few feet away from the shooter, and we all hit the deck. The rocket flew by our heads and blasted the hell out of the next recessed helicopter that couldn't move because the helicopter pad was blocked. That ended their copter fleet for sure! It appeared that the top floor was the home to numerous troops, as there was a dining room that could accommodate probably fifty or so with an adjoining kitchen, refrigerators, the whole nine yards. We cautiously proceeded down the hall with Andy, Oscar and Arm checking and securing each room as we went. One room appeared to be an office with secretarial desks with computers, and I wondered how the hell they were getting all this underground power? We moved on and, sure enough, one room housed the secretarial staff; at least fifteen women were in their nightgowns or pajamas hiding in the back of their beds. The women were visibly shaken and submissive, so Andy directed three of the troops to round them up and humanely detain them. We moved on and met further guards at the rooms at the end of the hall. Many guards were only partially clothed, indicating that our surprise attack did catch them off guard! Who could imagine that they had so many guards and staff, and this was just the top floor. We finally secured the top floor and went back near the entrance to what appeared to be an elevator, knowing that when we got there we'd have to be on alert for guards in the elevator or waiting on the second floor below. There were no floor lights above the elevator like conventional elevators have, so we were kind of in the dark.

The elevator door opened up, and so did guns from within the elevator; first through the slit of the door opening and then a barrage when the door opened wide. The shots took down two of our troops, but the three guards in the elevator went down almost instantly.

As the two soldiers on our side were tended to, eight of us, Arm, me, and six soldiers (leaving Andy and Oscar behind in case we went down, to avoid a lack of leadership) pulled the three bodies out of the elevator and entered the elevator.

We pressed Floor 2 and left instructions with Andy and Oscar to try and find stairs, while reloading the elevator with eight armed soldiers, respectively, to keep the second floor assault going as efficient and smooth as possible! We posed for an armed reception as the elevator stopped on floor two.

The door opened just enough for Arm to throw out a frag grenade, and I hit the "Close Door" button on the elevator (thank God it was a conventional OTIS type).

The grenade exploded outside, and I reopened the door. No shots came at us, as the four guards that were outside on Floor 2 were within frag range and were down. One moved, and I shot him where he lay.

Some shots came from down the hall where a red revolving light and siren was going off. The rooms on both sides of the hall appeared to be offices? A big, two-door wide opening was under the revolving red light and as we visually directed our soldiers to attack and clear each office, we proceeded to the big door. The two rooms adjacent to the big door opened their doors and sentries came out shooting. We all unloaded on them, but more from both rooms quickly replaced those fallen. Our troops shot as soon as a glimpse of anything emerged from either door and they soon ceased coming from either side.

Advancing, we didn't receive any resistance, so we quickly got to the double door opening and opened it. Inside was a larger laboratory than we'd seen before; half again as large as Suriname. There seemed to be more electronic centrifuges and analytic instrumentation. Things that only someone in Analytic Chemistry would know; things like Nitrogen Evaporators, Soxhlet Extractors, Viscometers of the digital kind, etc., all apparently used for the creation of the modified cocaine molecule. There were also cylindrical vessels and holding tanks with bottling dispensers and small conveyors to presumably bottle and ship condensed versions of the cocaine-like derivatives to other facilities.

But, what lies below on the third level down? We retraced our steps back to the elevator and met zero resistance. We loaded it with troops at the ready for a sinister reception as we arrived at Level 3. We opened the elevator door and there was nothing but a very large vat or tank, holding tons and tons of coffee beans! It was ginormous, and there was a packaging facility to the right of the vat looking into the large cavern from the entrance platform. I presumed they were packaging and sending boxes of tainted coffee from here, somehow?

There was no sound from this large holding and packaging area, so we went up to Floor 2 and double checked and coalesced with the other troops; then to the top level and took the stairs up to that small opening next to the helicopter where the first sentries came from. I thought, it would be hard to ship out of here with boxes and bottles? They had to do it somehow. Well, I guess we'd find out, but it was very perplexing as to how they shipped out of a pasture?

We all, except for two men, made it back outside to the area next to the Stallions. Arm, Andy, Oscar and I all double checked that everyone, except our fallen fellow fighters, were here and tended to, if injured.

I called Jack to advise status. "Jack Warner here," he said. "You won't believe what we found!" I said. "What?" Jack said. "Well, it's a hell of a big place and all underground, and nothing is apparent from above but pasture land. There is a helicopter landing pad apparatus, hydraulically driven, with a backup copter. Then, the first or top floor is guard quarters and offices, like a big business. The second floor was more offices and a big fucking laboratory. Much larger than any of the others, even Suriname. It had lots of sophisticated analytic equipment; like Evaporators, Viscometers and holding tanks and bottling facilities. I guess to ship the modified cocaine liquid for soaking coffee beans in? The bottom floor was mostly a vast cavern with a very large vat or tank filled with coffee beans. There was a packaging apparatus next to the big vat, presumably to package coffee beans that were already saturated with the addictive component!" I said. "My God, Paul, this sounds like the best-equipped and main operation, and a completely hidden one! I'll get a group of chemists, analysts and technicians to get there and get everything figured out. "Is the entire complex secured at this point?", Jack asked. "Yes", I said. Great job Paul! Tell Armando, Andy, Oscar and everyone "Great Job!" Jack exclaimed.

"Thanks, I will," I said, "Talk later." We continued to account for and split up the troops, who already knew to get back in the same super Stallion that they came in, although one had visible damage on its stern.

The flaming small helicopter at the pasture's helipad was just about out and the entire illusive, Teresina subterranean pasture operation had been neutralized! Hopefully, this is truly the last of the Coffee Cartel. A horrific empire started by an unlikely African miner with dictatorial and money-hungry inclinations, named Wongari Kamau, known as Kubwa Mkuu locally and the Big Chief or El Gran Jefe in South America and Cuba!

We all entered our respective Stallion and most sat down for departure. Most of the troops had a relieved, exhausted facial expression, reflecting the lack of adrenaline after the intense confrontation we all just went through. I was so relieved that I had made it, unscathed and in one piece (only an indentation on my helmet) – Thank you, God!

I addressed this group of fifty on this Stallion, and Arm was addressing the other Stallion group before we both left the groups to return to our car and go back to the Alfa to recover.

"God bless you all; you have just helped eliminate one of the biggest threats mankind has ever known," I said and left down the Stallion's rear ramp. I met Arm and we slowly walked to our car down on the side of the road, trying to retrace our steps, as another mine could be triggered. The slowly accelerating whir of the large Stallion blades groaned in our ears. Arm said, "Let's try to retrace our path from the car, I don't need another land mine in my life!" "Yes," I said. We gingerly advanced toward the car. It was almost impossible to retrace our steps in a pasture with six and seven-inch high weeds and grass with occasional bushes. We were nearly to the fence and, "Click!" but Arm was not the offender this time. I had stepped on another landmine and I had not only stepped on it, I had slipped off of it at the same time. It didn't explode, it was a dud! I knew then that God was intervening or condoning our activities and that this mission was condoned by our all-knowing higher power. It was ironic that we had killed numerous guards in this assault, but the greater good seemed to justify our killing those guarding a facility bent on severely hurting innocent coffee consumers. That was true, I believed, for all of the Coffee Cartel's installations on both sides of God's planet Earth.

Arm said, "Paul, you are the luckiest SOB on earth!" "Thank God, it was a dud. Only a few feet more to the fence, so let's ease on, my friend," I said.

We got through the fence and to the car and started back to the Alfa Hotel. "Paul, that was the strangest and toughest of these Cartel compounds we've dealt with, agreed?" Arm said. "Yes," I said. "Do you think this was their last stronghold?" Arm said. "I sure as hell hope so, and after your interrogation of El Gran Jefe, you do too, right?" I said. "Yes, I think we got it all, Pablo," Arm responded. "Yes, and we both stepped on landmines today and survived!" I said. "Unbelievable," Arm said, "I think you have something when you say, God is on our side." "Thanks," I said.

We made it back and we're ready for two or three days of sleep! (lol) We hurriedly get to the room and went to bed.

The super cell rang at 4 p.m. and I didn't know what was what! It took a while to be able to answer, "Paul here." "Paul, Jack Warner. I wanted to call and congratulate you and Armando for a job well done. The rest of my group here in DC wanted to thank you both for all you've done to eradicate this Coffee Cartel." "Thanks, Jack," I said. "I want you to continue to stay in Teresina, if you want, or go back to Cuba to your Sara, or whatever you want to do on Uncle Sam's dime. Yes, continue to use your FBI VISA card, and tell Armando to do the same. I'll be in touch with both of you soon," Jack said, and hung up.

Arm was still asleep, so I quietly made some coffee and wanted to let Sara know that the raid was a success and that I was okay.

I called my Sara. "Hello," she said. "Hola," I said. "Pablo, how are you, I've been worried sick," she said. "I'm fine, my dear," I said. "We had a hell of a fight on our hands here in the Teresina countryside. The place was a subterranean fortress under a pasture west of town. It had offices, secretaries, a laboratory like the CDC's and guards everywhere. The place could package and ship out liquid-altered cocaine for saturating coffee beans, packaging and shipping for treated beans, and a tremendous vat of nothing but beans on the third floor down. Arm and I are both fine and I believe the Cartel is finished," I told her.

"Thank God," Sara said. "What happens next, when can I see you?" she added. "I need a little rest, but I'll be there as soon as I can make arrangements!" I said. "I miss you and love you terribly," she said. "I know, I know, the feeling is mutual my Angel," I said. "I'll let you know as soon as I make plans, okay?" I added. "Okay," she said, and hung up.

As soon as I got off, I looked at a call I'd received while talking to Sara. It was from Jack again; I called him back. "Jack Warner, here," he said. "Jack, I was talking to Sara when you called," I said. "There was one thing I had forgotten to tell you before," he said. "Yes?"

I said. "I've obtained approval for you to have the 'Café Negro' Hatteras docked behind Pascal Padron's estate. All you have to do is show your credentials to our guards, who are now holding the Padron Plantation," Jack said. "Great," I said. "Paul, there is one contingency," he said, "You have to turn in all the tainted beans in her hull!" "Gladly," I said. "I'll have to figure out how in the hell I get them out to turn over to you and where? But that's a hell of a lot better than fighting Coffee Cartel guards all over the world!" I added, and hung up.

Wow, I still felt like a train had hit me from behind and sat on the couch exhausted. It was 5 p.m. and I wondered about going back to bed now, or staying up till 9 or 10 to get another good night's sleep. I opted to wait a while, as my adrenaline was pumping slightly at the thought of returning to Sara and of acquiring the "Café Negro." This boat would be a constant reminder to me of the Coffee Cartel and how I'd stumbled on the sinister operation.

How will I get those damn beans out of my new Hatteras? I'm sure I'd think of something, short of hauling beans out in buckets. Sara and I would have to go back to Trinidad to deal with her home and assets, so acquiring the "Café Negro" would be a comfortable side benefit while there. I could then take the empty yacht around Cuba to Marina Hemingway near Havana and dock it with the BFB.

I instantly thought of my friend Carl and how he was doing, so I called him. "Carl?" I said. "Paul?" he said. "How are you," he said. "Fine, Carl, I think I'm about finished with this assignment, as we raided and secured what we're sure is the last of the Coffee Cartel's operations," I said. "Boy, that's good! You've been through hell while I've been looking after the BFB and Loopee," he said. "How are they?" I quickly added. "They're fine," Carl quipped. "The BFB is good and Loopee is fine," he said. "That's great Carl. Are you in love?" I said. "No, but what I've got is just as good, I think?" Carl replied. "Oh boy, there you go again!" I responded. "So, what are your plans now Paul?" he said. "I'm still on assignment with Jack, but I think I'm about done. He did say that the powers that be have consented to give me the 'Café Negro' that we discovered. But I've got a hell of a lot of bad coffee beans to unload, and I imagine the engines and instruments are fine since Coffee Cartel money went into them. I'm thinking that you and I could bring it around Cuba to the Hemingway Marina and dock it alongside of the BFB. Would you be agreeable to make the trip?" I said. "We might work out a deal where you could charter one of them, and we both make money? Just a thought, my friend," I continued. "Both sound great to me Paul, just let me know and I'm there!" Carl said. "Great, I'll be in touch," I concluded, and hung up.

I thought about getting something to eat, when the damn phone rings again. "Hello!" I said. "Is this the world famous, ex-FBI mercenary, Paul Pilot?" the voice said. "Yes," I said, because I knew it was legit, or at least I hoped so. "This is Peter Kincaid and I work for Jack Warner at the FBI. He asked me to look into your coffee bean removal dilemma and I've found the answer for you, I think. I contacted a company there called 'Arboles Vamos,' or 'Trees-be-Gone' in English. They cut down and make shavings out of trees and bushes; really a land clearing outfit out of Trinidad. They assure me that they can suck out and blow the beans into a large dump truck and send them to a landfill to be buried or confiscated and trucked to wherever Jack wants them. It may smell like Starbucks around there for a while but I've hired them with Jack's blessing, and on the FBI's tab, to remove the beans from your new boat. They're just waiting on dates compatible with their work schedule to do the job," Peter said. "Fantastic!" I said. "I've been trying to figure out how to get them out myself, and it sounds like you've come up with an efficient and cost-effective (for me anyway) way to do it," I added. "Just let me know when you want to do it and whether you want to be there? You wouldn't really have to be there Paul, but Jack said it's your boat and that the entire premises is still heavily guarded," he said. "I'll have to let you know Peter, but I really appreciate the help," I said. "Should I call you?" I added. "Yes, my number is 202-643-1180 here in D.C," Peter concluded, and hung up.

Wow! What a relief, I'd never have thought about one of those mulch-making tree-blower things but that's the ticket, and they're paying for it! Fabulous, I thought. Did I want to be there when the coffee beans were removed? I thought, yes, just because the average guy that would do the extraction would probably not be as careful as he should, or that I would be, in the process. It was a gorgeous and expensive boat, save the empty hull portion, and they were not making this over-spec Hatteras anymore. I'd just coordinate with Sara to see when would be the best time for bean removal (strange conversation with myself, right; bean-removal timing?).

I was even more hungry now, so I decided to see if Arm wanted to go eat. I looked and he was still asleep, so I quietly put on some appropriate clothes just to go downstairs and eat at the Hotel's restaurant. I went in after the slow elevator, and after all the news and the thrill of getting to see Sara soon, the "Café Negro" and the coffee removal, and had to order a Macallan 18 and a glass of water on the side with ice. About half finished and here came Arm, looking a little bleary-eyed. I said, "Welcome comrade!" He said, "Wow, what a good sleep." It was 7 p.m. by now and I asked him if he wanted a drink? He said, "Yes, Café Negro." I laughed and said, "Funny you should say that. I've been talking to Carl and he agreed to help me take the 'Café Negro' from Trinidad around to Havana and the Hemingway Marina. That's a relief, and I thank the FBI and Jack for that acquisition."

"What are your plans, Arm?" I added. "I've got a life in Puerto Rico. My partner has been taking care of everything he can," he said. "Our little private investigation business has been doing pretty well, and it's a hell of a lot less stressful than fighting a Coffee Cartel! The FBI pays well however and, as you know, I love finding out the truth from criminals, murderers and the like. This past time with you, fighting such a menace has been very rewarding for me," Arm continued.

I finished my scotch and he his coffee. "I'm going to order dinner, want anything?" I said. "Yes, breakfast," Arm said. "We'll see what the waiter will do?" I said. I motioned for the waiter but no success, so I finally got up and ran him down. He apologized, and said, "Un minuto, por favor!" Even I knew that he meant "One minute, please," even if it was Portuguese! I went back to the table and said, "I think I got his attention, try ordering an omelet." In about two minutes the waiter came to the table and asked what we would like, in Portuguese, but Arm understood and ordered an omelet. The waiter said he would check? I ordered wine and a Ribeye, rare. The waiter left and both Arm and I were trying to get our circadian rhythm back after such an early morning out-of-synch, intense ordeal. We just sat and gazed at the restaurant's wall decorations and fixtures.

The waiter came back and asked Arm what kind of omelet he wanted and all was good; and he had my Stag's Leap Cabernet, which was just okay. I drank and thought of Sara with a relieved air about me.

Our meals finally came and we enjoyed them and the tranquility of the setting. No one else was in the restaurant that we could see, which added to the peaceful atmosphere. We ate our meals and enjoyed the atmosphere.

I motioned for the check and signed it to our room. I couldn't finish my Cabernet and Arm didn't care for any, so I left half a bottle and we left. I told Arm that I would go back to our room and maybe read or watch TV.

We walked to the slow elevator and to the room, entered, sat on the couch and turned on the TV. A movie with Bruce Willis was on and it was strange to hear him speak Portuguese. I watched as Arm went back to bed. I too was whipped and after a half hour or so, I turned off the TV and hit the sack.

I awoke to the slight light emanating from the window, even though the blinds were pulled. My first thought, after coffee, was to get the hell out of here and get to my Sara! I assumed that Arm would feel the same. I made the coffee, got a cup, and sat down at the dinette to look up on my phone flights to Key West. There didn't seem to be an easy way to get back on commercial airlines, let alone a direct flight. I finally found one with only four stops, so I jumped on it. I could leave Teresina at 2:20 p.m. this afternoon and get to Key West at 3:35 p.m. tomorrow. A little over 24 hours, but relatively speaking, great!

I hurriedly reserved my flights. All done, except I'd need Sara to pick me up or get a taxi to the Conch House when I arrived. Arm was walking around slightly dazed. I said, "Arm, I'm getting the hell out of here this afternoon." He said, "What is going on here?" "I want to go too, Pablo," he quickly added. "Well, have a cup of coffee and sit down and make reservations. It'll take me over 24 hours to get back to Key West," I said.

"Okay, okay! I'll get on it as soon as I wake up!" Arm said. He got up and drank his coffee while I went to pack what little I had here. One small Tumi bag was more than enough for my wardrobe. I went back out and

Arm was busy making reservations to go back to San Juan, Puerto Rico. I got another cup and was thinking about breakfast. I wrote Arm a note that I was going downstairs to the Alfa restaurant for breakfast.

I went down to the restaurant and ordered two eggs over medium, home fries, bacon, toast, and the ever-present cup of coffee, to remind one of the coffee nightmares we'd been through; and it probably would from now on! I sipped the dark brew and thought of the blessings I have and the biggest – I was still here!

Arm and the waiter both came to my table at the same time. I said, "Have a seat," and they both sat down! Laughing, the waiter got up and offered more coffee.

"How'd you do?" I asked Arm. "Good, I leave this afternoon at 4:20 p.m. and get home day after tomorrow at 2:10 a.m.," he said. "How many stops?" I said. "Four, and one is for three and half hours. It is what it is," Arm responded, and waived to the waiter. The waiter came back and Arm ordered his breakfast. A little more coffee and Arm got his breakfast. We didn't say anything more and enjoyed our meals.

We finished, paid, and both of us just walked through the lobby and went out onto the Avenue Rio Poti. We started walking east and enjoyed the shoppers and businessmen hustling along, just like any city in the US. Another reason to believe that commonalities among people prevail, all working to live, laugh and love!

We continued to walk off our breakfasts. It was great to walk down the street with little concern about a landmine, helicopter, or someone shooting at you. We didn't talk much, but body language told me that Arm was enjoying the peaceful stroll down the street as well. We walked and walked and it was about 11 a.m. when we got back to the Alfa.

I told Arm, I really didn't have anything to do except call Jack Warner and tell him what our plans were and my Sara to tell her I'd see her tomorrow evening.

I called Jack. "Jack Warner here," was his standard greeting. "Paul," I said. "I wanted to let you know that Arm and I are flying out of Teresina this afternoon; Arm to San Juan, Puerto Rico and me to Key West. I should get there tomorrow afternoon at 3:35 p.m. Arm will get to San Juan at 2 a.m. day after tomorrow," I said. "Good, no problem, I really don't see you or Armando being required, at least in the near future. My group and special CIA forces will follow-up examining all of the Coffee Cartel's neutralized locations," Jack said. "Keep your super cellphone and I'll be in touch, but relax and enjoy your new spouse. Tell Arm to relax as well, but keep his phone as well," Jack added. "That's about it Jack," I said. "Okay Paul," Jack added, and hung up.

I called Sara. "Hola," she said. "Hola, Angel!" I said. "Pablo, Pablo, what's up?" she said. "I've made reservations to get back to you as soon as I could. I'll be arriving at Key West International at 3:30 p.m. tomorrow afternoon. Can you pick me up?" I said. "Yes, absolutely, I've got the blue bomb right here, my love!" she added. "Great, I can't wait," I said. "I'm going to leave for a 2:20 flight as soon as possible to make sure I'll get the first leg. I've got four stops; Sao Paulo, Buenos Aires, Lima and

Miami, but I'll call if there's a delay or problem, Sweetie,"
I said. "Okay, my hero husband," she said, and hung up.

It was nearly noon and I told Arm, who had also been
packing what little he had, "I think I'll just go ahead to
the airport, turn in my rental car, and wait for my first
flight." "I'll go with you and chill until my flight later,"
Arm said.

"Alrighty then, I'm ready!" I said. "Une momento,
por favor," Arm said, and picked up his bag from the bed.
He said (as he returned in three seconds, not a minute as
he asked for) "I'm ready."

We looked at each other and left the room, walked
to the elevator and went down to the lobby via that very
slow elevator for the last time. I got to the Checkout desk
and handed them the key, checked the bill and charged
it to my FBI credit card. We walked out the back door to
my rental car, the KIA. We threw our bags in the trunk
and drove to get petrol, as I was supposed to turn the
damn thing in filled or get put in jail (joke). It was just a
short drive to the Teresina Airport, so the first gas station
would do. I saw a Brazilian WAWA gas station substitute
and drove in, filled up and got back on the road.

We pulled into the car return area. I turned in the
KIA with a full tank and no damage. I charged it to
Jack's FBI card, and we both got on the rental car shuttle
and went to the terminal. We got to the ticket kiosk and
Arm gave me a big hug, as I did he, and said, "Good luck
my friend. I'd fight anyone with you, you saved my life;
I think it's three times by now, but that land mine in a
Brazilian pasture was the best yet!" as he walked off.

I loaded my information in the kiosk and got all tickets to Key West, via Miami. I walked to security and I was fine, as we left our Barrett REC7's on Kamau's pasture. I got through security in a breeze; although I was held up a little by others not breezing through. I got to my gate at 1:10 p.m., so over an hour early, but things could have gone south easily.

I waited for my Sao Paulo Flight to board. I walked to a small book, snack, drink and memorabilia store and looked through to see if any new books by Michael Crichton or Dan Jones were out. There were none, so I researched the monthly's and such and found Big Game, Angler's Unlimited, and a Hurricane Awareness book in Spanish that I thought Sara could interpret. Cuba is certainly a recurring hurricane target. I paid for my magazines and went back to Gate 32 and sat down. I thought, hell, I looked for a book when I should have looked for something to eat! The Alfa's breakfast was long gone. I had time, so I picked up my stuff and looked for anything edible within walking distance. There was a Brazilian tapas kind of thing, but I was famished. So I got several beef & seasoning-stuffed burrito things? I carried the Brazilian hotdog and everything back to Gate 32. I sat down to enjoy whatever it was? The burrito things weren't half bad and I ate all of them too fast.

I thumbed through the Angler's magazine and thought of Carl and my BFB just north of Havana. Interesting article about new invisible monofilament fishing line, caught my interest in a while.

I noticed people were lining up; maybe I missed an announcement? Well, maybe it was in Portuguese? Probably, I thought. I did have priority loading status, I also thought, due to my FBI status. I picked up my bag and stood with the group and was called after the passengers with disabilities or children. I boarded and found my aisle seat. The flight was noneventful to Sao Paolo. I got to stay on the plane for the next leg to Buenos Aires. I got up and walked back and forth in the aisle, several times. I waited forty-five minutes and we took off. Again, a decent flight, but there was a plane change in Buenos Aires. I made it to the new gate and waited to be called, as the layover was short.

I was called, boarded and found seat 36C, an aisle seat, as I hated to bother someone to get up for a stretch or a bathroom visit. I tried to catch a nap on the way to Lima, but woke up hungry when the stewardess asked a question. I took a cheese snack pack and Apple Juice; consumed it, and tried to resume rest and closed my eyes again.

The Lima landing was rough, with side winds and a full plane, but successful. Again, a change of planes to a 747 for the big flight to Miami. I was groggy from the semi-sleep, twilight zone I was in on the last flight. I got some peanut butter crackers and a Snickers from a nearby machine and found my new gate. But, I had another long wait, so I pulled out my fishing magazines and munched my snack. My flight to MIA was six hours, so maybe I could get some sleep. A LATAM 747 should have a little more room, and it was a First-Class flight; thank God, as I was really getting tired.

They called it, and I boarded and sat in 3A again; again, aisle, and a relatively large and reclining seat. I asked for a scotch and water to help relax for a long winter's nap, even though it was summer. I drank down my scotch and reclined, only to be awakened for lift-off and to raise my seat. Damn!

We were off, so I again reclined and I hope my facial expression got the flight attendant's attention that I wanted to sleep. It worked, since I awoke about an hour from Miami, when the garbage pickup occurred.

I'd been in airports and planes for almost a day, so I was legitimately fucked up. Thank goodness I go some sleep on this big leg to Miami.

We landed after circling the large airport for some thirty minutes. A smooth landing ended by another wait to get to the unloading ramp, but I was up front and stood up upon the plane's final stop.

The door opened, and I deplaned and made my way to the Silver terminal to catch the last segment of my trip. Sara would be waiting and although I felt terrible and needed a bath, I was excited. I got to the right section after riding the Tramrail through five stops. I was twenty-eight minutes early and sat down, exhausted again. Almost went to sleep, nodding off occasionally.

Announcement; boarding began and after the needy, I got to board. It was a short forty-five-minute flight from Miami, so I had to revive somewhat for Sara. As soon as we took off, I ordered coffee, again that reminder.

The flight was good, weather great, and I couldn't wait to plant a big kiss on my ebony angel. Two cups of coffee and a trip to the head and I was ready. We idled up to the tarmac spot and deplaned down portable stairs, and I walked to the small terminal building. Sara was standing at the doorway waiving. I waved back and walked faster and grabbed her around the waist and planted that big one on her full lips. We kissed for about two minutes, or was it a lifetime?

We held hands as we walked away, oblivious of the travelers all around, and through the door to where Sara had parked the car. She opened the trunk and I threw my bag in. I closed the trunk and got in the passenger's side. It was wonderful to see her, in addition to just being alive after all those raids.

Sara drove directly to the Conch House and parked on Truman. We got out, I got my bag and walked to our room. We sat on the couch with hands clasped, squeezing intermittently. "I missed you terribly, Sara," I said. "Me too, you," she said. "I'll bet you're tired after over a day traveling?" "Yes, I am," I said. "Please go to bed, so you can recover a little," she said. "Okay," I said and went in to our bed as my two cups of coffee on my flight from Miami had worn off completely.

I lay there marveling at my blessings and thanking God for every one. I drifted off momentarily.

I woke up at 8 p.m. with a start, as I'd dreamt I stepped on a landmine like Arm had done. Sweat was pouring from my brow and arms. Sara was over me, soothing and loving her husband with the bad dreams.

"I'm okay," I said. "Thanks." I got out of bed and put on my robe, which Sara had left out for me. I walked out in the living room and sat down. Sara had started coffee. "Your days and hours will be mixed up for a while, until you get your circadian rhythm back again," Sara said. "Where did you learn about circadian rhythm?" I said. "I had security shift workers at the Mall and we learned about it then to better adapt to shift hours," she said. "Well, I agree that my rhythm is out of synch," I said. "In fact, the only thing I'm in synch with on this earth is you!" I added.

"What are your plans now?" Sara said. "I think we've stopped the Coffee Cartel and that my involvement is done. Jack Warner told me that the "Café Negro" Hatteras is mine, so we'll need to move it after I get the coffee beans out of it," I said.

"What would you like to do?" I said. Sara said, "I think we should decide where we want to live, don't you?" "Yes, but let's discuss and enjoy the process of looking," I said.

Costa Rica is still high on my list, but I'll be good with wherever you want. But I would like it to be on an ocean, so my two Hatteras's can be utilized and maybe even generate some income. Carl has expressed an interest in running one of them for charters," I said. "I want to live on the water anyway, so that's not a problem," she said. "What do you want to do with your home in Trinidad?" I said. "I think we should just sell it and put that money into our agreed upon destination," Sara offered. "Sounds good," I said. "We could even live on the BFB, if you're okay with that?" I continued, "We might rent a storage space, since storage is limited on my boat. But we could spend some time on the BFB, and some time in our home, and sometime in a resort, or sometime anywhere on this big earth that you would want to go?"

PART SIX

Washington, DC

My super cellphone rang, and I knew it was Jack. "Paul, is that you?" he said. "Yes," I said. "I have another assignment for you," he said. My heart sank, after all the talk of a new beginning and fresh start that Sara and I had. "I would like you and Sara to come to DC next Tuesday!" he said. "What's up?" I said. "I would rather let you both know after you get here, okay?" he went on. "I guess. I don't have a choice, do I?" I said. "No," Jack said. "Anything else?" I said. "No, I'll see you then. Call me when you get in; I made reservations for you at the Hilton on Connecticut Avenue," he said, and hung up.

"I don't know what the hell is going on?" I told Sara. "Jack Warner wants us both to come to Washington, DC next Tuesday," I said. "What? Why?" she said. "I don't know, except that it screws up our plans to go to Trinidad and start getting our life together, in order," I said. "Why am I involved?" Sara said. "I guess because you're my better half?" I quickly responded.

"The FBI has been extremely good to me and are giving me a million-dollar boat and they were paying all of our expenses, so let's go see what's up!" I said with conviction. "I know, I know," Sara said. "I'll make flight reservations for Monday, okay?" I said. "Si, me amore," she said. "I really don't care where we go, where we are, or anything, as long as I'm with you Pablo," she added.

"I feel the same way, Sara," I said, and turned the conversation to maybe getting brunch, since Jack called and made us miss breakfast. "Let's get brunch? Are you hungry?" I said. "Famished," she said and we went downstairs, where there was enough buffet breakfast left from the earlier eaters. There was Quiche, bacon, home fries, toast, the whole nine yards. I overfilled my plate, after Sara filled hers. We sat at a small table for two on the veranda and it was wonderful. A breakfast can be beautiful, if you have the perfect environment. We even ordered a Mimosa to enhance the moments even more.

We finished, thanked the hostess, and went back up to the room and I looked at possible flights for Tuesday. "How does leaving at 2:17 p.m. and arriving in DC at 5 p.m., non-stop sound?" I said. "Fine," she said. "I don't have any nice clothes to wear." "This is Saturday, maybe there's a few nice places open on Duval today and again on Monday," I said. "Let's go shopping on Uncle Sam!" I continued. "Okay, okay, let's go," she said.

We got in the blue Chevy and I said, "Hell, we don't need to drive, let's walk, it'll be good for us!" "That sounds good," she agreed. "I probably should get something as well," I said. We walked down Truman to Duval and towards the Pier House on the north end of the island. There were a few clothing shops, a Coach shop and so on. She picked out a couple of nice summery dresses, some shoes, a Coach purse, some blouses, etc. I found a shirt and high-cut pants by Tommy Bahama.

She said, "I feel a lot better about going to your capital now." "Good," I said. "I wish I knew what Jack is up to?" I added. We enjoyed the walk, the shopping, the tourists, and we got lunch at The Hard Rock Café. A cheeseburger and French-fried sweet potatoes for a change. We both had beers; her Dos Equis and me, a Corona Light with lime. I asked her if she had enough clothes to feel okay?" She said, "Yes, I think so, but another pair of shoes would do it."

We left and went back to a Banana Republic store, which had a nice pair of high heels.

"Do you think either of us need anything else prior to our DC visit," I said. "It really depends on what Jack has on his mind? If he wants us to dress formally for a dinner or something, we're not ready," Sara said. "I doubt that, but I really don't know, sweetie," I responded.

"By the time we walk back to the Conch House, I'll be ready for a nap. How about you?" I asked. "Yes," she said. We sauntered back to our room, disrobed and lay down together. Sara said, "Thank you for coming back to me, Pablo." "Thank God!" I said. We both slipped off into unconsciousness.

We'd been asleep for quite a while when that damned super phone rang. Guess who? I thought. I answered, "Paul here." Jack responded, "Ha, Ha, Jack Warner here." "You always answer the phone, "Jack Warner here," so I thought I'd try that salutation on you for a change," I said. "I know and you got me on that one," Jack said. "I called to give you a heads up on your visit. Many of those involved directly with the Coffee Cartel affair have been invited to a dinner Tuesday evening and it will be attended by several staff members and Harvey Hyde, the Assistant Director and the Director of the FBI. I thought it only fair to let you know that a suit and tie and evening dress would be required. If you can't find them in Key West, then text your and Sara's measurements and I'll have appropriate attire awaiting you at your hotel in DC," he said.

"Key West is not noted for its formal attire; in fact, it's noted for no attire at all!" I said. "Ha, Ha, that's two in one conversation," Jack laughed. "Just text me both of your sizes, and I'll have your clothes waiting at the Hilton," he said. "Thanks, Jack," I said, and hung up.

I explained to Sara about the dinner, guests and clothes requirement and got her sizes. I texted Jack the statistics and told Sara I was sorry that Jack interrupted her nap and that this Monday's trip was unexpected.

I made us a cup of green tea, and sat down at our dinette table. "After the Washington, DC dinner and business is over we can go back to your home, right?" I asked. Sara said, "Yes." "What do you think about going with Carl and I to deliver the 'Café Negro' around

Cuba to the Hemingway Marina?" I asked. "I'm not an experienced boater but I can swim well, and I love you and know you love fishing and the sea, so yes!" Sara said. "Great," I said. "I'm also thinking that I know of a little Cuban restaurant that is good and I think you'd enjoy it for dinner. It's not very fancy for Saturday night, but we might go dancing afterwards at Rick's on Duval," I said. She said, "Perfectamundo, Pablo."

I called "El Siboney" for dinner reservations, but they didn't take any. So, we'd just go and wait if there was a line. "What time would you like to go, they won't take reservations," I added. "Six thirty," she said, and since it was 5 p.m., "I'll take a shower," I said and did.

We finished getting cleaned up, poured ourselves a drink, and sat on the couch in front of the coffee table. "Hopefully, your mercenary missions are finished forever!" Sara said. "I will tell Jack that I'm retiring again while we're in DC, my angel," I said. "Life is too short and now that I've found you, it's shorter!" I added. "Thank you, Pablo, that's the best thing you've ever said to me since you said that you loved me," she said.

"Okay, that's settled then; let's go to dinner," I said, and got up. Sara put our glasses in the sink and we walked out of the room and down to the carpool Chevy. We got in and to "El Siboney" we went to get a table. It was very busy at this time of night, and there were two couples ahead of us.

It was only about ten minutes and we had a table for two. We ordered an avocado salad and Ropa Vieja over rice, with a small side of plantains. The salad, small talk, homey atmosphere, aura of love covering Sara, and the Ropa Vieja were all very satisfying . . . to say the least.

We ordered a light flan for dessert, and that truly capped off a wonderful dinner. Sara loved it and told me about her mother teaching her how to "slow cook" the Ropa Vieja when she was a young girl.

We tipped well on the bill and left to go leave our car at the Conch House and walk down to Duval and go to Rick's to dance and have a toddy or two!

We parked, got out, locked the car, and walked down to Rick's without stopping.

There were only a few people dancing, but it was nice and they played music with a good downbeat that made you feel like dancing. We drank and danced the night away, as they say. Very nice evening so far, so we walked home and went to bed and to sleep. There was an unspoken feeling that we had had such a nice fulfilling evening that sex was not required.

I awoke at 7 a.m. to use the restroom and was up for good. I quietly slipped out of the bedroom in my pajamas and closed the door, so as to not wake Sara. I headed for the coffee, as almost everyone on this planet does and again thought of the Coffee Cartel. "But, it's all over, isn't it?" I said to myself.

Sara joined me at the table after she made her coffee. I told her, "Love you!" She said, "You too." "I'm so looking forward to our life together," I said. "We certainly can survive on my pension, your pension and maybe even have income from the very boat that held the secret coffee formulation in its hull. I've talked to Carl about chartering it and he was excited," I continued. "It will be exciting to look for our new home together," Sara said. "Very much so, my dear Pablo."

"Does Costa Rica have a big charter boat and fishing business?" Sara said. "Yes, there are plentiful pelagics and bountiful species for the table. There are resorts like Los Suenos and towns like Jaco that are sustained by beaches, charters and fishing. After outfitting, our new "Café Negro" would fit right in, if not too competitive there to get started. But I know two captains working out of there that could tell me what we need to do. Maybe we could go there and find out about homes and the charter business?" I offered. "Sounds like a plan, Man!" Sara responded. "Okay, honey babe, how big of a home do you want?" I said. "Well, one good question deserves another. How many children do you want?" she quipped. "You cut right to the chase, don't you," I said. "I can't figure out how big a home I want without asking; you started this," she said. "I really don't want babies or children at this point in my life, I want you!" I responded. "I've always wanted children and I'm only thirty-five years old, my love," Sara said. "I know, sweetheart, I'm only fifty-eight," I responded. "Yes, I would like to have at least one, just one," she said. "I'm glad I finally found this out, not even a month after we got married!" I said – PAUSE – "You asked me what I wanted and I told you, but you are really what I want too," she said. – ANOTHER PAUSE – "If you want a baby, I'll do my best," Paul said. "I love you, Pablo Pilot!" she responded. "Okay, now that, that is settled, how big of a home do you want?" I asked. Three bedrooms, but I could live with two and two baths, a living and dining room, with a nice kitchen and a carport or garage for two vehicles, and a pool! Any more questions?" Sara said. "Ha, Ha, no more questions. I asked and you told me, didn't you?" I said. "Thank you, my love," she said.

We were asleep for a couple of hours when that damn super cell rang and I knew without answering, that it was Jack. I thought to myself; I'll be happy to throw this damn phone to the garbage as soon as possible. Jack said, "Paul, I just wanted to give you an update. Several teams from more than the FBI have been analyzing, investigating, interrogating, reconciling and verifying the information. In essence, it shows that all of the Coffee Cartel's operations are all down and nullified. Your assumption that the one in the Brazilian pasture, near Teresina, was probably the first to start and the last to go down, was correct. I thought it might be comforting to know that it's really all done. I wanted to also add that the President has also been brought up to speed and is, as I and all of the country, in your debt. I should also note that Tuesday's dinner is mandatory, and you must be dressed appropriately. Your attire will be waiting at the Capital Hilton in DC, as I mentioned before. Thanks again, Paul, you're the best!" he said, and hung up. Damn, I thought and said aloud to Sara, since the call had awakened her as well. "Jack says that many parameters by several teams have verified that the Coffee Cartel is down, destroyed and done," I told Sara. "He also said that the dinner Tuesday afternoon was mandatory, as several dignitaries will be there and reiterated about our clothes being at the Hilton, when we get there tomorrow. I think we get to DC at five, and we should get to the hotel by six, for sure," I went on.

"After that Tuesday dinner is over we can make arrangements to go back to Trinidad and deal with your home, work and the "Café Negro." Then get Carl to help us take it to the Hemingway Marina. We'll get to Costa Rica and find out about chartering and homes as soon as we can," I continued.

I went to the fridge to find a cold beer, but none were to be found. I told Sara, "Would you like something from the Mercado, I'm going to get a couple of beers." She said, "A nice Chardonnay, por favor."

I walked down to a little market and got two Coronas and a chilled Cakebread Chardonnay. It was a nice walk, but hot and humid. I got back to our room and Sara had turned on the TV. They were talking about local politicians running for office. Sara said, "You'll never get in politics, will you Pablo?" I said, "No way, Jose." "It's sad, but I think politics give power, and power breeds corruption, in Cuba and in the US. Yes, everywhere in the world!" she said.

I asked Sara, "Do you want to do anything or go anywhere?" She said, "No, Paul, we've got a big day tomorrow, packing and going to your capital city." "Why did you say, Paul, when you always call me Pablo or maybe even Pablito?" I said. She said, "I just wanted you to know that I know that is your real and proper name, and I was presumptuous in calling you Pablo." I hesitated and then said, "Sara, I really prefer Pablo coming from you. Strange, huh?" Sara said, "Strange, You're not strange, you're my soulmate Pablo."

We both walked to the bedroom and took off our clothes to get into our pajamas, or clothes for me. My pajamas consisted of shorts and a T-shirt. Sara had real pajamas on and although loose fitting, there were definite curvatures protruding that unmistakably belonged to the sexiest woman alive. I didn't want her to think that all I wanted her for was sex, so I tried to ignore the curvaceous protrusions.

I went to the fridge and found a mango that I'd taken from the fruit board in the lobby and cut it into chunks. I placed the pieces of mango in a bowl and placed a few toothpicks in them. I took the bowl and asked Sara if she wanted any? She took a few and said, "Perfect dessert for our Cuban dinner." We looked at each other in adoring glances and subtle eye and eyelash movements. "We're going to start a new chapter in our relationship tomorrow and I'm very excited about going to your capital, the Capital of the greatest country on earth!" Sara said. "Yes, I guess you're right, my dear, I've just taken my country's greatness for granted most of the time," I answered.

We finished the mango and both walked to one side of the bed and got in. We lay there, staring at the ceiling, without uttering a word. We closed our eyes and slipped into unconsciousness.

Again, the glint of the sun's rays pierced the edges of the curtains in our bedroom. I covered my head with the sheet, but after a few minutes I realized I was awake. I looked at my watch and, yes, no wonder, I'd been asleep over nine hours. I carefully and quietly slipped out of bed and put a T-shirt on, then slipped into my flipflops. I headed for the coffee maker, as always, and made a cup. I stepped out to the balcony overlooking the pool. Everything was quiet, peaceful, and a little foggy, which is a rare occurrence in Key West. The inversion caused my coffee steam to look like a smelter chimney. Such a peaceful setting, I'd have to thank my buddy Sam for the wonderful accommodations and memories made here. I'd call him, but 8:05 a.m. was probably a bit early. He had several properties around Key West and was probably on "Key West Time," which is an hour or two later than expected.

Sara had gotten up, made her coffee and joined me in that alluring, loose-fitting pair of pajamas. "How could I be so lucky?" I asked myself. "Hi there, my love," she said. "Hi there," I answered. "We never have fog in Trinidad," she said. "I know, it's very rare here as well," I added. "Want anything from the kitchenette? I'm going to make another cup of java," I said as I left the balcony. "No," she said as she stared down at the empty pool.

I made my cup and came back to Sara. "What do you want to do for breakfast, Sara Sonata?" I asked. "I'll go down and bring you breakfast in bed, or we can go to Goldman's or whatever," I added. "Breakfast in bed, sounds very nice, sweetness," Sara said. "Alrighty then," I said, as I sipped my hot coffee. I thought, I'll go now to get her breakfast and when I get back, she'll be happy, and my coffee will have cooled to drinkable.

I went down to the Bed and Breakfast's breakfast spread. I got Sara scrambled eggs, brown sausage and hash browns, with orange juice and white toast. I asked for a tray for bed service for my darling, and the attendant gave me one with a small rose in a vase. "Just leave it in the room," she said. I cautiously went back to the room and she was expectantly, in bed. I presented her the tray and she said, "I could get used to this!" I said, "Okay, I'll do it as often as possible." "Wow," she went on. "The rose is the topper," she continued. I told her to enjoy, while I left to go back down to get my breakfast.

It was 9:15 a.m. by the time I got back and I removed her tray and said I wanted to call Sam, the owner of the Conch House, and thank him for such a beautiful stay. I called and Sam answered. I thanked him for the beautiful stay and that I'd built some lasting memories. "The Hostess, attendants, service, breakfasts, and everything was first class," I said. "You are very welcome, old friend. Please come back anytime," Sam said. "Thanks again, Sam," I said, and hung up.

"We better pack and get ready to go. Our flight is American Airlines at 2:17 p.m. We'll arrive in DC at 5 o'clock," I said. "Okay, I'll be ready, and thanks again for the beautiful breakfast," she said.

We packed and I said, "Would you like to shower first?" She replied, "You go ahead." We both showered in turn.

We grabbed our bags and threw them in the trunk of the Blue Beast. I walked around to open the door for Sara, but she beat me to it. "Gracious, Pablo," she said anyway. "It's all in the gesture, whether results are achieved or not," I said to myself; so true in life.

The phone rang. Sara and I looked at each other, questioning? I answered, "Paul Pilot here." Jack said, "That's my line, Paul." "I wanted to call and let you know again about dignitaries being at the dinner tomorrow evening," Jack said. "I know Jack, you already told me. Sara and I will look okay, if you had our clothes sent to the Hilton," I said. "What I didn't tell you is that two of the dignitaries are the President and Vice President of the United States!" he said. – PAUSE – "Wow! Really?" I answered. "Yes, really!" Jack said. "What kind of a dinner is it?" I said. "Just be there, on your best behavior and bring your lovely wife, Sara," he said, and hung up.

"A fine time to tell us, when we're halfway to the airport!" I said to Sara. "Tell you what?" she said. "That the President and Vice President will be at the dinner, among other dignitaries, including some from the FBI," I said. "No!" she said. "Yes," I said. "I cannot believe that we, let alone I, are having dinner with the President of the United States!" she said. "I knew I married an important person, but this is ridiculous," she added. "I hope you like the clothes he picked out for us or we'll have to go shopping tomorrow morning and pay a tailor big bucks to have things ready," I said. "It will be OK", she said.

We arrived at the Key West International Airport and I intentionally parked the Blue Beast in the open, long-term parking lot just southwest of the main airport, so NAS security could retrieve it without a ticket hassle.

We got out, after putting the key under the passenger's seat, and walked to the airport. We found the American Airlines ticket counter and entered our confirmation number in the kiosk, and it spit out our tickets. We were over an hour early, so we leisurely walked toward security.

When we got to security, Sara got through okay with her passport, as she didn't have a driver's license for this country. But when I showed my license and ticket, they pulled me to the side. I then showed my FBI credentials, and it got worse. They were convinced I had forgeries. We were both detained while they verified my credentials, or whatever the hell they were doing. I was getting hot. If the smalltime guards only knew what I'd been through the past month to protect them and the entire planet from the "Coffee Cartel." Oh well, they didn't know and were only doing their job. I wondered what triggered their rejection and interrogation?

After an eternity (probably 20 minutes), a small man, about sixty-five, came towards me and said, "We apologize, Sir! Your driver's license had expired and we doubted your FBI connection." We called and verified that you were hired by the FBI, then were retired from them and then rehired. Again, I apologize."

Thank God we were so early, as now it was 2:05 p.m. and our plane leaves at 2:17 p.m. We both ran and got to the gate as the last passenger handed the gatekeeper their boarding pass. We gave him our boarding passes and walked onto the tarmac to the plane. A little excitement goes a long way, but all was okay now. We found our adjoining seats and sat after putting our bags in the overhead.

"All that hassle caused by my expired driver's license?" I said. "They thought you looked suspicious, as well," Sara said. "Why?" I asked. "You are dressed like a bum, not an agent or representative of the FBI!" she said. "Just because my pants are full of holes and my shirt has a patch of dried blood that wouldn't come out!" I responded. "Oh well, we're here on the way to have dinner with the President," she said. "Did you tell them that?" Sara added. "No, I thought it would make things worse," I said.

We took off and the flight attendant went through her instructions. I held Sara's hand and started relaxing, as my blood pressure came down. We closed our eyes until the attendant came. We got our drinks, sipped some and closed our eyes again.

An announcement preceding landing was the next thing we knew and hurriedly drank our drinks and threw the plastic glasses in the attendant's trash bag. We landed and waited to deplane. As we walked toward ground transportation, a big Japanese man with a big sign, "Paul and Sara Pilot," was standing on the side. I said, "I'm Paul Pilot," to the man. "Okay then, please come with me. May I carry your bags?" he said. "Yes, thanks," I said and Sara and I turned over our bags (me a little reluctantly). We walked behind him to a stretch limousine, just like in the movies and this guy looked a lot like "Odd Job" in the Goldfinger movie.

"Odd Job" opened the side door for us and then put our bags in the front passenger's seat beside him. He said, "My instructions are to take you to the Capital Hilton." I said, "Yes, that's correct." He said, "There are drinks and glasses on the side, along with snacks, if you desire. It was Mr. Warner that instructed me." "Okay," I said.

"This is our capital city, Sara. I'm really glad we were summoned here on Uncle Sam's dime, so we could see the capital city together," I said. "Could you point out points of interest to us, as we go?" I asked "Odd Job." He said, "Fine." "We're just passing Arlington, Virginia, as Ronald Reagan Airport is just south of it," he said. "Soon I'll take you by Arlington National Cemetery, it's on the way and will be on your left; you'll see lots of small white crosses of our fallen heroes." "Wow," Sara said. "The Pentagon will be on your right as we pass," he said. "I've always heard about these places, even growing up in Cuba," Sara said. "There it is," Odd Job said. "In a minute we'll cross the Potomac River. Then I'll go a little out of the way to show you the Washington Monument," he went on. The White House will be on your right after we leave the Washington Monument." "Okay, there's the monument," he went on. "Wow," Sara said. "There is the White House coming up on your right, I'll slow down," he said. "Fantastico!" Sara said. "Your hotel will be ahead on the right. I'll let you out at the main entrance," Odd Job said.

He pulled up to the gorgeous Capital Hilton and came around to let us out. Then he gave our bags to the bellman. I asked Odd Job if I could pay or tip? He said, "No, Mr. Warren took care of me, well!" I said, "Thank you for the pleasant ride and super tour." "Your more than welcome," he said. The bellman took us to the check-in counter. I told the girl my name and she immediately said, "Yes, Mr. Pilot, your suite is ready. Just follow George and he'll take you there. Here are your keys, the room bar and everything is covered." "Did I marry the President?" Sara said. "No, my dear, just one of the President's men," I said. We followed George. He just carried our bags, as they were small enough to go in an airline overhead.

He had a master key and opened the door. I had never seen a more gorgeous suite, I was impressed and Sara was overwhelmed. I gave George a $20 bill and he said, "No thank you, Sir!" I stuck the twenty in his jacket pocket and said, "Take this or I'll take you, and I'm a 10th Degree Black Belt!" He took it and left, saying, "Again, thank you Sir."

What a place and what could be better for my Sara. She just walked and checked, and walked and touched. I went to the bedroom and there was a TV controller on the nightstand, but no TV. I pressed the "on" button and the largest TV I'd ever seen came out of the foot of the bed. It must have measured 5' long. Sara said, "Wow, talk about a TV!" I said, "That is class." Sara went to the restroom and there were two commodes. Upon inspection, it was obvious that one was a bidet.

This was a fantastic room. We put our clothes in the closet, and low and behold there were clothes already there. On the right a suit, shirts, ties and shoes; the whole enchilada. Her dresses, shoes and lingerie were on the right side. I said, "I guess we should try on everything to make sure it fits." "I agree," she said. We took off our traveling clothes and I tried on the suit without the shirt, as I didn't want it to wrinkle, to see if it was the right size. The pants were a little longer than the top of the shoe break I was used to, but still OK. Waist was perfect and the jacket fit better than any I'd ever had. One tie in particular went well and I asked Sara, "This tie?" She was halfway into her evening gown and said, "Perfectamundo, Pablo!" She pulled up and I zipped up her evening gown. Perfect fit, and it not only fit her curves but accented them. Our shoes were just right. Jack had done well.

I called Jack, as it was only 6:30 p.m. and he said, "Jack Warner here." I said, "Paul Pilot here." "Jack, I just wanted to call and tell you that the accommodations are super and the clothes fit us perfectly." "Good," he said. "Enjoy your evening and I'll see you at the Capital at 5:30 p.m. tomorrow, dressed to the nines. Okay?" Jack said. "Okay," I said, and hung up.

"Sara, what do you think?" I said. "This is the most fantastic experience I've ever had, Pablo. It could not be any better," Sara said. "I feel the same, my angel," I responded.

"Are you hungry?" I asked. "Yes," she said. "Let's change into something less formal, but after this day I'd like to take a shower," she added. "Okay, you first," I said.

We both showered and got ready for dinner. I said, "This hotel has a nice restaurant and it's very convenient." "Yes, that sounds good," she said.

I made us a drink. They had Macallan 18, of all things; this was a first in any hotel that I had ever been to. Sara wanted a Lemon drop and a small covered plate of sugar was already there. They also had a similar plate of salt; what class, I thought.

We sat at a formal dining table. Sara said, "This is unbelievable!" "I know, I know," I said. "Because of your performance and success in destroying the Coffee Cartel, we're enjoying this beautiful suite, perfect attire, and are going to see President Trump tomorrow," she said. "Thank you, my dear, it is great and I thank God for the fact that I'm even here to enjoy it. There were several life-threatening encounters," I said.

We finished our drinks and went down to the restaurant. The host sat us at a table for two. A waitress asked what we'd like to drink. We ordered the same drinks we had in the room. The menu was complete and Deep Sea Scallops caught my eye. Sara thought Chilean Sea Bass would be good for her. The waitress returned and I ordered a nice Sauvignon Blanc to pair with our scallops and bass.

We enjoyed the atmosphere and a few other couples were also enjoying the evening. It wasn't busy, probably since it was Monday night. We sipped our drinks and our glances said it all. The Pachelbel Canon was playing in the background at just the right decibel level. Our meals were properly presented from over our right shoulders and we were asked if we had anything else we wanted? "No thank you," I said. Our dinners were wonderful. Consumptive silence prevailed.

We finished and were visually satisfied, smiling and shaking our heads in affirmation. The waitress returned with dessert menus, but we were just filled to the brim and our wine wasn't finished and would conflict with the sweetness of desserts. We charged the meal to our room and I left a thirty-five percent tip.

We were a little tired physically and emotionally from the thrill of all we'd experienced today. We walked to the elevator and went to our room.

We didn't hesitate disrobing and slipped into bed. I turned on the TV just to see it come up in front of us, and a torrent of color engulfed us. We looked in amazement, and within a minute I asked Sara, "Off?" "Yes," she said. We again were so satisfied that sex would have been redundant. No alarm was set, and we closed our eyes and recounted our experience since landing at Reagan. "Thank you, Paul", she said.

This time Sara got up before I did; at least she wasn't there when I awoke. As soon as I gained some degree of consciousness, I detected the aroma of coffee. I got up and as soon as I went to the small kitchen, Sara put another Keurig cone of Starbuck's coffee in the maker. "Good morning," she said. "Good morning, how long have you been up?" I said. "For a while, I had to go to the restroom and couldn't get back to sleep; thinking about the dinner, the reason for it and meeting President Trump." "I think the dinner has something to do with the Coffee Cartel, or why would you and I be invited?" she went on. "You're probably right, but I don't really know. Logic tells us that my only connection to the government is through the FBI and destroying the Cartel," I agreed. "Want to get breakfast, I've been up long enough to get hungry," Sara said. "Yes, let's just go downstairs to Starbucks, they have nice breakfast sandwiches," I responded. "Okay, I won't have to get too pretty," she said, as she went to the bidet room where her makeup was. I went to a half bathroom, where my toiletries were. In a flash we were ready and left our beautiful suite.

The restaurant was set up for a buffet breakfast, so we signed up. Black coffee and orange juice preceded the feast.

We looked around and a few recognizable Senators and Representatives were having breakfast; the Buffet, no less. I was thinking it would be great if they were as frugal with taxpayer's money as they were getting an "all you can eat" economy buffet. Most of them didn't have a clue about the horror and near-death experiences, or even the "Coffee Cartel." Their knowledge would have caused panic in the US, and probably the world, in short order. Oh well, I thought, eat your breakfast and try to stay focused. I did point out Orin Hatch and John McCain to Sara. She had no idea who they were, which actually I thought of as a blessing.

We got back to the room after a stroll down Pennsylvania Avenue and headed straight to bed. "Don't forget to set your alarm; I'll need a couple hours to get ready, but I'll work around you my love." "Jack left me a phone message that someone would pick us up at 5:30 p.m. at the front lobby door," I said. "So I'll set it for 3:30?" "Okay," she said.

It felt like I'd just fallen into sleep when the alarm went off. We both got up. I said, "You want to shower first?" She said, "Yes." So, I went for the coffee pot again, made a cup and laid out my red tie, light blue shirt and maroon suit, underwear, socks and brown shoes. Whoever picked our outfits out knew what they were doing; size, color coordination, the whole nine yards. Sara's outfit was beautiful; both sexy and subdued. It was an evening dress out of a fashion magazine, with lace over a lavender dress along the neckline. Her shoes were high-heeled, but not too high. I don't know what you call them? I just rememberd the half bath with my toiletries and it had a small shower.

Sara came out wrapped in a towel and said, "Do you want me or the shower?" I said, "I want you but I'd better get a shower, especially since I just remembered that I had a small one in my bathroom. Sara laughed and headed for the closet for her clothes.

I grabbed my underwear and went to my half bath, half shower bath room. I showered, shaved, brushed and combed, brushed and rinsed, dried and donned my Duluth Trading Company underwear. I went out and Sara was back in the big bathroom; I assumed to put her makeup on.

She finished and emerged looking absolutely gorgeous. She asked me to again zip up the back of her evening gown or dress, which I did. She put on her shoes and was ready. "I'm so lucky to have found you and knew you were very pretty, but your absolutely, damn gorgeous!" I said.

I put on my outfit and new shoes and we were ready. It was 5:15 p.m., so we just made it. "I don't think we have to take anything and hopefully Jack will tell us where to go, where to sit and whatever." Sara even had a matching purse of a slightly darker shade of lavender. "Let's go," she said.

We went down to the lobby and then to the front doors and rotating cylinder entrance. Sara said, "Should we go out or stay here?" "I don't know?" I said. "Okay, it's 5:32 p.m., I'll go out, you stay here," I added. I went outside and saw no one that looked like our ride. A few minutes later a large, stretch, Lincoln Limousine drove up. I didn't want to be presumptuous, so I waited for him to make a move since two other couples seemed to be waiting outside. The well-dressed driver got a sign from his front seat and showed it to all of us outside. The sign said, "Pilot Party." I went inside and told Sara, "The driver is here, my dear."

We were escorted and put in the rear door of the limo. We were only a short drive to the Capital, but it was surely a classy one. Sara was thrilled, as was I. The driver was very professional and told us that he was hired to stay until we were ready to go back to the Hilton. "Nice," Sara said. I said, "Muy bien." Sara chuckled. We arrived at the Capital and were met by one of Jack's staff who had followed my Cartel involvement. He escorted us to a large room inside the capital with a stage-like raised platform, with our flag behind it and curtains all around. There were rows of chairs facing the stage-like platform and as we entered, I saw Armando sitting at a chair in the front row. He saw me, got up and shook my hand, and said, "What's the deal here?" "I don't know?" I said. Sara said hello and we were directed to sit next to Arm. Andy Pellerito was the next to come. We all greeted each other and Andy was seated by his aid next to Arm. Jack Warner and Harvey Hyde came down from another entrance and said, "I'm very glad that you all made it!" "Thanks, it's good to see these guys in a better setting," I said. "What's the deal? Did you make a movie or something?" I went on. "No, Paul, just sit down and be patient," Jack said as he and Harvey moved off to the right and sat down in the second row. Sara was shaking her head in disbelief and sat down next to me. The room was filling rapidly and I imagined if President Trump was going to be there, it would surely fill up; but why? This whole thing appeared as a setup for something involving my team, Armando and Andy. The room was now full and a recording started playing, "Hail To The Chief." Oh my, Trump was about to make an entrance. Sara took my left hand in hers and squeezed. President Trump walked in and took the podium. "Good evening, Ladies and Gentlemen," he said. "We're here this afternoon to honor a few of America's unsung heroes," he continued. "There are events that take place in the course of governmental affairs that do not reach the public domain. There are good reasons that light is not shown on these events. Let us merely say that it's in the public interest to keep these events hidden, and please have confidence that their very nature are such that we're better off not knowing the details." And in my opinion, should never be. With that said, we're also here to honor a specific individual who deserves our highest praise for uncovering, and ultimately playing the major role in stopping, what may have been the biggest threat that the United States of America and maybe the world has ever known. His name is Pilot, Paul Pilot. Please join me Paul."

Oh Boy, I got up and moved to the platform with President Trump. I stood beside him, while he proceeded. "Mr. Pilot, I would like to present you with the highest Medal of Honor that a President of these United States can bestow on a civilian . . . The Presidential Medal of Freedom," he said as he moved behind me and placed the medal on my neck. "I, the United States and, indeed, all of mankind are in your debt, Paul Pilot!" Trump continued. An attendant gestured for me to move to the side. Mr. Trump again spoke, "It is also my pleasure this evening to honor two other individuals that courageously helped terminate the threat that faced us all. First, Armando Ortiz; please join me. Second, Andy Pellerito. Mr. Ortiz faced almost insurmountable obstacles, while steadfastly pursuing destruction of the same threat that Mr. Pilot uncovered. I would like to present both of you with the Distinguished Service Cross for your efforts and valor."

Mr. Trump stepped behind Arm and hung the Medal around his neck. The aid motioned for Arm to move next to me. "I now call Andy Pellerito to join me." Andy got up and stood next to Trump. "Mr. Pellerito was also a key participant, along with Mr. Pilot and Mr. Ortiz in stopping the same threat I've been alluding to. You are also a recipient of the Distinguished Service Cross for your efforts." Trump stepped behind Andy and placed the Medal around Andy's neck. "There were countless other people involved with stopping this menace; the FBI was instrumental; namely, Harvey Hyde and Jack Warner, who oversaw numerous activities to neutralize this menace to mankind. Other people, within the government and without, all contributed to the success of these missions," Trump continued.

"I thank you all for coming here tonight and sharing this great honor!" Trump finished and we stepped down. Sara came and hugged me as I stepped off the stage. Arm shook my hand, Andy as well. Then a barrage of congratulatory Congressmen, Senators and media; NBC, ABC, FOX, they were all there and they were all after the specifics of the threat. I know it would come out someday, but I honored President Trump's resolution that the details of the threat remain unknown.

Jack, again, made his way to me. "I know I didn't warn you, but I thought it best to remain a surprise. Again, please don't tell the press anything or it will not be good. I've warned everyone else that I can think of as well," he whispered. "You should come with me as several have been invited for dinner in an adjoining room. The media will not be present." Sara and I followed him. Other aids directed those invited to the next room and table. Guards restricted entry of unwanted guests. All the places were identified by small Name placards on gold rimmed charger plates. Sara and I were placed next to President Trump and Melania. Sara was seated next to Melania and appeared thrilled beyond words. Several notables were seated at the same table; Harvey Hyde, Anthony McGregor (Acting Head of the FBI), Jack Warner, Andy Pellerito, Armando Ortiz, Senator Hatch, on and on until the head table was filled. Some had spouses or dates, some did not.

Dinner was served immediately and impeccably as soon as Mr. Trump and his table's guests were seated. A well-made spinach salad was carefully placed at each plate. Red or white wine was served, along with Pellegrino. President trump asked that we bow our heads, and said, "God bless those among us that fought to rid ourselves of a large, demonic threat to life, as we know it, and bless this food to the nourishment of those seated at this table that stopped the threat, as well as those who had little to no knowledge of the threat at all."

We ate our salad, followed by a nice prime rib, garlic potatoes, and asparagus drizzled with hollandaise. Perfect! I held Sara's hand off and on throughout the dinner; neither one of us could believe the entire experience. It was quiet, except for a string quartet playing in the background.

President Trump got up after the main course and came over and whispered in my ear, positioning himself so that Sara could hear as well, and said, "I want you to know that I truly appreciate your effort to uncover and help destroy this Coffee Cartel. This Medal was the only way we could figure out how to recognize your heroism without telling the world what was happening. We're still treating those addicted in Key Largo and elsewhere. I thank you Paul from the bottom of my heart!" I said, "Thank you, Mr. President."

Sara looked at me in amazement and adoration and gave me a big kiss. I was overwhelmed with everything and wanted us to leave as soon as we could, it was almost suffocating, but dessert was served. A chocolate souffle with syrup décor and whipped cream on top. "Not too sweet, just scrumptious," Sara said.

The President said "Goodnight all," after the dessert, and we were "out of there." Sara said on the way out that Melania was so nice. "We had a kinship, being from another country and all," she said. "She's as nice as she is beautiful," Sara added. "You both are, but I'm prejudiced. You're the most beautiful and nicest woman on God's earth", I said.

We finally got to the steps of the Capital and could see our driver waiving beside his limo. We reached the limo and our driver politely opened the rear door for us, and we got in. This evening was a culmination; an experience that gave meaning to my life here on earth. Sara broke down crying with appreciation and exhaustion. We rode back to the Hilton, ready for the remainder of life, together!

Printed in the United States
By Bookmasters